The Body on the Train

Also available by Frances Brody

The Body on the Train

A Kate Shackleton Mystery

FRANCES BRODY

CROOKED LANE

NEW YORK

Published in the United States by Crooked Lane Books, an imprint of The Quick Brown Fox & Company LLC.

Crooked Lane Books and its logo are trademarks of The Quick Brown Fox & Company LLC.

Library of Congress Catalog-in-Publication data available upon request.

ISBN (hardcover): 978-1-64385-160-0
ISBN (ebook): 978-1-64385-161-7

Cover illustration by Helen Chapman
Book design by Jennifer Canzone

Printed in the United States.

www.crookedlanebooks.com

Crooked Lane Books
34 West 27th St., 10th Floor
New York, NY 10001

First North American Edition: November 2019

10 9 8 7 6 5 4 3 2 1

*To Judith Murdoch
and Rebecca Winfield*

Eyes Only

Riga
15 February 1929

A J Cook
Miners' Federation of Great Britain

Fraternal Greetings Comrade,

    The time is ripe to work for the election of a British government that will lead to the resumption of diplomatic relations with the Union of Soviet Socialist Republics and solidarity between the working classes of our countries. Our emissary will make his way to Friends in the North. Ensure good use of gold. May the shade of your Vernal Parliamentary Election blaze the colour of the people's flag.

We salute you,
Grigoriy Yevesyevich Radomyslskly

Unloading The Rhubarb Special

King's Cross Railway Station
Saturday, 2 March, 1929, 2.15 a.m.

Steam, smoke in your eyes. Rattling, shunting engines, thundering in your King Lears. Fingers numb. Nice light boxes, lift 'em from the truck. Splinter of wood in the flesh of your thumb. Try to bite it out with your new gnashers and off it breaks. Daft how a tiny hurt can pain that much. Heard a story. Lad in the school hall, P.T. lesson, vaulting, spell in his finger from the vaulting horse. Turned septic. Lad died.

Young. Old. Never know when your time's up.

Speedy job, unloading rhubarb. Perishable. Due at Covent Garden, due at Spitalfields, due, due, due. Always one eye on the clock. Who'd be a porter?

He would. Railways in his blood. King's Cross. Centre of the world. Stomp up from all corners of the globe. Bankers and country bumpkins. Penniless foreign royals. Swanking riff-raff.

But he belongs, proud to belong. Known here. On York Street born. On York Street he'll die.

By two in the morning, he'd murder for a pint, murder for his bed.

Best thing about this special? The smell. Lean into the truck and reach for the crates lined with blue paper, blue setting off the red of the rhubarb. Breathing in takes him back to the country. A

3

boy again, on the hop-picking. Setting off for Kent with a slice of bread and marge sprinkled with sugar, a bottle of water.

Magic to be here in the smoke and steam and in the same instant back in a field of hops, back in an orchard of English apples.

Slam the door of the empty truck. Open the next one.

Reach out. Touch what shouldn't be there, not on the rhubarb special.

The minute he touched it, he knew. Or that's what he said afterwards, when he described the cold shiver. This didn't grow in any farmer's field.

Chapter One

No matter how many times I come to London, I still love to look about me, even if it is only at the shops and the risk-taking pedestrians on Gray's Inn Road. Young DC Martin Yeats left me to my gazing, which I curtailed a little so as not to be classed as a country bumpkin. The driver wove in and out of the traffic until we drew up at the grand granite-faced building on the Embankment that is New Scotland Yard.

Once inside, we exchanged the smoke of the city for a fug of cigarette fumes, mingled with fried bacon. Someone must have been sent to bring sandwiches.

As befits a man of high rank, Commander Woodhead had his office on the top floor, reached by a juddering lift. I first met him and his wife when Mother and I were staying in London with Aunt Berta. As young men, he and Uncle played in the same rugger team. I remembered him as tall and broad, with a shock of dark hair.

The man who stood as I entered his office was slightly stooped. His hair, though still plentiful, had turned white. He looked ancient beside the young detective constable.

As my father often said, the war robbed institutions of a middle generation. Now old and young worked side by side, looking at each other across a sometimes incomprehensible divide. That absence of the men in the middle benefited youngsters like Martin Yeats. He surely must be entrusted with greater tasks than escorting a lady detective from King's Cross.

The commander came round to my side of the desk to shake hands. "You'll have had refreshments on the train, Mrs. Shackleton?"

If that was his polite way of telling me not to waste his time over tea and buns, it worked. "Yes, thank you."

He took a seat and motioned to DC Yeats to draw up a chair. In spite of his haste in wishing to jump to the business in hand, he observed the usual courtesies, asking about my mother and aunt.

He had probably seen my aunt more recently than I had, but the less said of that the better.

It did not take long for him to meander almost to the point. "How much do you know, Mrs. Shackleton?"

"Only that you wish to talk to me about a special assignment, connected with a crime thought to have been committed in the West Riding."

He nodded. "That is so."

I waited. If this was a game of drip-dripping information, two could play. Let him start. He began by telling me something that I already knew.

"The LNER runs a special express train from Ardsley to London during the forced rhubarb season. It carries up to two hundred tons of rhubarb to supply the London markets."

I knew about that train, timed to arrive in London before dawn, daily between Christmas and Easter. It doesn't always do to begin by correcting a person who ought to be well informed, but that did not stop me. "The starting point is Leeds Central Station, Mr. Woodhead." Ardsley was the major junction for the surrounding areas.

He glanced at his papers. "Quite so." He frowned and waited. When I didn't give him a recipe for rhubarb pie, he continued.

"When King's Cross porters unloaded the train last Saturday morning, they found a body, thought to have been put on the train at Ardsley." He picked up and handed me the only piece of paper on his desk: a watercolour head-and-shoulders artist's portrait of a middle-aged male.

The man's features were refined but unremarkable. His hair was a mixture of dark brown and grey. He had a lined forehead neither too high nor too low, the usual number of eyebrows, deep-set pale blue eyes a little on the small side, a rather narrow nose and somewhat full lips. The lips made me guess, irrationally, that here was a man who loved his food. His chin jutted a little and yet his jaws so smoothly blended into his neck that it might have been called a weak chin.

Was he some poor tramp who had stowed away, eaten poisonous rhubarb leaves and died?

"Who is he?"

"That is the question, or one of them. Who is he, and who put him there?"

The commander gave DC Yeats the nod.

The younger man leaned forward. "He is in his middle years, five feet seven inches tall and in possession of his own teeth." The commander gave another encouraging nod to DC Yeats.

"He was found without –" Yeats hesitated. "He was found without identification. He appears fit, well-nourished, probably a professional man, or a gentleman."

There was something neither of them wanted to mention. I had not come two hundred miles, rattling for over four hours on a train, to hear part of a story. DC Yeats had been going to say something else before he changed his words to "without identification".

Had the man been horribly mutilated?

"What other details do you have?"

The commander scratched his ear.

Yeats scratched his nose. Was there a flea in the room?

Yeats said, "The gentleman wore only his underwear. He had been placed in potato sacks, tied with cord."

For a moment, silence held. The image gave me a shudder. I felt suddenly cold.

The commander spoke first, looking at me with compassion, as if remembering when we first met and I was just a child.

"Perhaps not at all the sort of case for you, m'dear. Though being local to that neck of the woods, and being that we need someone undercover –" He seemed ready to usher me from the room as if his summons to me might have been a foolish whim, a whim he regretted.

I guessed his thoughts. How could that nice girl turn into a woman who does not turn a hair at such a story?

I ignored his unwillingness to believe that even nice girls grow up.

Someone must have thought that the man might be identified by his clothing, a tailor's label, a bespoke shirt, or handmade shoes. "Was there anything at all to give a hint of his identity?"

"The underwear was a type widely available."

"How did he die?"

Now Mr. Woodhead spoke with a trumpeting pomposity that made me wonder what my lovely aunt ever saw in him. "Shot through the stomach don't you know. Bad business."

So there would have been blood at the scene, but not as much as if he had been shot through the heart. The killer had taken no chances.

"Mr. Woodhead, what is it that you think I might do that the railway police, Scotland Yard and the local CID cannot?"

"You have a reputation for winkling out information." He once more turned to his constable.

"Up to two hundred growers from across the rhubarb growing area despatch goods on that train. That night, there were crates from just seventy-five growers—the season is drawing to a close. Officers from Wakefield and Leeds have questioned every grower, as well as railway staff. No one knows a thing."

Then somebody must be lying, or be very cunning. "Does the train stop anywhere after Ardsley?"

The commander shook his head. "No scheduled stops, being an express. It was held up for signals outside Grantham, but the signalman saw no suspicious activity."

"And what about King's Cross, might the body have been put on the train there?"

"We have sworn statements from the porter who found the body, and from his fellow porter who was by his side within minutes." He turned to his DC.

Yeats handed me a photograph of the interior of a railway goods truck stacked with boxes, the sort used for oranges, and with a bulky sack in the foreground.

Whatever the unfortunate man weighed in life, he would have been a dead weight once life ebbed. "It must have taken two strong men to put him on the train."

Yeats seemed reluctant to speculate. "There may have been a clumsy attempt to make the sack look like a sack of potatoes, which doesn't suggest careful planning."

There had been nothing in the press. Here was an artist's portrait of the deceased, and yet secrecy surrounded the death. That seemed odd. Somewhere in the back of my mind was a connection, evading me now, but it would come.

"You must have questioned growers, and the railway staff, and showed the portrait."

The commander moved a cup from desk to windowsill. "There were the usual enquiries. It would be unwise to reveal the full facts. The portrait was shown to a few trusted individuals with a stake in the area."

"Then I need the names of these trusted individuals, and the full facts."

The commander lit a cigarette. "You will have all the information you need."

That was not the most satisfactory answer. "Mr. Woodhead, that might be interpreted as all the information you believe I would need." I gave him a smile. "I need to be fully briefed."

Woodhead glanced at DC Yeats with what seemed to me to be a shifty look. "Yeats, you will ensure that Mrs. Shackleton is fully briefed."

Yeats nodded. "Yes, sir."

Something about this assignment did not feel right. Yet I have wages to pay.

"Mr. Woodhead, you would have the usual contract drawn up, covering my time, my assistant's time, and disbursements?"

"Would you need an assistant for this task?"

What a cheek, when he could draw on the entire resources of Scotland Yard!

"Of course. As you know, I work with Mr. Sykes."

"Yes, I know the name. Reports speak highly of him."

Several questions came to mind. Murder cannot be kept quiet, and yet I had heard nothing about this. "How is it that there has been no report in the newspapers?"

"To go public at this stage would bring us the usual deluge of letters and calls from cranks and people hoping to trace a long-lost husband, son or brother."

This did not make sense. Newspaper reporters sniff out a serious crime faster than my bloodhound picks up the scent of a squirrel.

"You placed an embargo on the story."

"We asked newspaper editors to show restraint."

"Why?"

He began a long explanation, the gist of which was that the less I knew, the more likely it would be that I could investigate with an open mind. There was also the hint of some threat to national security. The mention of national security must have allowed him to impose silence on the press. During this long explanation, I glanced at DC Yeats, to read his face. I could not.

Yeats rested his hands on his thighs. Perhaps he had jittery legs and must keep them still. He stared steadily at his feet.

"Mr. Woodhead, please tell me what you are thinking so that I don't go into this investigation with one hand tied behind me." This was risky, but I said it anyway. "We have known each other a long time. There are those who will vouch for my discretion, and that I can hold information while still keeping an open mind."

DC Yeats lost interest in his shoes. He sat up a little straighter. Perhaps he too had been kept in the dark.

"The answer lies somewhere within the Yorkshire coalfields. I'd stake my reputation on that."

"The coalfields?"

Looking relieved at having a reason to move, DC Yeats rose and crossed to a cabinet. He produced a map. After waiting for a nod of permission, he spread the map on the commander's desk.

The commander indicated an area almost like a triangle edged by Leeds, Bradford and Wakefield. It was full of blue and black dots. "This is an area of thirty square miles. Coal and agriculture, as you'll know." He tapped with his nicotine-stained finger. "There's Leeds, where you boarded today. There's Ardsley where we believe the man's body was put on the train."

"What is the significance of the dots?"

"Blue for every railway station that closed during the strike –"

"But that was all of them, and it was three years ago."

"Black for every mine where men went on strike."

I did not trouble to point out that his dots must then represent every single pit. "You are pinpointing the coalfields and the railways, rather than agriculture?"

"Indeed."

"What connection might there be between the 1926 strike and a body found on the rhubarb train three years on?"

"Who was at the heart of the General Strike, Mrs. Shackleton?"

"The miners held out longest."

"Quite so! Railway workers and miners tried to hold the country to ransom. They failed in their attempt at revolution."

"Revolution?"

"The threat never goes away."

It occurred to me that if miners committed murder, they would be capable of making sure the body would never be been found. Railway workers would not put a body on a train. "Do you believe that disposing of the body in such a public way was deliberate, some kind of warning? If so, who was being warned by whom?"

"I am privy to intelligence the public will never be troubled with. Often that information is partial. The defeat of the General Strike was the end of a battle. It would suit foreign powers to foment unrest."

"You think the man on the train may have been a secret agent, murdered for money, or assassinated?"

Mr. Woodhead frowned. His nose twitched disapproval. I had set off in the race before waiting for the starting pistol. "That is one line of enquiry. It does not help that in the aftermath of the strike, police are perceived as the enemy. We can expect no cooperation."

This did not surprise me. Miners and their families had been starved into submission.

But rhubarb growers?

He waited for my response.

Did he imagine I might wave a dowser's wand across his map and the tip of my wand would touch the place where some deadly deed originated? "Are there other lines of enquiry?"

"We hope that is what you will uncover. Who knew he was coming, and why."

"The carriage where the body was found, do we know which growers' produce it contained?" Of course, as I spoke, I realised that a guilty party would be unlikely to put a body in the same compartment as their own rhubarb.

"DC Yeats will give you details. All the growers have been questioned. That might be a waste of your valuable time."

"What about the murder weapon?"

"It's thought to be a .25 calibre handgun."

DC Yeats folded the map and slid it into a folder.

I took the folder. "There isn't a great deal to go on."

"I think you might find a way, Mrs. Shackleton, if you agree. We are still following normal enquiry procedures, albeit with reduced resources. New lines of enquiry will emerge."

"I'll need a list of growers whose produce was on that train, and of all who have used the train this year." It seemed to me more likely that a grower who was *not* loading produce that night might have risked disposing of a body.

Sykes would be good at questioning the growers. He might discover something that the police had missed.

Although this particular suggestion of the commander's smacked of the proverbial haystack and needle, the mystery intrigued me. More importantly, I hated the thought of this man— whoever he was, and whatever he may have done—losing his life, and in death being treated so ignominiously.

"Do we know when the man died?"

DC Yeats made the slightest of movements. There was something he wanted to say, yet he did not speak.

The commander did. "We can't say for sure. It would be guesswork. Do you need time to think this over? I shall understand if your answer is no."

What was the matter with him? Did he think I was not asking the right questions, or was I asking too many? Perhaps he was simply being clever, and challenging me to say yes.

"If I may be fully briefed, and with the contract drawn up by the end of today, I shall start immediately."

That would please my bank manager.

Was it my imagination or did he seem disappointed? Perhaps not disappointed in me as a detective, but as my mother's daughter, my aunt's niece. This was not a task for a "lady". And yet, he had summoned me.

"Thank you, Mrs. Shackleton. Welcome aboard. You will have my appreciation and that of the force for your efforts."

For my efforts! It seemed to me that he expected I would fall at the first hurdle.

The commander took a file from his cabinet. "I'm so sorry but I have another meeting. May I hand you over to DC Yeats? He will give you all the information you need." He passed the file to Yeats.

I ignored his urgent wish to be elsewhere. "You want me to go undercover?"

"Yes."

"The railway police and local detectives must have asked direct questions of the railway staff and the growers. There could have been no line of questioning without reference to a body and a train."

"That is correct. But we wish you to be discreet."

"Why the secrecy? Surely the people who have been questioned may be allowed to know my mission?"

"Prefer this to be QT. You see, m'dear, there are influential men in the north, industrialists on whom our economy depends. It would not do for them to imagine Scotland Yard –" He paused, thinking of how to phrase this. "It would not do for them to think of Scotland Yard as grappling too long with unanswered questions and that we are bringing in outside assistance."

He did not want important people to think that Scotland Yard had turned to me.

He smiled. "And Mrs. Shackleton, I have arranged for you to have afternoon tea at The Savoy with a lady who has similar interests to yourself. I hope you will enjoy that." With apologies and polite remarks, he moved towards the door.

There are not many female detectives. I quickly guessed who that person might be. She would understand that I wanted to go straight home and start work.

"One more question, sir."

"Ah of course, you want the lady's name."

"That wasn't my question, Mr. Woodhead. I'm guessing the lady is Mrs. Kerner?"

"Dashed clever, Mrs. Shackleton. And I wanted to surprise you."

"How best shall I communicate with you?"

He nodded towards Yeats. "You and Yeats will come up with a way, I'm sure. Good day, dear Mrs. Shackleton."

He made his escape. He wanted me to take on the job, or he did not. He wanted me to succeed, or he wanted me to fail. I could not make up my mind about him.

Chapter Two

∼

The chill in the cellar corridor of St Pancras Hospital seeped into my bones. Our footsteps made an unholy racket on the stone floor. DC Yeats needed no escort, having been here before.

"Are you sure you want to view the body, Mrs. Shackleton? I can tell you all you need to know."

"I am not being ghoulish, Mr. Yeats. I owe it to the man, and to myself, to see him."

Of course, the man in question might have considered being viewed by a strange woman one more indignity to add to the rest. "I would be paying my respects."

With so little to go on from Commander Woodhead, my one-sided meeting with the deceased might help.

I can count on one hand the people I trust completely. Mr. Woodhead was not one of them. Men of his breeding and generation err on the side of protecting female sensibilities. I needed to be sure that I started with knowledge of the facts.

Yeats had telephoned in advance. The waiting mortuary attendant led us to a table by the wall. There was a dim light from the cellar window. A pale overhead gaslight cast a soft glow. With great gentleness, the attendant drew back the white sheet to the level of the shoulders, revealing the man's marble features. The artist who had drawn the sketch of our unknown man had given him life and colour. There was no life or colour now.

At a nod from DC Yeats, the attendant folded back the covering sheet.

A scar on the abdomen marked the place where a bullet had left its mark.

Yeats drew my attention to the man's hands. "There are no signs of his ever having done manual labour, but you'll notice callouses on the thumb and forefinger of his right hand."

"Yes."

"And a trace of what might be ink."

Perhaps this gentleman had held a pen, wrote many letters, drew up plans and schemes. I said nothing, being reluctant to discuss the man in his presence—even though he was beyond hearing.

His right elbow was slightly swollen, and also his knee. This was something or nothing. DC Yeats read my thoughts. "Not so much as an appendix removal, and no battle scars."

Perhaps he had led a charmed life to the very end.

As I grew accustomed to the light, I altered my first impression of someone without colour. There was a suggestion of shading, of variation. He did not have those entirely pale legs that we English are blessed with.

I indicated to DC Yeats that we could leave the man in peace. The mortuary attendant was close by. We waited until he had once more covered our gentleman, and then took our leave. There was a lift. Without discussion, we ignored it. That lift had carried too much tragic weight. Neither of us spoke until we reached ground level.

Police and hospital staff are frequently on good terms with each other. DC Yeats was no exception. He and I sat in the staff canteen. Stewed tea steamed from thick white cups.

Yeats took a drink. "I thought our man might be a writer, because of callouses on his thumb and forefinger. I took the head-and-shoulders drawing to publishers, and to bookshops, all along Charing Cross Road. No one recognised him."

"That was a good thing to try though."

"Yet he gives me the impression of being a fit man, someone who spent time outdoors, not a man who lived his life entirely at a desk."

That was my view too. "He has enjoyed sunshine, perhaps wearing shorts or a bathing suit."

Yeats nodded. "Still discernible, that difference in his skin colouring."

"He has been abroad then." The puzzle was what brought him to the place he met his end, wherever that was. "You have thoughts on time of death?"

"He was placed in the sack before rigor mortis set in. The pathologist examined him early on Saturday and thought he had been dead for less than twelve hours." Yeats placed an attaché case on the table and gave it a tap. "There's additional background material in here. Shall we find a more congenial place, The Savoy where you'll be having tea?"

"Yes, let's. But I'll telephone to Mrs. Kerner and we can rearrange afternoon tea. She'll understand." I took one more drink from the thick cup.

He did the same, but a much longer drink. "I don't like to offend the kitchen staff. They occasionally oblige me with a late-night meal." He smiled. "How did you know it was Mrs. Kerner that the commander wanted you to meet?"

"I would love to say that female detectives are so numerous we have formed a club, but that wouldn't be true."

The truth is that Annette Kerner introduced herself to me a couple of years ago. We got on very well. She dubs herself the Mayfair Detective, loves to take cases for people of high social standing, and also works with Scotland Yard. Mr. Woodhead must have had a word in her ear, and would expect her to pass on his insights. But since he had already made up his mind, and agreed a press embargo, I thought it better to start from scratch.

We pushed our chairs from the table and rose at the same time. "Mr. Yeats, depending on how long you and I need for the briefing, I'd like to catch a train to Leeds this evening."

He nodded. As we made our way back to the entrance, he took out a notebook. "I thought you might say that. There's a 5.45 p.m. from King's Cross to Leeds Central, with a restaurant car, arrives 9.35 p.m. I'll ask the receptionist at The Savoy to make a booking. Is there anyone else you'd like me to ring?"

This young man would go far. "My housekeeper, Mrs. Sugden."

She would arrange for Sykes to meet me at the station. We could make a start, come up with a plan of action.

While we waited for the taxi that would take us to The Savoy, my curiosity got the better of me. "Mr. Yeats, you're young and new to the force I think."

"I was at Exmouth a year before coming here."

"How did you come to be assisting Mr. Woodhead?"

His expression was at once both bashful and droll, like the romantic but bumbling hero in an amateur play. "Oh he asked for me, after something came up in the briefing."

I gave him an enquiring look, but he was a man who waited for a prompt. "Go on then. Let me in on it."

He cleared his throat. "I happened to know a bit about what was in the sack, which had held potatoes. There were two spuds still in there. I identified the variety."

"Which was?"

"Arran Victory."

This is a shocking admission, but when he named the potato, we laughed, like giddy schoolchildren. It must have been a reaction against the distress of seeing that unfortunate man. All the same, I felt bad about laughing, and so did he. Our taxi came into view.

"We'll make it up to the poor man. We'll find out who did this to him."

Chapter Three

❧

As it happened, Annette Kerner had other plans than afternoon tea with a sister sleuth. She had left a note for me at The Savoy reception.

Kate, m'dear, Fiddlesticks to cream tea. Will you dine with me and a couple of embassy chums? Later, we'll be at the tables. I feel sure you'll have a newcomer's lucky streak.
Annette.

It was tempting, but work came first. I wrote a friendly refusal to the suggestion that I gamble away my Scotland Yard fee before earning it.

DC Yeats and I took a table by the window in the Thames Foyer, sufficiently far from the American jazz band so as to hear each other but not be overheard.

He opened his attaché case. "I have some documents for you."

There was a copy of the map we had looked at earlier, additional copies of the watercolour of our unknown man, and a carbon copy of a closely typed sheet, noting the investigation to date, and listing the rhubarb growers.

In chirpy mood, the band played "Me and My Shadow".

DC Yeats lit a cigarette.

As might be expected in an investigation involving the railway, timings were meticulously noted. The rhubarb was booked in between 3.30 p.m. and 6.30 p.m., with a clerk and one porter on duty.

"And no one noticed the sack?"

"No. The sidings are extensive and there's a small workforce at Ardsley, a clerk and a guard. They saw nothing unusual."

That might be true, or not. Word of a body on the train would spread quickly between stations. By the time railway police asked questions in the north, amnesia would reign. No railway worker would want to risk coming under suspicion, any more than they would want to lose time off work by attending an inquest.

"What about the inquest?"

"Opened and adjourned."

I quickly read through the progress report, which amounted to no progress at all.

The last pages indicated who had been shown the sketch of the unknown man, mainly mining officials, and mine managers.

"Why have so few people been shown the artist's sketch?"

"The investigation may be widened."

"What were the criteria for deciding who sees the picture?"

"I'm afraid I can't answer that, not being party to the decision."

"Oh, come on, Mr. Yeats, give me a helping hand."

He hesitated. "If you'd met Mrs. Kerner, I believe she may have told you that she has been asked to keep an eye out for gentlemen from Russia, Bolsheviks. She moves in embassy circles."

"I see, well actually no I don't. Why would a murdered Russian Bolshevik be put on a train in Yorkshire?"

The band struck up "I'm Looking Over a Four Leaf Clover".

"If, for instance, he was trying to foment unrest, bringing Russian gold."

The document's pages had been hole-punched and were held together with a metal clip. At the back, there was a scrap of paper attached to the clip, where there had been another sheet.

"Mr. Yeats, don't you want me to succeed?"

"Pardon?"

"The missing pages?"

"Ah."

"Who typed this?"

"I did." He fished in his pocket and produced a flimsy folded sheet of paper. It was a pale carbon copy. "They are the sort of people the commander wouldn't want bothered, and whose word can be trusted. They have already given full cooperation."

From this list of important people in the locality, one name jumped out at me.

I placed the documents in my satchel.

"Mr. Yeats, just so that we are all clear, would you please pass my message to Mr. Woodhead? I accept the assignment."

"I hoped you would."

Our taxi reached King's Cross with time to spare. Mr. Yeats came onto the train, to see me settled in the carriage. My trusty satchel held the precious notes. I would not take it from my shoulder for the whole journey.

"Is there anything else I should know, any other titbit of information we may have missed?"

"I can tell you that the body on the train has baffled our department. At first some officers treated the incident as comical, absurd. 'If this body came in on the rhubarb train, who might we find on the liquorice train and the coal train?'—that sort of thing." He hesitated. "There must be people who cared for him, who will want to lay him to rest. He has a look of my Uncle Bob, and so I really would like to know that he will be identified."

"So would I. I will need to show the sketch to more people than have seen it so far."

His bright blue eyes looked troubled. He ran his hand through his neatly oiled hair. "I believe the prohibition is on telling his story."

"I don't know his story. None of us do. But by now hundreds of people will know how he was found. It won't remain a secret."

He did not answer, simply looked through the window at the station master taking up his position. We shook hands. "Thank you for your help, Mr. Yeats."

I went with him to the door. Stepping out onto the platform, he made way for an American couple, excusing themselves, hurrying to catch the train. I stepped aside to let them on.

DC Yeats waited. I stayed by the door, with the feeling that he was not quite ready to say goodbye. Was there something else he wanted to tell me?

"Wouldn't it be interesting, Mrs. Shackleton, if a dead person could utter just one more sentence?"

"That depends on the sentence."

"He might have accused the man who killed him."

It was an intriguing thought. There may be something he had left undone. He meant to change his will, pay back a loan, or return a borrowed book.

The train began to move. I expected Yeats to wave and turn away, but suddenly he was trotting alongside the carriage. I leaned forward to hear what he wanted to say.

"As well as the spuds there were gold coins in the sack—two spade shield George III guineas."

We gave a last wave. Not wishing to be decapitated as the train left the station, I ducked back. Perhaps what our man had left undone was the start of a workers' revolution, funded by Russian gold of British origin. Two guineas wouldn't go very far.

Had Yeats forgotten, until now, to tell me about the coins? Unlikely. This must be one more titbit of information that Commander Woodhead had intended to keep from me.

He was not to know that Yeats and I would forge a bond over an unseemly fit of the giggles.

* * *

Martin Yeats stepped from the fug of the station. He wished he was going north with Mrs. Shackleton, to follow her lines of enquiry.

She put him in mind of his mother and sisters, women who stood no nonsense. Women who earned their place in the world. He was glad he had told her about the potatoes, and the coins. Mr. Woodhead was growing forgetful.

Chapter Four

The American couple, who had caught the train at the last minute, were to be my companions for the journey. Their name was Loomis. They were from Connecticut, here for the Ryder Cup Golf Tournament.

Mr. Loomis offered to put my satchel on the rack, in a rather persistent way that made me determined to keep it close. Had I been alone in the carriage, I would have looked through the papers.

I escaped to the restaurant car and requested a table for one, where I could look through the documents privately.

In the description of the victim, there was no mention of callouses to the thumb and finger, those marks of a persistent scribe that DC Yeats thought might mark him out as an author who wrote by hand.

The disposal of the body on a train was so bizarre as to seem an act of stupidity, or panic. Yet someone had taken the time to strip him of his clothing. If I wanted rid of a body, I wouldn't put it on a train to one of the busiest stations in the Empire.

Yet perhaps there was symmetry. If the man had come north from the capital, was he simply being sent back like an unwanted parcel, possibly as a warning? But if so, a warning to whom? And who had lifted and carried such a dead weight without being noticed?

Gold coins in the sack made an interesting addition to the mystery. If Mr. Woodhead's theory about an envoy bringing Russian gold was correct, had someone interrupted the transaction, kept the lion's share for himself, and sent two gold coins back with the messenger?

When I returned to the carriage, the American couple smiled a welcome and enquired whether I had enjoyed my supper. They had eaten an enormous lunch and looked forward to a light supper at the Queens Hotel.

We talked of what they might see while they were in the area, as the golf tournament was not due to start for at least another month. I told them that they must visit the Yorkshire Dales. I named the place that is the nearest to heaven on earth that mere mortals will ever find. I told them about York and Harrogate, and the arcades and markets in Leeds and Bradford. They no longer struck me as dubious characters, but one never knows.

While we were talking of what shops might interest Mrs. Loomis, I came up with a plan that would allow me to wander about the area surrounding Ardsley without arousing suspicion. My preference would have been to go in as what I am, a private investigator. Since Mr. Woodhead insisted on my being undercover, I would be a photographic journalist, writing about the district, creating for myself a licence to be curious.

It was then that what niggled me earlier in the day came to mind. I remembered the newspaper article from last weekend, giving an account of a murder very close to the setting off point for the train that carried the unknown man.

Chapter Five

⌒

My dining room doubles as an office. Mrs. Sugden had taken off her apron. She and Sykes sat at the table. Mrs. Sugden keeps a pencil behind her ear and is never without her small leather-bound notebook.

"Mr. Sykes, Mrs. Sugden, we are working for Scotland Yard."

I explained about the unidentified man, ignominiously treated as cargo, carried to King's Cross on Friday night and into the early hours of Saturday. I placed his picture before them. "He was shot through the stomach."

Mrs. Sugden let out a sigh. "Poor fellow. There must have been an awful lot of blood."

Sykes, used to police briefings where no one speaks until the final full stop, glared at Mrs. Sugden.

"We need to know who he is, who killed him and why he was put on that train. I know it's late, so I'll understand if you want to read the file tomorrow."

Sykes reached out for the papers.

Mrs. Sugden put on her glasses. Sharing the document, they began to read the account of Scotland Yard's investigation to date. Both are quick readers but Mrs. Sugden likes to linger on a detail here and there. A little friction emerged, regarding how soon to turn the page.

I left them to it.

We have a decorative cold scuttle, too elegant to use for coal. It is where we stuff old newspapers. I took out a bundle of papers, hoping that the pertinent pages hadn't been used to light the fire.

Fortunately, what I wanted was still there.

By the time I went back into the dining room, Sykes and Mrs. Sugden had finished reading. Sykes produced Ordnance Survey maps. Had he stayed in the police force he should, with his ability, have risen through the ranks. That would have been my loss. He spread the map on the table. Once he had pointed out Ardsley, and the railway station, I placed the two rescued articles on the table, one from Saturday's first edition:

SHOPKEEPER FOUND DEAD

Police were called to a shop in Thorpefield late Friday evening. The shopkeeper, whose name has not yet been released, had been fatally wounded. The death is being treated as suspicious. At present police are releasing no further details.

The next article was on Monday, 4 March.

SHOPKEEPER MURDERED FOR PALTRY TAKINGS

Police have named the dead Thorpefield shop-keeper as Mrs. Helen Farrar of the Corner Shop, Silver Street, Thorpefield. She was found to have wounds to her head. The shop was ransacked and money taken from the cash register. A tin cash box had been broken open and emptied of its contents. Wakefield police are questioning Stephen Walmsley, aged 20, in connection with the murder and robbery. A worker at the local pit, he has lodged with Mrs. Farrar for some years. Police are appealing for witnesses. No one else is sought in connection with the death.

Mr. Sykes and Mrs. Sugden each read them.

Mrs. Sugden spoke first. "Isn't Thorpefield where your old friend lives?"

"Yes. And I do believe that it is time for me to pay her a visit."

I fished out my notebook, while Sykes measured the distance between Ardsley and Thorpefield with his finger and thumb. "The shop is a couple of miles from Ardsley station. The closest village is Rothwell."

It puzzled me that neither Commander Woodhead nor his DC had mentioned this murder. "Surely it's too much of a coincidence that on the same night, within an area of a few miles, there were two murders?"

"I'd say so," Sykes agreed.

DC Yeats and I had arranged that I could contact Scotland Yard on the line from my father's office at Wakefield Police HQ, but at this time of night that was not practical. Martin Yeats had said that his landlady did not allow telephone calls after 10 p.m., but that his room was on the ground floor, near the telephone. I took the risk.

Perhaps my clever collaborator had expected a call. The operator came back to me quickly. "Connecting you now, caller."

We had agreed on first names for any such calls.

"Martin, Kate here."

"Thought it might be."

"Does the name Mrs. Farrar ring any bells?"

There was a long pause. "Yes, but no connection."

Even if Scotland Yard didn't know the local geography, somebody should have pointed it out. Perhaps someone had, and any link had already been investigated and discarded. If so, I would be going over old ground.

"Martin, would you be so kind as to arrange for me to visit Stephen Walmsley? He's in Wakefield."

"Wakefield?"

I did not want to say on an open line that Walmsley was a resident of His Majesty's Prison. "Yes. George King is such a good host I hear."

"Ah, yes, so he is. How soon do you want to visit?"

"Soonest possible, tomorrow?"

"Will be in touch."

"Thank you." I hung up.

This was not an ideal way to communicate, but at this time of night it was preferable to finding a police station with a secure line to Scotland Yard and going through the rigmarole of an explanation before being told to ring back in the morning.

Eager Martin Yeats would enjoy his journey back to Scotland Yard, and his latest task.

I came back into the dining room and told them of my planned visit to Wakefield prison, to meet the man accused of murdering the shopkeeper. "DC Yeats says there's no connection. The motive for the murder of Mrs. Farrar appears to be robbery, but that feels too neat."

Mrs. Sugden licked her pencil and made a note. Sykes stared at his fingernails. He hates it when a person licks an indelible pencil.

Mrs. Sugden sometimes makes a little whooshing sound when she has a good idea. She did so now. "You say this man was put in a sack?"

"Yes."

"Was there ash? Might he have been some sort of penitent?"

Sykes held his tongue with difficulty. I never pooh-pooh Mrs. Sugden's odd suggestions. She sometimes has an uncanny way of coming up with a useful line of enquiry, but to keep us on track I told them Mr. Woodhead's suspicion that the man might be a foreign agitator.

Mrs. Sugden pounced. "Mediterranean, probably a Catholic. That would tie in with sackcloth and ashes."

"Except there were no ashes," Sykes said rather abruptly, "it was a sack, not sackcloth, and the man was shot."

"True, on the face of it," Mrs. Sugden agreed. "But we're not theologians." She gave him a hard stare. "And there are lots of people who are anti-Catholic."

To shift the conversation, I told them of Commander Woodhead's suspicions and DC Yeats's guesswork.

"One line of enquiry is that he was carrying cash to encourage another miners' strike, and that he was murdered for his money.

DC Yeats's thought he might be an author, because of callouses on his thumb and finger."

Mrs. Sugden made a note. "Why would anyone murder an author?"

Sykes hates it when Mrs. Sugden interrupts. "Even an author might occasionally have money."

Perhaps convening at this time of night was a mistake.

Mrs. Sugden had not finished. "I read a story where a playwright murdered a man who knew that his original play in English wasn't original at all. He'd translated it from the German without letting on." She paused for a moment. "There's a word for it."

"Whoever he was and whatever he did or didn't do, someone must miss him."

Sykes pointed to his map, tapping Ardsley. "Anyone wanting to dispose of a body round here would be spoiled for choice. Within a five mile radius, you have disused mine workings, slag heaps, fields, reservoir, woods. Go a bit farther, there's the river."

Knowing the area, I had already thought of that. "You're right, but the villages are heavily populated. As well as mines and farms, there's a mill, a school—lots of children who'll wander the fields and woods. Perhaps whoever did it wanted to give himself time to be clear of the area."

Mrs. Sugden frowned. "What happened to the man's clothes?"

It was a good question, and one of many. If we could find the man's clothes, we might find his killer.

It was getting late. My niece Harriet would be back from the second showing at the cinema very soon. "Let's all sleep on it. We'll talk again tomorrow."

Mrs. Sugden decided that it was a good idea to make cocoa. Sykes preferred a drop of whisky, and so did I.

Mrs. Sugden went into the kitchen.

Sykes pointed to the page that listed some of the people who had been told about the body, and presumably the commander's suspicions. "Your cousin is on this list."

"Yes. James isn't the only person on the list who works in government. A friend's husband is on there, too. Benjamin Brockman, a mine owner." Benjie Brockman's name was near the top of the list. "I've known Gertrude Brockman for years. We first met at riding school when we were eleven."

"Isn't Mr. Brockman something to do with the county bigwigs?"

"He's deputy to the Lord Lieutenant of the County."

"That's where you're going to invite yourself to stay!"

"Yes, though given that I'm undercover, I'll have to hope that Gertrude or Benjie will be indiscreet and confide in me."

"Will Mr. Brockman have told his wife?"

"It would be useful if he has. Commander Woodhead is keen that I don't barge in, saying that I'm investigating because Scotland Yard and CID have hit a brick wall."

"Because there's nervousness about another miners' strike?"

"That was the impression the commander gave me."

Sykes scratched his head. "Then with respect, Mrs. Shackleton, you may not be the best person to be there."

"How so?"

"If there's a need to infiltrate, it would take some horny-handed son of the soil to gain the workers' confidence."

"That would rule out all three of us, you, me and Mrs. Sugden. Shall I tender our resignation?"

He gave a small chuckle. "Where do we start?"

"Railway staff have been questioned, but if you want to go in there as LNER's visiting security inspector, I'm sure that can be arranged."

He pulled a disagreeable face. Knowing Sykes, this meant he was already considering something more devious than dressing up as a railway inspector.

"Do we have the usual expenses budget?"

"Yes. But bribery and corruption? You shock me, Mr. Sykes."

He laughed. "Shock the unshockable Shackleton? I don't think so, but there is a possibility I'll find a porter with a loose tongue and an empty pocket who likes a drink."

"That sounds like as good a start as any."

He caught the uncertainty in my voice. "You have another idea?"

Sykes is an avid supporter of cricket. He once explained how slippery ground might delay play. I felt we were on such slippery ground now, and said so.

"I'm used to slippery approaches, Mrs. Shackleton."

My next idea seemed as unlikely as some of Mrs. Sugden's notions. I mentioned my fellow passengers on the train, Mr. and Mrs. Loomis, here for the Ryder Cup. "It might just be that they are friendly Americans, but they did seem over-curious. It set me wondering if the Ryder Cup really is the main purpose of their visit."

Sykes looked suddenly cheerful. He always does when I become suspicious. "You're thinking that they could be Russians who learned to speak English in America."

"It's more to do with a possible golf connection. The dead man has callouses on his thumb and fingers—my father has the same, from playing golf."

He raised an eyebrow. "Oh?"

"Dad complains of pains in his joints. I've made poultices for his knee and elbow. The victim had swellings to his knee and elbow. DC Yeats thought he had been fit and active."

"A revolutionary who might take time off to watch the golf tournament?"

"You've heard about it?"

"The papers are full of it. Will you ask Mr. Hood to call at the golf course?"

"I won't ask Dad. I'm asking you."

"Should be interesting. I won't pass as a golfer."

"You'd pass as yourself."

"Anything is worth a try. But if Commander Woodhead believes our unknown man was here with Russian gold, he must have intelligence to that effect."

"I'm sure he has, but there was no offer to share it."

"Then I'll visit the golf club. Given all the secrecy, am I allowed to share the picture?"

"Probably not, but go ahead. We have to do this our way."

"Extra copies from my discreet printer friend?"

"Indeed."

What Mr. Woodhead didn't know wouldn't hurt him. If we succeeded, he would not dare rap my knuckles. If we failed—but I wouldn't think about that possibility.

* * *

Sykes left before Harriet arrived home from the cinema. She went to bed, blissfully unaware that we were once more on a case. Mrs. Sugden let the dog out for his last stroll about the wood, and then retired for the night. I sat at the dining room table, making a few notes. Jotting down thoughts helped me to keep those thoughts from spinning around in my head.

Finally, I took out my writing case and penned a letter to Gertrude Brockman. She knows I am a keen snapper and that I had an article in the *Amateur Photographer*. It would not surprise her to know that I intended to take photographs and write an article about Rothwell and the surrounding districts. After all, the place is rich in history. It even has the remains of what some call a castle, where the kings of old came to stay while gathering taxes and hunting wild boar to extinction.

I warmed to the idea, telling Gertrude that it would be lovely to come and stay with her, if she could put me up for a few days.

If this letter caught the first collection, it ought to be with Gertrude by tomorrow afternoon. Mad as it was at this hour, so long after midnight had struck, I put on my coat and walked to the nearest post box, on the lane. Although I tried to be quiet, Sergeant Dog heard the door open and came to accompany me.

As we were on our way back, a motorbike overtook us. Ours is a quiet street. It is unusual to hear any sound at all after 10 p.m.

The motorbike stopped by my neighbour's gate. He shone a light on the street number, and then turned away. I caught up with him as he was entering my gate, calmed the dog, and followed the man onto the path. I recognised the police motorbike and that he was a despatch rider. By some instinct, and my reassurance, Sergeant Dog decided hostilities were not in order.

"Hello, can I help you? I'm Mrs. Shackleton."

"Evening, madam—or should I say morning? I have something for you. You need to sign for it."

We went into the hall.

The envelope he handed me contained a permit signed by the Prison Governor, allowing me entry to His Majesty's Prison at Wakefield, to visit Prisoner 87513, Stephen Walmsley, at 11 a.m. later that morning.

Chapter Six

❧

Philip Goodchild met me at Wakefield railway station. He has tufts of light brown hair that turn gold in summer. He still lives next door to my parents' house, with his widowed mother. Philip was always shy, the kind of person easily dismissed as lacking by those who did not know him. When I telephoned and said I would like him to drive me to the prison, he expressed no surprise. He knows the way. He knows his way everywhere. Not only is he the best mechanic in the West Riding, he carries maps in his head. Once having completed a route, he never forgets.

As children, we simply took him for who he was. If anyone ever asked his name, he would say, "Philip and it is not an F, it is a Ph, which is a chemical symbol and stands in for F in certain words, such as phantom and philanthropy."

He ought to have been a professor. Instead, he learned everything about the maintenance of motor vehicles.

We were travelling in a van he had repaired for a grocer.

"I have to make sure the van is running right before I deliver it back. I call this a test drive. I do it every time. My customers expect it."

Through my father, Philip has repaired the vehicles of police and prison staff. If he had a proper business, he could easily find himself contracted to repair official motors.

We drew up by the prison gates.

Philip cut the engine. "You are allowed to get out. I am not permitted to stay here. This area is in the vicinity of the prison.

Civilians cannot park here. I will take the van somewhere else. When I have done that, I will come back and stand by that street lamp. I will watch for you to come out."

"I'll look for you, and come across to the street lamp." It is best to accept what Philip says. He thinks everything through and makes a plan. I guessed that he had discussed this with his mother. To suggest some other arrangement would upset him. "Thank you, PH."

He smiled. It was our childhood nickname for him. Everyone else who was part of our merry band has gone from the street. I am the only one who sometimes calls him by that name.

It was oddly comforting to have him with me.

He frowned. "You will come out, Kate?"

"Yes. I will come out."

"And you will come out of this same gate?"

"If they send me out of another gate, I will come round to this one."

He was satisfied.

Under the watchful eye of the guard, Philip drove away.

As I took the first step towards the prison, a sense of dread swept through me. Perhaps it was to do with the size of the building, the iron gates, or some memory in the air of the thousands of people brought here, heavy with fear and despair.

An earlier version of me might have heard gates clang behind me. When young and marching for the vote, I was with the suffragists. We took part in peaceful demonstrations but not everyone avoided arrest. I knew the experience of imprisonment through the stories of suffragette friends, the brutality and attempts to strip away the self. I had no wish to be a martyr; played my part, but was secretly relieved not to be incarcerated.

I took a deep breath and gave myself a little shake. I walked towards the man on the gate, permit in hand. One more deep breath and I became someone else, a person who will not be cowed by men in uniform, no matter what their rank or station. Nursing experience always stands me in good stead. And I have excellent models among my old suffrage friends, and my family. Women from my mother's and aunt's rank in life quite naturally carry an air of authority and entitlement. There is a way of shifting the shoulders and straightening the back.

The gateman had one of those faces that will always look youthful, plump cheeks, pale blue eyes, and strands of fair hair showing beneath his cap.

After a few moments I was taken across a yard towards to what appeared to be a little house. Another uniformed man pointed to a battered chair and asked me to wait. Polite and courteous, but what lies beneath?

After what seemed a day and a half but could not have been more than ten minutes, another officer entered. This man was tall and so cheerful he might have just come up trumps in a sweepstake. The sound of his boots clattered us to the main building. After that, everything merged into an opening and shutting of doors, the turning of keys and endless brightly lit corridors.

One prison officer gave way to another.

At last, I found myself ushered into a cold, whitewashed room with a high barred window. Two wooden chairs, placed with mathematical precision, stood on either side of a wide table. The prisoner sat with his head bowed. It occurred to me that this is the kind of place where one should bring cigarettes or chocolate. I had neither.

"Stephen?"

The prison officer cleared his throat. "Kindly address the prisoner by his surname, madam."

Stephen Walmsley raised his head and looked at me. Puzzled. His dark eyes were red-rimmed. He appeared confused, and why should he not be, at the sight of a stranger? The newspaper account had given his age as twenty, but he appeared younger. There was a yellowing bruise on his cheek and a cut near his lip.

"Officer, I need to speak to Mr. Walmsley alone, and will you please remove the handcuffs?"

"Can't do that for security reasons."

"I will take responsibility."

He hesitated, pursing his lips. Whatever edict had come from on high, the importance of my visit must have been made clear. I doubted it was Commander Woodhead I had to thank. More likely, DC Yeats had found a way to send a message that carried the commander's authority.

After a hesitation, he unlocked the handcuffs. "I'll be by the door, madam." He left the door open.

I closed it, imagining his ear against the other side.

Stephen rubbed his wrists, first one and then the other. There was a painful looking mark on each wrist where the handcuffs had been too tightly fastened.

"Mr. Walmsley, Stephen, I'm Mrs. Shackleton. Kate Shackleton. How are you?"

He did not answer. Neither would I in his situation. What an idiotic question. I sounded like some patronising do-gooder who might make things worse for him.

Still he did not speak.

"How are they treating you?"

He did not look at me, nor did he answer.

The sketch of the unknown man was in my pocket. I had formed an idea of showing it to him, saying that if he helped me, perhaps I could help him. That plan no longer held water.

"Have you seen a solicitor?" I should have known that. I should have found out.

It took several moments before I realised he was refusing to talk.

"I'm sorry you are in here."

At that, he looked across at me. So was he, of course. More sorry than I.

I pressed on. "Do you understand why you are here?"

He placed his hands on the table and looked down at them as if seeing them for the first time. They were workman's hands, clean, tiny cuts, the nails cut straight. "Who are you?"

"Someone who wants to find out what happened on Friday night."

"Are you here to see if I'm daft? If I'm to be sent to the loony bin?"

"Why do you think that?"

"I would have to have been more nuts than crackers to do what they say I did. Mrs. Farrar was good to me."

"Did you kill her?"

He sighed. The question was an old one now. It had been thrown at him a hundred times, along with fists. "I would never have hurt Mrs. Farrar. Everyone knows that."

"Who knows it?"

"Everyone. They came to the prison the night after I was taken. I heard them."

"Who?"

"My workmates, pals from the band, Milly and Joan."

"Milly and Joan?"

"I heard Eric playing the trumpet. I didn't hear the tambourine but I know Joan would have been bashing it. Milly would be there."

"What did they play?"

He shrugged. "Eric stopped in the middle of a note. He must've been moved on."

"Will you tell me what happened on Friday?"

"I've telled it overmuch."

"To the police?"

"Aye."

"And a solicitor?"

He gave a snort. "He were in a hurry, had better things to do."

"If you didn't kill Mrs. Farrar, tell me what you can. Perhaps I can help."

"No one can. They've made up their minds to blame me."

"At least let's try. Were you at work on Friday?"

Slowly, the story slid from him and filled the small room.

He finished his shift at the pit where he worked on the winding machinery. He went back to where he lodged, above Mrs. Farrar's shop, bringing fish and chips for them as he did on a Friday night. While they ate, the water was heating for his bath. It was band practice night. He filled the tin bath. He always did. It was too heavy for Mrs. Farrar. He took the bath into the house. She was moving about in the scullery.

While he took his bath, he noticed that everything that would polish was polished. The house smelled of lavender. She had brought in daffodils from the garden, arranged in a painted jam jar. Everything shone, as though she was expecting someone. The brasses gleamed. She had starched the antimacassar. It had been like that for a few days, no dust allowed, but she hadn't said what brought it on, and he hadn't asked.

He was glad she was cheerful because a while before she had seemed miserable. But of course, they all had.

Apart from that, all was usual. He called to her when he was ready for his back washing. She washed his back, and then left him to it.

He emptied the bath where they'd planted potatoes. He hung it back on the nail outside.

The suit he wore to band practice had been Mr. Farrar's. It fitted him right well. Mrs. Farrar was glad that there was use for it. He took his trumpet and set off for practice. He played with the Temperance Band.

After band practice, he walked Joan home. She lived on Silver Street. He wouldn't say she lodged there because Mr. and Mrs. Arkwright were more like mam and dad to her, just as Mrs. Farrar was like a gran to him. They were both lucky, him and Joan. They had been lucky up until last Friday.

"Is that where I'd find Joan, on Silver Street?"

"Number 42. She works though, at mill."

"What happened next?"

He seemed reluctant to continue. I urged him to pick up the story, wanting him to keep talking, remember the details of that evening, and that night.

They went inside, he said, him and Joan. Mrs. Arkwright had baked, she always did. As he was walking back towards Mrs. Farrar's, with buns wrapped in a tea towel, he saw two of his pals. They were going into the Miners' Institute. He didn't go with them because he knew they'd be drinking. He'd signed the pledge when he joined the Temperance Band, although he'd really only joined for the trumpet playing.

He shouted goodnight and went on his way, going round to the back of the house, the shop door being bolted. The back door was wide open. Mrs. Farrar lay on the floor by the fender. He knelt down beside her, at first thinking she'd had a fall. He went to pick her up and that was when he knew. She was dead. He didn't know what to do. He thought someone had broken in. He looked around to see if anyone was still there. No one was, but in the shop everything was chucked about, cash drawers pulled open, cash tin gone. He covered Mrs. Farrar with the counterpane from her bed. He was shaking, and lit a cigarette to calm his nerves. He knew she would hate for the place to be a mess. She kept everything just so. He began to clear up. He mopped the blood. Then he knew from the mess that it would take too long to put everything as it was. So he went for help.

Police and ambulance came. He had blood on him. They took him to the station and kept on at him all night, trying to make him say that he'd killed Mrs. Farrar.

I believed him when he said that he had not.

"Stephen, you said that Mrs. Farrar had seemed miserable, but on that day she was cheerful. Do you know what made her unhappy, and then what might have accounted for her change of mood?"

"People have their ups and downs."

"But that night was different. She'd brought flowers in the house. Did she do that often?"

He thought for a moment and then seemed suddenly interested. "No, she never did. She said they belonged outside, growing as God intended."

"Was there anything else about how she was that evening?"

"When I came in with fish and chips, she was singing. She was singing, I don't know, daft stuff. "The Grand Old Duke of York." I thought it was a bit funny for her to be singing a nursery rhyme."

"Do you think she was expecting someone?"

"She never said."

"Did she get many visitors?"

"Not really."

"Any?"

"Only neighbours coming in the shop."

I took out the sketch of the unknown man. "Have you ever seen this person?"

The question took Stephen by surprise. He looked carefully at the image.

"No." He looked at me with the same care. "Do you think he did for Mrs. Farrar?"

Without warning, the officer opened the door. "Time's up, madam."

I looked at my watch. "My time isn't up, officer. Please leave us."

Surprisingly, he did.

"Has anything unusual happened lately?"

He sighed. "I don't know. I don't know nothing since I been in here."

"Try and think. Have there been strangers about?"

"Not right round by us but the home was closed, and there's been work going on nearby." He leaned forward, suddenly eager to tell me something else. "Mebbe that's why Mrs. Farrar were upset that time. She didn't want the Bluebell Children's Home to close. None of us did. She allus visited, went to see the kids."

"The children's home?"

"Where I was fetched up. A lot of us was."

"What happened in your family?"

"Dad died. Mam went off. Mrs. Farrar allus said, 'Don't blame yer mam too much. She'll be sorry. She'll blame herself well enough one day.'"

"Mrs. Farrar sounds a good person."

He gulped, fighting back tears. "I woulda been lost without her. She took me in when I was thirteen."

The officer opened the door again, this time looking at his fob watch. "Time's up."

The officer produced handcuffs.

Stephen held out his hands. He spoke without prompting. "Tell mi friends not to fret."

The officer stood back, so that I could leave before them.

I stood in the corridor.

As he came out, Stephen said, "It musta been that made her sad, made us all sad, the home closing."

"Thank you, Stephen." I needed to come again. I should have specified that I needed more time with him. "Chin up."

It was a ridiculous thing to say to a man who must go to sleep with a noose at the back of his eyes. Words are easy to say when you are going in one direction along a corridor and a prisoner is going in the other.

Another escort appeared. I stood aside while Stephen was led away.

I turned back to look. So did he. He cast a glance of hope, and pleading, and then unaccountably began to sing, and though the prison officer barked at him, he kept on singing.

"The Grand Old Duke of York, he had ten thousand men. He marched them up to the top of the hill and he marched them down again. And when they were up they were up, and when they were down they were down, and when they were only halfway up they were neither up nor down."

My escort led me back the way we had come.

When we had left the corridors behind and were in a high-ceilinged open space, I turned to him. "I need to see the governor."

A single crumb of comfort came from the fact that Stephen Walmsley had not yet been charged with murder.

Chapter Seven

❧

Ged Adams of Middleton spared Sykes the longest time. He was one of the smaller growers, and grumbled that earning a living from the rhubarb came hard. There were so many in the game and the big boys had the advantage. They sat in the doorway of a little hut that held spades, candles and a couple of long leather aprons. Ged poured strong sweet tea into tin mugs. He looked out across all the land they could see, mist just clearing from the frosted and furrowed earth.

"Why would I put a body on a train, with acres of land to choose from?"

When they had finished the tea, and Sykes had learned how the rhubarb was taken to the station, he asked to see where the forced rhubarb grew.

"Looking for a body?"

"Just interested."

Ged lit a lamp. He opened the door into a shed with such a low ceiling that Sykes had to bend. It was warm inside, heated from a stove at the back and pipes that ran the length of the shed. In the eerie lamplight, he saw row upon row of crimson stalks with large heart-shaped leaves.

Beginning to feel he would learn nothing at all of value, Sykes next talked to Stanley Ambler of Hope Farm. Stanley tended his raised strawberry beds as he talked. "Don't believe a word of it, gov. It's a tale to give government an excuse to send spies in and see how much we're growing."

By noon, Sykes had visited nineteen of the growers whose produce went on the train that fateful Friday night. He learned that the growers started work at dawn, finished at dusk, and that nobody knew a thing, and not a single man among them noticed anything unusual.

By then, the car was filthy, the windscreen decorated with dead insects. Sykes stopped for petrol, and to have the car washed.

He drove home for a bite to eat and to warm up. Rosie was out. That's why she doesn't want a telephone, he thought as he cleaned his shoes. She thinks it would do nothing but ring when she goes out and stop the minute she comes back.

Opening his road map on the table, he checked the route to Moortown Golf Club.

He drove out of the city towards the suburbs, a pleasant enough journey. Green space, lots of trees, fresh air. This made a change from his insurance jobs. It beat visiting stuffy offices. The drive gave him time to think of how they should best go about this odd business of the man in the sack, but no inspiration came.

He had never visited a golf course. As far as he was concerned, golf was for people who didn't understand cricket. Hitting a small ball with a long stick seemed to him the worst kind of pointlessness. If the unidentified man had suffered a head wound, attributable to a blow from the sharp end of a golf club, that would be different. It would be a reason for being here. As things stood, Sykes had no great faith in Mrs. Shackleton's idea that the unknown man might have been a golfer. Golfers, guns and Russian gold did not make a good fit.

Mrs. Shackleton was blindly feeling for a starting point in the investigation, he told himself. When he did not bite at her suggestion that he go undercover as a railway security inspector, she came up with this.

The way in which the man's body had been dealt with smacked of revenge, and suggested financial shenanigans, wheeling and dealing. Perhaps the man had reneged on a debt and paid with his life. Lawlessness was rife these days, ever since the war. Even so, in all his years on the force, Sykes had never come across a link between crime and rhubarb.

The minute he drove through the gates of Moortown Golf Club, Sykes had the measure of this place. It was for people with more money than sense. All good chaps together, being jolly, scratching each other's backs. And now men were crossing the Atlantic to knock small balls around in a different country. Had nobody anything better to do these days?

For a moment or two, he stayed in the motor looking about him, considering his approach. He combed his hair, put on his hat, and climbed from the car. He told himself not to look at the bigger cars round about. First a person is pleased to be that rare creature who owns a vehicle, and then he sees all the others, newer and bigger, that belong to men who are no better than he is. Still, for all they knew, this was his Friday car.

With that cheerful thought, Sykes walked towards the clubhouse, a modest single-storey building with tiled roof. Once inside the comfortable room, with tables dotted about and a bar by the far wall, he caught the attention of a young waiter.

"A word with the senior steward, son."

"Right, sir!"

Sykes was glad there was none of that, "Who shall I say wants him?" business. He waited, looking out of the window at the vast stretch of green. A few Americans had arrived. He could pick them out. Unlike the British players in their varieties of tweed, the Americans wore a sort of uniform in navy. They sported V-neck sweaters and smart caps with a deep neb. One had draped a second sweater over his shoulders. He must be feeling the cold. In another ten minutes, they would envy the Englishmen's tweed jackets.

A player strolled into the bar, walking as if the world belonged to him. His skin was brown from the sun. He looked healthy. Perhaps Mrs. Shackleton was right. The unknown man in the artist's portrait might have been an American golfer.

The steward approached. He was a thin, balding fellow whose shoulders made points in his jacket. He spoke pleasantly enough, though seemed slightly wary. "You wanted to see me, sir? I'm Jack Braithwaite, senior steward."

"Jim Sykes, private investigator." Sykes produced his card. It had Mrs. Shackleton's telephone number. Mrs. Sugden sometimes annoyed Sykes, but she had a manner of answering the telephone that could not be faulted.

The steward stared at the card. He turned it over and looked at the back. "What can I do for you, Mr. Sykes?"

"This is a routine enquiry, Mr. Braithwaite." Sykes produced the artist's portrait of the unknown man. Let the dog see the rabbit was Sykes's philosophy. What Scotland Yard didn't know wouldn't hurt them. "I wonder if this face is familiar to you?"

The steward looked carefully at the portrait and shook his head. "No, sir, never seen him before. Should I have?"

"We think he may be a golfer."

"A wrong un?"

"We have no reason to believe so. He is a man we are trying to trace."

"Name of?"

"Unfortunately, we do not have a name."

"I get it. You think he might be one of the American players, or an American visitor?"

"Nothing so precise."

"Is this a kind of warning?"

"Not exactly."

"I get it, sir. I'll keep an eye out for him."

Of course the man didn't get it. He was guessing, playing the part of the helpful fellow. There was no possibility of Mrs. Shackleton's unknown man being recognised, unless he had a twin brother, or unless the dead revisit the earth at the time of a golf tournament.

"You won't see him here, but someone who plays golf may recognise him." This was ridiculous. Sykes began to feel like an actor in amateur dramatics, an actor who had forgotten his lines. "He may be a golfer and that is why I thought it wise to elicit your help, Mr. Braithwaite."

Having gone to the trouble and risk of paying for extra copies, Sykes made a bold decision. "I'll leave this portrait with you. Will you please show it to members of the teams?"

"I will, sir."

"Use your discretion. This isn't for the general public. We are very keen to hear whether anyone closely connected with the game recognises him. Contact me directly if you have information."

"I'll be glad to help, sir. And do you play?"

Sykes never liked admitting certain things were beyond him. "I'm a cricketer."

As he left the clubhouse, and glanced at the figures on the course, he had another reason for being profoundly glad he did not play golf.

There would be a day when everyone knew the story of the body on the train. While Sykes felt satisfied at having accomplished this morning's mission, he imagined a time when some golfer would point him out.

There's that private investigator chap. He came to Moortown Golf Club hoping to find a dead man swinging a club.

Chapter Eight

My request to see the prison governor must have been expected.

"Governor's in a meeting, madam. I can ask the senior officer if he will have a word."

"Very well."

I waited on a hard wooden bench. The atmosphere now seemed stifling. I felt my heart racing. Now I thought of questions I might have asked Stephen. As to the mystery of the man whose portrait sat crumpled in my pocket, I could think of nowhere to go with it. I had wanted justice for the unknown man, justice in some abstract way, given that it was too late for him. Now I also wanted justice for this gentle young man. Unless the real murderer of Mrs. Farrar could be found, the police would not give up on Stephen Walmsley.

After several moments, the senior officer appeared. "Can I help you, madam?"

He sat down beside me. I wished I knew what the prison governor and his staff had been told about my visit. Without that knowledge, I thought it best to keep a neutral tone and limit my questions. As someone with "high up" connections, I should not need to ask what solicitor was representing Stephen, but I did.

The reply did not surprise me. I recognised the name of a man who would take his fee and go through the motions, listening to whatever the police told him.

As if explaining one syllable words to a child, he said, "Walmsley was found with blood on his hands, madam."

"What was his motive?"

"Robbery."

In a way this was a relief because it sounded so absurd. Stephen was in work, would have a pay packet. Mrs. Farrar looked after him. He loved her like a granny. He played in a band, had friends and neighbours who would rally round. If he had battered the old woman to death, I would swallow the cherries from my mother's red hat.

"How bad was the injury to Mrs. Farrar?"

"She was struck on the back of the head with a heavy object."

"What sort of object?"

"A two-pound brass weight from her own weighing scale."

Something strange happened as I listened to his words. The shadow of a blow rippled down the back of my head, turning my neck stiff and my shoulders to iron.

It was a great relief to step out of the prison doors into the yard and an even greater relief to come through the wicket gate. Yet that weight remained. It grew heavier, as if by dark magic.

What also came out into the cool air with me was the unimaginable ache of men who had lost all hope.

* * *

Philip must have been waiting nearby, because after a couple of minutes, he appeared on the other side of the road, by our designated lamppost. He did not wave, or call, but simply stood. Waiting.

I crossed over.

Without a word, the two of us walked to where he had parked the grocery van.

When we climbed in, he asked, "Where to, Kate?"

I wanted to say, just take me home.

But I was on a case, and this might be the most important case of my life. Dear Philip, dear PH, so much passed him by. He shut out matters that might confuse him. He was waiting for instructions, a look of bovine complacency on his sweet face.

"Would you take me round where we used to play, round by the rhubarb fields? I want to do a bit of reccy."

He frowned. I had not been specific enough.

I tried again. "I want to go by the farms we used to cycle to, along the lanes that lead to the big pit. I want to go beyond Ardsley Station. There's a children's home, we saw it once."

He nodded. "It had big gates. There were swings and a slide. It was private."

"And I want to go by that shop where we bought halfpenny drinks and liquorice and lollies. It won't be open. I just want to see it."

"Why won't it be open?"

"Because the owner died."

He hesitated. "Can I ask you something before we go?"

"Of course."

"Mam keeps telling me about a big garage where I can mend the cars."

"Nearby?"

"Not far from us, along the Wakefield Road. The owner is retiring to Morecambe."

"And what does your mam say about it?"

"She wants me to think it over. The owner, Mr. Battersby, he wants me to think about it too. Why should I go to another garage? I like to be in my own garage."

"I know you do. Your mam knows you like your own garage. You are used to it."

"Yes. I'm used to it. Is she fed up of me? Is she fed up of seeing me when she looks out of the kitchen window?"

"Oh no! She thinks you might like a bigger garage."

"Well I won't."

"No one will make you move. Your mam will never be fed up of you."

This satisfied him. Without another word, he started the van.

Perhaps I had said the wrong thing. His mother must be trying to plan for when she was no longer here. What Philip would do without her, I couldn't imagine.

Whenever I drive myself in the Jowett, I attract attention. I congratulated myself on the good idea of exploring the area this way. No one would look twice at a passenger in a grocery van.

Chapter Nine

As we left Wakefield, driving along winding lanes, a vivid memory came to me from childhood. We used to cycle to the rhubarb fields, do battle with sticks of rhubarb as swords.

"Do you remember, Philip, when we played at the Trojan Wars?"

"We played at the Battle of Waterloo. Sometimes we were supposed to be fighting marauding Scots."

"And when we got hungry, we could eat our rhubarb swords."

Philip drove on, passing the fields with the sheds where the forced rhubarb grew, each shed with a track leading from gate to shed.

"I am in the process of counting the rhubarb sheds," he announced, "all of them."

"How long will that take you, driving round?"

"I am counting them on the Ordnance Survey maps. After that, I will drive round to confirm my findings. I have counted three hundred and five so far."

That was a lot of rhubarb. Was there rivalry among growers, perhaps? Or some nasty landowner who had decided he did not want unsightly sheds to mar his view? New and daunting possibilities sprang to mind.

We passed the first coal mine, its winding gear stark against a sky streaked with grey.

"I've written about that pit," Philip said.

"Are you counting coal mines?"

"Not yet."

"What did you write?"

"All its facts. How deep it is, how much coal it gives, the names of men who died there."

"Just that pit?"

"For now. I will write about them all. I have written about rhubarb, all the facts."

"Philip, what you said ties in with an idea I've had."

He smiled. "Do you want to read my facts?"

"Yes. I'd like that."

"Which ones?"

"The facts about the rhubarb, to begin with."

We drove on. I asked to do a short detour, passing Ardsley Railway Station. It had a small station office, and extensive sidings.

Philip stayed in the van. I took my camera, went into the station, making a show of looking at the timetable for passenger trains. I then walked along the platform to where a goods train stood. A truck door was open. This may have been where the unknown man was brought. Perhaps someone had conveniently left a truck door open on that day, too.

If I asked questions, I'd stick out like a sore thumb. Already attracting attention, I put the camera back in my satchel. This part of the investigation would be best left to Sykes.

We drove on. Philip pulled in to the side of the narrow lane, allowing a herd of cows to waddle to their milking parlour.

As he set off, a horse and cart loaded with a bed, a couple of chairs and a table came dangerously close. The wobbling furniture, not very well secured with rope, seemed an apt image for the enormity of my task. With little to go on, and hampered by the instruction to investigate with discretion, I felt like a person playing with dice loaded in favour of the tables.

I had always thought of Thorpefield as a village, but of course it is just a hamlet. We came in on the back lane and came close to the

Corner Shop that we used to call the halfpenny drinks shop. "Slow down, Philip, please."

"It's closed," Philip said. "No drinks today."

The shop stood alone. The large rear garden bordered adjacent fields. It would be possible for someone to come across those fields unnoticed and enter the house part of the building from the back.

"Keep going, Philip, just drive up one street and down the next."

"Someone robbed that shop," he said. "Someone killed the halfpenny drinks lady."

"Yes."

He drove up Silver Street, the first in a row of workers' cottages. Number 42, last in the row, was where Stephen walked with Joan after band practice. I imagined the police going door to door, asking questions. But perhaps they had not needed to ask questions, when they found Stephen Walmsley with blood on his hands.

"Kate, why would someone rob a little shop when there are big shops?"

"I don't know. What do you think?"

"There are no big shops in this village. Everywhere else there are Co-operative Stores. Here there are none."

"I hadn't thought of that."

"Are you investigating?"

"I know you can you keep a secret, Philip."

"I never told how far we used to come, and how we got sick on the rhubarb."

"I hope to be back here very soon, to start investigating."

He nodded. "Is there anything else you want to see?"

Stephen Walmsley had mentioned the children's home. "Philip, where is that orphanage with the big gates? I can't get my bearings."

He turned left onto a narrow lane. It wound round behind the area of housing. The way grew dusty, and I soon saw why.

The gates were gone, and so were the swings and slide. The ground was churned.

Philip stopped the van.

The only sound was the creaking of wheels as a woman pushed an old pram along the lane.

I glanced out to see the baby, but saw only the stone figure of an angel with a chipped wing. The woman saw me looking. "It's a crying shame," she said. "Something has to be saved from that fine place."

She didn't stop.

Philip drove a few more yards. Where a house once stood, there was nothing. The children's home was gone. Piles of rubble made a sad pattern across the grounds.

I had seen enough. We turned back.

Philip was enjoying our drive. He stopped by a lane where in summer the trees reach across and touch each other, forming a green canopy.

"We called this the fairy way, do you remember, Kate?"

"Yes. Thorpefield Manor, my friend Gertrude's house, is up there. I don't want to be spotted snooping."

"Why not?"

"Because I've written to her, inviting myself to stay. She would think it odd if she sees me before she has had time to reply."

"Does she know that you are investigating?"

"No."

"Will you be safe?"

"Yes."

He took one hand from the wheel. "Thorpefield Manor is very old. In the wall, there are bee boles. I'll leave my treatise on rhubarb in the third bee bole from the gate. The bees don't go there now. They prefer a different hive."

"Well, thank you." It was always a good idea to go along with Philip's suggestions. Alternative ideas might lead to upsetting confusion.

"And if you need me, Kate, leave a message in that same bee bole."

Chapter Ten

❧

Success! I came home to a message on the hall table. Gertrude had telephoned.

> *Mrs. Brockman delighted for you to come. Telephone her about a time.*

I put in the call to Gertrude before taking off my coat.

The butler answered. I remembered his sonorous voice. Over the telephone, he sounded as though he might be speaking from beyond the grave.

Gertrude was not long in picking up.

"I'm thrilled that you're coming to stay, Kate. We've so much to talk about. Can you come tomorrow?"

"That would be perfect."

"Now, I wanted to ask, will you be bringing a maid?"

"Gertrude, you know that I don't have a maid."

"Ah, I'd forgotten. Not to worry."

"And I don't need a maid."

"If you say so!" She continued. "I've arranged a small dinner party for tomorrow evening."

"That sounds lovely." I sensed the appearance of a man without a wife, to be carefully seated within pass-the-salt distance.

"Oh, and we will go riding. I have just the horse for you."

Preparing the ground, I told her more about my magazine commission, making it up as I went along. Riding would give me the opportunity to see places of local interest, but then she mustn't think me rude that I would need some time to explore alone.

Naturally she was keen to help me in this imaginary endeavour.

Sykes arrived as Gertrude and I wound up our conversation.

My bloodhound lay on the kitchen floor, appearing to listen. I swear he senses when I am planning to go away, although he does have a permanently sulky impression which he cannot help.

Sykes, Mrs. Sugden and I sat at my kitchen table with cups of tea. Sykes gave a cheerful account of having strayed into the foreign territory of a golf club, and a less than cheerful account of visiting rhubarb growers.

We checked which growers he had called on, and the farms still to be visited. I made a note of some names. "Since I'll be staying at Thorpefield, I'll call at some of the local farms. Growers may be more relaxed about talking to someone who will take their photograph and show an interest in the business."

"Good luck with that," Sykes grunted.

Mrs. Sugden pushed her notebook towards me. "I consulted the directories, like you said. These are the names and addresses of estate agents in the area. Shall I ask to be notified of any corner shop or general store that becomes available?"

I thought for a moment. The shop would be owned by Benjie and Gertrude. Everything in Thorpefield was their possession. Yet estate agents would be unlikely to pass on a familiar telephone number to Gertrude. She would not be dealing with such a matter herself. "Yes, you do that Mrs. Sugden."

I told them about my visit to the prison to talk to Stephen Walmsley. "I have a feeling we are onto something, but I don't know what."

Mrs. Sugden made a note. "And did this fellow do it? Did he kill the shopkeeper?"

"I don't believe he did."

Sykes tried to disguise a sigh. When he is about to question my judgement for not rushing to a guilty verdict, he prefaces the comments with two words. I glared at him, waiting for the words: "With respect".

He thought better of it, adopting a position of patient thoughtfulness, making a steeple of his fingers. "Stephen Walmsley had blood on his hands. The puzzle is that he hasn't been charged."

"Perhaps the puzzle is insufficient evidence. He went to Mrs. Farrar's assistance, as he thought. Isn't that a normal reaction from a young person who was close to her?"

Sykes appeared to consider this, but said nothing.

Eventually, he came round to what worried him. "A clumsy deadly assault and robbery is a different type of crime altogether from the man shot and put on the train. I'm not sure considering the shopkeeper's case will take us closer to discovering our man's identity."

"All the same I want us to find out more. Perhaps I'll be in a position to do that at Thorpefield."

Sykes wore his Doubting Thomas face. "You said yourself Mr. Brockman is unlikely to confide in you. As deputy Lord Lieutenant of the County, he'll have signed the Official Secrets Act. Suspicions about political activity will make it difficult for him."

"Gertrude hasn't signed, as far as I know. And it's the best way in that comes to mind."

"I don't like the sound of this, Mrs. Shackleton. Wakefield CID and Scotland Yard have painted themselves into corners. Now they bounce you centre stage."

Sykes was right, but he can be a bit of a nay-sayer at times. He would have been more optimistic had he come back with some useful titbit from the rhubarb growers, or the golf club. "I want us to do well on this. It might be the biggest job we've had. If we succeed where others have failed, the credit will be greater."

Sykes had been looking again at the reports of Mrs. Farrar's murder. Now he glanced up. "Stephen Walmsley. What's he like?"

That seemed like changing his tune, but it was how we worked when we came at a case with our different prejudices. I described Stephen, his youth, his quiet demeanour, his sincerity.

Sykes spoke with infinite and annoying patience. "Did he say anything that would convince a jury that he was not guilty?"

"None of us can answer that. It would depend on what sort of case can be made against him, or for him. He had been roughed up, yet he stuck to his story. I believed him."

"I'm sorry to say this, Mrs. Shackleton –"

"No you are not."

"You would believe him, because you want that to be true."

Of course I wanted that to be true. I hated the thought that someone who seems perfectly decent and truthful could commit a violent act. "If you met him, I believe you would also doubt his guilt."

I knew what worried Sykes, before he said it.

"You can't bear the thought of some likeable young chap going to the gallows. That's why you are a detective, and not a judge." Rewarding himself for this magnificent insight, he took a gulp of tea.

"There may be other reasons that I'm not a judge. If an appointment to the King's Bench comes my way, I might just say yes."

Sykes laughed so suddenly that he spluttered his tea.

"Meanwhile, I will presume young Walmsley not guilty, and so should you."

Chapter Eleven

I drove the scenic route, through Rothwell. Beyond Carlton and Robin Hood, an old stone sign by the side of the lane announces THORPEFIELD. I turned up the lane.

All this land was part of the Brockman estate. The family seemed never to make up its mind whether to give the area entirely over to coal, or go on with the agricultural uses that pre-dated mining.

Suddenly finding myself in the wake of a horse and cart, I slowed. Horse, cart and rider turned off by the common.

Thorpefield Manor came into view as I rounded the bend, and then disappeared and reappeared, in a game of hide and seek as the lane twisted and turned. There is a wood across from the house and grounds. With the promise of spring, the leaves had begun to turn green.

The gates to the manor house stood open. A long and winding drive led to the house, which came into view as the drive made its final curve. It is an imposing early Victorian villa built of local stone. Weak sunlight cast the shadow of the house onto its forecourt. Slowly, I drove into the shadow. The stone balustrade had deteriorated since my last visit. Paint peeled from the door. This surprised me. Gertrude was such a stickler, conscious of her social position.

Someone had heard the car.

Moments later, as I was getting out of the car, a young man appeared. A slight young chap, he had black curling hair, the face of an angel, and the brightest of blue eyes. He brought with him the scent of hay and horses. Something about him was oddly familiar.

"Mrs. Shackleton!"

"Yes."

"I was looking out for you, madam. I'll take your car to the garage."

"Thank you. We haven't met before?"

"I'm Alec. I look after the horses and I'm learning to be a mechanic."

He didn't look old enough. "That's a big responsibility for a young chap."

"I'll be sixteen next month!" Smiling, he picked up my camera bag.

By now, someone else had heard my approach. The big oak door creaked opened. There stood the imposing figure of Benjie's loyal, long-serving butler.

"Hello, Raynor."

Alec deposited my camera bag on the top step and hared away without a word.

Raynor picked up the bag with his little finger. He presents an imposing, almost formidable, figure. In the days when butlers were said to be paid according to height and breadth, he would have earned good money.

Raynor inclined his large head. "Welcome back, Mrs. Shackleton."

I once saw a play based on the Dracula story. Raynor, with his, long pale face and deep-set eyes, looked so like the leading man that it was uncanny. On a previous visit, I had to repeat to myself: his name is Raynor. He is not Count Dracula.

Gertrude came smiling down the broad staircase to meet me. Tall and slender, she wore a light jersey sweater and skirt ensemble in a combination of grey and pale green.

"Kate! It's been too long."

"Lovely to see you, Gertrude."

I hate to feel a hypocrite but it would be worse to tell the truth: it is good to see you, but what I really want is to solve the case and go.

"I thought I would never entice you here again. Not that I blame you. We are as godforsaken and isolated as ever."

"I'm sure that's not true. What do you say, Raynor?" I shrugged off my motoring coat.

Raynor was quick to take my coat. "We shall never compete with Piccadilly Circus, but people come and go. Only yesterday we had a person driving farm to farm, questioning the rhubarb growers."

Raynor looked at Gertrude, and then at me. It seemed as if he was warning her, or me.

"Really? I hope it's not someone else writing about the area, and beating me to it."

Gertrude had been about to say something, but Raynor walked away. Even in soft shoes, he has a way of making himself heard.

It was a good thing that Gertrude did not press the butler for more information. I felt sure that if Raynor told us about the visitor and his odd enquiries, the stranger would turn out to be a man who drove a Jowett car, wore black, and looked like a policeman. I say very little about my work as a rule, but over the years I may have mentioned my assistant.

She led me into the music room. "Raynor can be a little odd these days. We make allowances. Benjie relies on him."

"Yes I suppose he would."

Raynor has been with Benjie since he was a boy.

Sykes would be mortified to know that his discreet enquiries had become a focus for attention.

We sat by the window, agreeing that it was not too early to have a cocktail, which Gertrude mixed. "And you have an important mission while you're here?"

"If you call a photographic essay important."

"Oh I do. And you hinted you might abandon me."

"Not abandon."

"Good, because I have such plans for us, Kate. And as soon as you've freshened up, you must tell me all about your exciting idea."

After we had chatted and finished our cocktails, Gertrude rang for the maid.

A fair-haired young woman with a nervous manner came into the room, straightening her cap.

Gertrude turned to her. "Milly, show Mrs. Shackleton to her room."

Milly thought about an answer and finally muttered a reply.

"Milly's looking forward to taking care of you."

This statement took Milly by surprise. She began to blink rapidly.

I tried to put her at her ease as we walked upstairs, asking how long she had worked here. Not very long.

It interested me that Milly was one of the names Stephen Walmsley had mentioned. His pals had come to the prison on the night he was arrested—his friends from the band, and Milly and Joan.

There was jug and bowl in the room. As Milly hung my clothes, I washed the grime from my face and combed my hair.

I took out the photographs I had brought to show Gertrude. There we were, at the age of twelve, with our ponies.

In the photograph of their wedding, Gertrude and Benjie looked so well matched and happy.

Milly stared. "Goodness, how could he have been at that wedding?" She was pointing to Benjie's younger brother, who had been his best man.

"I shouldn't think it's anyone you know. You weren't born then."

Yet I guessed who she thought it was, and I was right.

"He looks just like Alec Taylor. Or I suppose I should say Alec Taylor looks like him."

I whipped the photograph away. "You mean the stable lad who took charge of my car? Perhaps superficially, but I don't think so."

She gave me an odd look, and why not? The resemblance was striking. Benjie's brother, Michael, and the stable lad, Alec, could have been twins, or father and son. Except that Michael died young. He did not live long enough to father a child who was now going on sixteen.

"I have a better one of Mr. and Mrs. Brockman's wedding." It wouldn't do to remind Benjie of the brother he loved.

Millie perked up when she saw the cameras.

"You take photographs, Mrs. Shackleton?"

"I do." Might as well rehearse my story. "I'm going to write a piece about people who live in the area, how they spend their time, where they work, what hobbies and such like, and I'll take pictures."

"I'd like my picture taking but there's nothing interesting about me."

"That can't be true. I'm sure of it, after knowing you for just a few minutes. What do you do on your day off?"

"I'm a Sunday school teacher at the chapel."

"Well then, there you are. Very interesting. I'll take your picture tomorrow in your Sunday best."

"Thank you."

She looked far from pleased. Either a girl with mercurial moods or my mention of Sunday clothes upset her.

She turned away, and began to inspect my clothing, pouncing on a skirt and blouse that she claimed would benefit from having an iron run over them. She would have dashed from the room. I stopped her with a question.

"Where were you before you came to work here?"

It would be too good to be true if she said she lived on a rhubarb farm, and last time she visited home, had helped put a body in a sack.

"At home with mi mam and brothers, in Robin Hood." She said that as if she would have preferred to stay there.

"And what about the young groom, Alec? Where was he before coming to live here?"

"He was in the children's home. They fetched him out of it, or Mr. Brockman did."

Unable to admit that I had been snooping about the area, and seeing the deserted ground where the orphanage had stood, I said, "Are there many children there now?"

"Oh no, madam. You see they all had to be moved."

"Why was that?"

"Subsidence. There's mine works all under that area. The children had to be moved away so that the earth wouldn't swallow them."

Chapter Twelve

Gertrude and I settled ourselves in wing chairs by the bay window in the music room. "Now tell me about this plan of yours, Kate."

I outlined my idea for an article about the area, illustrated with photographs of local people and places.

"We're rather dull here, not exactly *National Geographic* material."

"Nonsense! The minute Benjie comes home I want a picture of you in your place of choice—the lord and lady of the manor. I hope you can rustle up a dog and a gun."

"And country tweeds?"

"Not necessary, but if you insist."

She sighed. "Not sure about a portrait. We're looking a bit shabby just now –"

"You are not!"

"We might brush up well enough but the house isn't at its best. Don't tell me you didn't notice."

"In a house this age and this size, there'll always be something to do."

"You're right there. We took a hammering with the death duties, hanging over from when Benjie inherited."

"I'm sorry to hear that."

"Nothing to be done, Kate. One puts on a brave face but the strike added to our woes. We saved on wages of course. I can't tell you how much we lost by having to leave coal in the ground. After the neglect there was a huge amount of maintenance. Royds pit was in no fit state to re-open, just not viable."

I felt a wave of sympathy for Gertrude. "It must have been hard to see your workers and their families struggling to survive."

"As Benjie likes to point out to me, they had donations and money from all over the place. Don't start him on this. He'll tell you all about a delegation of Labour women going to Russia."

"From here?"

"From the Northeast, but it's all the same to him. Of course Raynor is gung-ho along with him. They spent hours in the study, plotting against the plotters."

Much as I appreciated Gertrude and Benjie's position, I felt greater sympathy for the miners and their families. "It's a pity the miners had to look abroad for support."

"According to Benjie, they got support aplenty. He'll tell you those women came back with vodka, caviar, Russian gold and instructions for sedition."

Russian gold. Where had I heard that before? Commander Woodhead and Benjie Brockman would get on very well. "And what do you think, Gertrude?"

"I just wish that strike had never happened." She poured tea.

I changed the subject. It was too soon to start probing and arouse suspicion. "Do you remember this?"

"Indeed I do!"

It was a picture of Gertrude and me with our ponies, taken on my camera by our riding mistress. I brought out one of her wedding day. I had snapped her with her bridesmaids, a cousin and her little nieces. In another candid and slightly grainy snapshot—not one of my best—Gertrude was standing with her mother on their lawn.

For a little while, we reminisced.

When the right moment came, I asked her what had happened to the children's home. "Milly said it was demolished?"

"Yes. It turned out to be in danger of subsiding. We couldn't take the risk of just leaving it."

"Where are the children?"

"They're in good hands. I saw to that."

"It was a grand old house. We used to look through the railings when we cycled out this way as children. Wasn't it called the Bluebell Home?"

"Everyone called it that, because of the Bluebell Wood nearby."

"Couldn't it have been shored up in some way, to make it safe?"

"Benjie had already looked into all the possibilities. And so did our fellow trustee, Eliot, but no. It would have cost more to preserve than to re-build. There wasn't sufficient money in the trust fund to do either, unfortunately."

"So, where did the children go?"

"To a very well run orphanage in Wakefield." Her eyes widened. "Oh, Kate, you're interested in adopting. I never thought, or I would have asked you over before the children left."

Adoption never occurred to me, and I said so. "I've semi-adopted my niece Harriet, that's enough for me."

And then suddenly, without preamble, she said. "I'm barren, Kate. We have tried so determinedly to have a child, which has been a great pleasure for both Benjie and me, but there it is."

I was so taken aback by her sudden intimate confidence that I did not know what to say. "I'm sorry."

"Don't be. You are in the same situation, childless, but with good reason."

"Have you seen a doctor?"

"Several, and the best. I stayed with an infirm old aunt in Surrey, taking care of her. She told me about the daughter of an acquaintance who went to a clinic run by a Harley Street chap, and I gave it a try."

"I'd no idea." This was a side to Gertrude I had not seen. It surprised me to think of her taking care of an old aunt. As to children, she has always put herself and Benjie first. I suppose having an heir was important, but neither she nor Benjie had seemed to mind.

"I've been poked and prodded and operated on, to no avail."

"Do you think it might Benjie's difficulty rather than yours?"

Her look of surprise seemed to say that this had never occurred to her. "Heavens no! Even if it is, it couldn't be admitted, if you see what I mean. So I have made a decision to adopt. Do you think that's shocking?"

"It would be odd if I thought that shocking. I'm adopted."

"Never!"

"I don't go around saying it, but it's not something I would hide."

"Then I'm glad I've told you. You are the perfect person to stand by me and persuade Benjie that I'm doing the right thing."

"Why, what does he say?"

"He refuses to discuss the matter. I have visited the National Adoption Society's office in Baker Street. I intend that we should choose a baby."

"Why London? Aren't there children nearby that you might consider? What about all the children who have just gone to the orphanage in Wakefield?"

She hesitated. "This may sound hard-hearted, but I don't want just any child. It could be from some poor creature who got herself into trouble up a back alley on a dark night and ended up in the workhouse. I want an intelligent child. The Adoption Society takes family histories. They have babies whose lineage is impeccable."

I could not think what to say. No one would describe my heritage as impeccable, yet I had turned out well. "You would be giving a child a good chance in life, Gertrude."

"And taking a big risk myself. No, Kate, harsh as this may seem, I want a baby from a good source. There wasn't one Bluebell child I would have wanted, none I could have taken to my heart."

I tried to think fast, and avoid involvement without seeming unkind, or shocked at her callousness. After all, I had never considered adopting. It must be something that begins to loom huge, large as life—because that is just what it is. Life.

"Then if you're set on it, I'm sure you'll persuade Benjie."

"One infant might jump out straight away, so to speak. Benjie would be more detached than I in considering lineage and so on."

I doubted anyone would be more detached than Gertrude.

In one of those sudden insights that might turn out to be completely wrong, I wondered if the existence of Alec confirmed Gertrude's feeling that barrenness was her burden, and not Benjie's. Benjie had brought Alec to Thorpefield Manor. He was a potential heir. Gertrude could not have missed the Brockman family resemblance.

Fortunately, she left that subject hanging and asked me about my fascinating project.

"Let me take a picture of you, on the window seat—that outfit is just perfect. And as soon as Benjie comes home, if the light's still good, I'll capture the two of you for posterity."

"He'll like that. He's had rather a lot on his mind lately."

I resisted the urge to appear to curious and ask what was on his mind. There would be a better moment for that.

"You both take a good photograph. I think young Milly will too. She tells me she's a Sunday school teacher, so perhaps I'll photograph her in her Sunday best."

"Oh take her in uniform, her best is rather shabby. But I suppose that won't show up in photographs."

"Everything looks better if the light is kind."

"Did Milly look after you?"

"Perfectly."

"If you're not accustomed to having a maid, I suppose you won't mind her clumsiness."

"What is her background?"

"She's the late child of a feckless widowed mother. For a short time, I had a girl from the children's home, where they were properly trained, but she turned into a rude minx when she realised she could find work in the mill."

A shaft of light made the window seat the perfect spot for Gertrude. I chatted, hoping to make her feel less self-conscious when I took her photograph. "It's such a shame that the Bluebell Home had to close."

"Yes it was a blow."

"I would have liked a picture."

"We might have one somewhere, in the Trust Fund files."

"That would be good. And there's a camera club in Rothwell. I've met some of the members from there. I'll probably say hello to one or two, offer to include some of their pictures. Snappers can be jealous of their own territory."

Gertrude laughed. "You'll endear yourself to them I'm sure."

Benjie arrived home while the afternoon was still light. He is one of those men who must bend over backwards to prove that his wife's widowed friend is the person he is most delighted to welcome into his home.

He did not look like a man who has had rather a lot on his mind lately. But then, I probably did not look like a woman working for Scotland Yard.

"Kate m'dear, so lovely to see you. Your name came up today."

"Oh?" I am used to Benjie's banter but hadn't expected him to tell me that I was mentioned at a county event.

"You've gathered quite a reputation over the years. The missing maharajah, the library business, and then that unfortunate incident that marred the day in Haworth."

"I didn't realise I was so under discussion, Benjie."

"So what mystery brings you to our neck of the woods?"

"No mystery. I'm here on an assignment —"

"I'm sure you are."

"For a magazine."

Gertrude tutted at Benjie. "Stop teasing. Kate is here to take photographs and write about this neglected part of Yorkshire, and why not? It's all Harrogate and York and picturesque coastlines, and the importance and grandeur of Bradford. We matter too."

He gave a mock bow. "You must be right, Gertrude. Kate is not here undercover for some nefarious reason. She would not do such a thing in the house of her old friends."

"Absolutely not," I said. "Benjie, you ought to be writing novels."

My heart was beating a little too fast. He knew.

I picked up my camera. "Benjie, you look handsome as ever. Now don't prevaricate."

Gertrude winked at me. "He always comes back from these official dos full of himself. And I don't know why. It's usually overseas businessmen here to pick British brains. Hope you didn't tell Johnny Foreigner we're putting the mill on short time."

At the mention of short time, Benjie looked suddenly glum.

I looked at my friends through the camera. As they put on their best faces, not a whit of discord or anxiety showed. They were, for that instant, lord and lady of the manor, without a care in the world.

After the photograph, Benjie rang for Raynor. The two retreated to the library.

Gertrude sighed. "What other husband would regard his butler as chief financial adviser?"

"Quite a few I should think."

"It's not as if I came empty-handed into this marriage. That mill was my father's. It just happened to be on Benjie's family land."

Gertrude is an expert embroiderer, and that seems to be her refuge. She moved to her usual chair and picked up her needle.

Glancing through the window, I noticed the light, and the shadows made by the poplar trees.

"Gertrude, I'm inclined to take a stroll, while we still have the afternoon light. Will you come?"

"You go, Kate." She smiled. "Never let it be said that I come between an artist and her inspiration."

I needed to think. Gertrude was unlikely to be of much help. So taken up with this new idea of adoption, she had probably paid no attention to someone coming to talk to Benjie about a body on a train. He was behaving abominably, by hinting that he knew I was on a case. Either he should come out with it, or keep quiet. So much for the Official Secrets Act.

Chapter Thirteen

I walked through the grounds to the walled garden, making my way towards the bee boles. Philip had indeed left his treatise on rhubarb in the third bole. The sheet was rolled, tied with a narrow strip of ribbon and with a small square of paper tucked into the ribbon. Good old Philip. If Gertrude asked me about my plans, I would at least have all sorts of information about rhubarb for my imaginary article.

The voice startled me. "Are you interested in bee boles, Mrs. Shackleton?"

I turned to see Raynor. He must have seen me from the library window, and followed. He could not miss that I held something in my hand, but had he seen me pick it up?

"There were bee boles where I stayed last year." I pushed Philip's roll of paper up my sleeve. "Such a pity these aren't in use any more."

"The hives are far more practical, but I do agree. There is something poetic about ancient beekeeping."

Time to divert him from what might appear odd behaviour, and a feigned interest in the living quarters of bygone bees.

"I've been explaining to Mr. and Mrs. Brockman that I'm creating a photographic essay about people and places, including this house and its occupants. I should love to take your photograph."

He gave a small embarrassed laugh. "I am not considered an oil painting, Mrs. Shackleton."

"But you have character, Raynor, and to my mind that is far more impressive."

"I don't know what to say. I am overcome at the thought of a portrait."

Perhaps it was my imagination, but there seemed a mocking edge to his tone. Gertrude may not have known that Benjie was asked about the man on the train, Raynor most certainly would know. I had always had the impression that there were no secrets between Benjie and his butler.

"Raynor, wait here while I fetch my camera."

"The bag in the music room?"

"Yes."

"Then let me, Mrs. Shackleton." Raynor smiled agreement at his own sudden decision, all at once eager to have his picture taken.

When he had gone, I read the message that Philip had tucked in with his treatise on rhubarb:

Leave a note if you need help.

What on earth did he imagine might happen?

But he was making a good point. I should have set up some code, some way of keeping Sykes and Mrs. Sugden up to date on my progress, or lack of it. Of course there was a telephone here.

I had a long time to consider this as Raynor did not come back as quickly as he went. His lengthy absence could be accounted for by the amount of pomade on his hair, a fresh starched collar and a pair of patent shoes that he admitted to wearing infrequently on the grounds that they nipped.

We chose his favoured spot, by the sundial in the walled garden, another by the gate.

"Shouldn't I have one with the house in the background, as an indication of my position?"

"Yes of course, if that's what you would like. But let's try taking a picture in the wood if we can find the right spot."

"I know just the place. There's a glade where I sit sometimes, just for a few moments' contemplation." He began to walk, leading the way to his private place.

In the centre of a clearing was a carved seat carefully wrought with a back and arm rests.

He turned to me. "It's not too dark?"

"It will be in another hour, but not now."

"Jimmy Noakes the gardener created this, when he came back from the war. The dream of it kept him going during his time in the trenches. He lived for the moment when he could come back, and make this chair from a tree that fell before it all began. He thought of sitting here, listening to birdsong, hearing a gentle wind disturb the leaves."

"This is a beautiful spot."

"He said for me to feel free to sit here whenever I want, even though I passed the war in the admiralty with Mr. Brockman." He sat down.

Sometimes the very first shot is the right one, and I felt that. All the same, I took a few more, just to be certain.

When we were finished, and walking back to the house, I asked Raynor about using the telephone to speak to my housekeeper.

"Of course. You can use the telephone in the hall, unless you would like privacy."

"The telephone in the hall will be fine."

"I'll leave you to it." He opened the door to Benjie's study. "Some papers for me to sort for Mr. Brockman."

He closed the study door behind him."

I put in the call, and waited for the operator to ring back.

After a few minutes, I was speaking to Mrs. Sugden.

I kept the conversation short. Would she let my mother know I would not be there for Sunday dinner? She would, and assured me all was well at the house, and with Harriet and the dog. We said goodbye. She hung up. I waited. There was a click on the line.

Someone had listened in.

It would not be safe for me to make calls from Thorpefield Manor.

Later, I asked Milly. "Are there many telephones in the house?"

"The one in the hall, Mrs. Brockman's bedroom, and Mr. Brockman's study."

Benjie had set Raynor to spy on me. It was nothing to worry about. We were on the same side, after all, but I needed to stay in touch with Sykes and Mrs. Sugden. Perhaps Philip's idea about my leaving messages in the third bee bole was not so outlandish.

I went up to my room, to read Philip's schoolboy treatise on rhubarb. He must have scoured his dictionaries and encyclopaedias, probably after one of our illicit cycling trips to the rhubarb fields. We were all so very young, thought we knew everything, and that grown-ups were extremely dense.

Chapter Fourteen

RHUBARB by Philip Goodchild, age 11, of Wakefield, Yorkshire, England, Great Britain, the World

Rhubarb, roó barb, n. a plant whose leaf-stalks are used for
culinary purposes, and its root used in medicine as a purgative.

A perennial long-living herb (Rheum rhaponticum) native
to Siberia and related to dock; heart-shaped, wavy leaves can
be poisonous; 6-petalled small white flowers; edible stalks, red
or green. (Family: Polygonaceae)

In the Opium War (1839–42) the Chinese authorities
stopped exports of rhubarb in the belief that British soldiers
would give up the fight when constipated. They were wrong.

I am proud to live in the heart of Yorkshire's Rhubarb Country in the frost pocket below the Pennines where market garden-
ers know what to do with the land to make it fertile. Some say
the ground is like the ground of Siberia. We have much rain,
plentiful coal and coke to heat the rhubarb sheds and shoddy
from the mills that contains nitrogen and does the roots good.
It is as if they are covered by a cloak that feeds them.

First of all the plant was used as a medicine for the gut
and inner organs. Marco Polo brought the drug to Europe and
to Britain where it did not work as a medicine. Only rich people could afford it as it was three times as expensive as opium
and gave them the runs. It was used to bake pies instead.

Some people write that in Chelsea Physic Gardens in 1817 rhubarb roots were accidentally covered by a plant pot over the winter. When the plant pot was moved in the spring, tender shoots were discovered. This was the start of the rhubarb we now grow and call Forced Rhubarb. This is poppycock. I happen to know the real fact. A gardener from Rothwell found this out, not a person from Chelsea. These roots were then forced in sheds in the dark.

Forced rhubarb is pink or red and is good for you. Here is my own experience of going into a rhubarb shed with my next door neighbour Kate Hood and our friends.

It was February. The ground was frosty. There was frost on the hedgerows. We left our bikes by the road and walked along the edge of the fields. Bobby's uncle works with the rhubarb so we know things about being careful. Outside the shed were two very heavy spades. This is because rhubarb roots weigh as much as a robust child or even more. Only heavy spades can lift the roots which must not be damaged. It was completely dark in the shed and warm as well because no air comes in and the rhubarb likes to be hot and heat comes along the pipes from the stove. We brought a whole box of matches and a candle. Candles are what the men use when they lift the rhubarb. Kate said that the rhubarb knows there is light above the roof and that is why it reaches up and grows. We each took it in turns to hold a candle under our chins, to look like a terrifying creature.

We did not break off the shed rhubarb. The rhubarb in the sheds is special. Kate says perhaps it hears us. We hear it, when it pops. Some children eat raw rhubarb because they are hungry. Some boys and girls pretend a stick of rhubarb is a sword.

My mother bakes rhubarb pie. She buys a big orange and squeezes juice onto the rhubarb. I do not like rhubarb pie. My dad does not like rhubarb pie. We eat it. Dad says, "That was up to your usual standard, love."

I say nothing.

Chapter Fifteen

The oak-panelled dining room at Thorpefield Manor is mock Tudor. The fireplace would hold an ox. Plentiful coal ensured a huge fire. A certain amount of smoke belched into the room. The heat did not travel as far as the long table where we took our seats. In spite of the chill, and the need for shawls, it is a magical room. The chandelier above the table holds fat candles whose dripping wax had created intriguing shapes.

We were five for dinner. Benjamin sat at one end of the table and Gertrude at the other. The thought came to me that when they grew old, they might need speaking trumpets to hear each other across that distance. Opposite me was their friend and business partner, Eliot Dell. If you saw Eliot on the street, you would know he was well off. His suits are made by the best tailor on North Street in Leeds, who it is said knocks all London tailors into a cocked hat. Their money comes from land. He is flaxen-haired, with deep-set blue eyes, a generous nose, slightly pointy ears, and an expressive mouth. When listening, he tilts his head as if that might help him catch every word that comes his way. I would have suspected Gertrude of matchmaking, but he and his mother are still in mourning for his wife. During our drinks before dinner, I had expressed my belated condolences to them.

Old Mrs. Dell sat beside me. She dresses plainly, without so much as a jet pendant, her only jewellery being her wedding ring. She gave the impression of having spent her life in mourning. "My left ear is the sharper," she confided. "I will try not to ask you to shout, my dear."

I noticed that Eliot and Gertrude exchanged a small smile when she said this. It made me feel slightly uncomfortable that they seemed to patronise Mrs. Dell, just as I had felt uncomfortable when Gertrude talked about the second-class orphans from the Bluebell Home.

The exchange between Eliot and Gertrude had not gone unnoticed by Mrs. Dell. "I make the numbers odd," she said quietly. "The vicar would have been here but he is with his ailing father. I should have liked to see him." She gazed across at her son. "So would you, Eliot."

He looked across at her. "I would what, mother?"

She spoke rather loudly, as deaf people sometimes do. "It is a pity about the vicar not being here. He would have visited the children."

"Oh he did, mother."

"Not recently." She turned to me. "Gertrude would have invited the curate, but he is painfully shy and excels at excuses."

I warmed to her. "Mrs. Dell, five is an excellent number."

"And I am glad you speak clearly. These days, so many young women mumble."

Benjie, the perfect host, tasted the wine, giving the nod to Raynor in that intimate way they have of communicating, more like friends than master and servant.

As Raynor poured, Benjie did his usual teasing. "You won't be safe here, Eliot, Mrs. Dell. Kate has a tendency to produce a camera from up her sleeve when you least expect it."

Naturally I had to respond. "Don't pretend, Benjie. I know you love to have your picture taken."

Eliot leaned towards me, confiding that he had a camera somewhere in the house, but couldn't remember where.

I smiled and looked beyond him to the sideboard, which was marginally more interesting than he. Its mirror, speckled with age, reflected the flickering candlelight.

Raynor set down the wine.

Since I had taken his photograph, he seemed to have grown taller. He strode to the door and took a tray of soup from a kitchen maid, balancing it on one hand.

While placing our dishes of oxtail soup, he appeared more than usually self-contained, as if bestowing a privilege rather than providing service.

I racked my brain for some topic of conversation that would draw out Eliot Dell. He has interests in mines, shares in railway companies. It would not do, after a cocktail and a glass of wine, immediately to talk to him about railways. Because I knew from Commander Woodhead's list that, like Benjie, Eliot had been shown the unknown man's portrait. I might just find myself saying: why don't you talk to me about the body?

A topic came to me. Golf. "Do you play golf, Eliot? My father does and he's so full of the fact that the Ryder Cup will be held in Leeds, and in only its second year."

Eliot Dell blinked, as if I had asked a trick question. "No, I don't play golf. Never thought to take it up."

So much for that.

With Harriet working at the cinema, I see more pictures than I otherwise would. Eliot, Benjie, Gertrude and Mrs. Dell kindly listened patiently to the plot of a film I had seen.

None of them went to the pictures.

That put me in my place. Was I losing my touch, my ability to fit in?

Horses did the trick. Gertrude and I reminisced about our ponies. Benjie and Eliot joined in.

Soup was followed by casserole of hare.

Shortly, I would bring the talk around to railways, and perhaps to crime, hoping to elicit a confidence. But first I complimented Benjie on his cars. He always seems to have a new one.

Eliot said solemnly, "There is too much traffic these days."

I glanced at Gertrude. She was gazing at Eliot as if his every syllable on the subject of heavy traffic was a word to be treasured.

Eliot is considered good looking. He looks pale by candlelight, a lean man with as much colour in his cheeks as an unbaked scone.

By contrast, Benjie's normally ruddy complexion had turned scarlet, thanks to the drink. He wagged his finger at Eliot. "Get a bigger car. They'll all give way."

Just as I was about to begin a subtle enquiry about the train line to London, Benjie said, "So tell us what great investigations you have been involved in lately, Kate?"

"Nothing to report, Deputy Lord Lieutenant, but if you need my services do let me know."

I wish nobody knew my occupation. If I were a typist, I would not be pinned in a corner and have questions fired at me about how one erases neatly on a carbon copy.

Eliot broke in. "As it happens we have had some trouble. Took a call from one of my railway managers. Seems our area director has taken it upon himself to appoint a fellow to look into security, at the suggestion of the police." He caught Benjie's thunderous look and tailed off. "Subject to our approval of course."

Benjie glared. "Save that for the brandy, old chap. You can tell me what he's going to cost."

Eliot turned pink. He looked across at me. "It's to do with the pilfering, especially on trains that bring the Scotch whisky."

He was lying, yet I could not shake the feeling that one or other of these men was baiting me.

Benjie steered us back to his question. "I know you don't talk about your work, Kate. Confidentiality and all that. I'm curious. It's none of my business, but do you earn money at it?"

I gave him my sweetest smile. "You're right, Benjie. It's none of your business."

Mrs. Dell laughed. "Good for you, my dear."

Gertrude put down her knife and fork. "Darling, Kate doesn't need to make money. She is a woman of independent means who just happens to like helping people in trouble."

Benjie bowed. "Just jesting. Kate knows me better than that."

I suddenly wished I had not come to stay here, but it was too late now.

Eliot's was a simple remark about the security man. He was trying to make conversation, or was he?

Perhaps I was being over-sensitive but I felt suddenly uneasy, as if the three of them had turned a spotlight on me.

Mrs. Dell said little after that. She looked from one person to the next as they spoke, and I felt sure that she was lip-reading as well as listening.

Gertrude said to Eliot, "Kate has turned her hand to photographic journalism."

"It's an assignment for a feature on people and places."

Even Eliot managed to look engaged. "Round here? Not somewhere more picturesque?"

I was glad of having read Philip's treatise. I talked about this being the hub of the country, the cradle of industry, about coal, and the miracle of rhubarb.

Eliot swallowed a mouthful of food. "You must see the sinking of the pit shaft. It will be a unique opportunity." He glanced at Benjie. "We want the world to know we'll be opening a new mine."

Gertrude groaned. "Kate won't be interested in that."

I assured her that I would love to see the sinking of a pit shaft.

Benjie perked up. "A photograph in a magazine, or in newspapers, would let people know we are open to investment." He looked at Raynor, once more pouring wine. "Good idea, don't you think?"

"I do, sir."

Gertrude signalled, no more wine for her.

Later, Mrs. Dell, Gertrude and I withdrew and left the men to talk. The drawing room smelled of lavender polish. Daffodils and tulips filled a cut glass vase on the occasional table.

Gertrude and I sat on opposite sofas near the hearth. Mrs. Dell had gone to powder her nose.

Since our being in this room earlier, for cocktails, something had appeared on the low table between the sofas. It was a prospectus for a new mine, the kind of document that is circulated when the owners are drumming up investment.

I picked it up.

"It would be an excellent investment, Kate. It's to have all the latest equipment."

Is that why I had been welcomed here so quickly? The widow of independent means. Last year, Gertrude discovered that I own a Rolls-Royce that I never drive. Perhaps that promoted me from Girlhood Friend to Potential Investor.

"Eliot's on the board. He has a good head on his shoulders."

I glanced at the names. Mr. B Brockman, Mrs. B Brockman, Mr. E Dell.

Not old Mrs. Dell, then.

"What do you think of Eliot?" Gertrude asked.

"I did meet him before, you remember."

"Yes, before his wife died."

"He seems a perfectly nice man, and fond of his mother."

"Oh he is." She confided in me that he was naturally concerned about his mother, especially after what happened to his wife.

I did not know the circumstances of her death, and enquired what had happened.

"Well you see, Kate, she was a hypochondriac." She glanced at the door, but there was no sign of old Mrs. Dell. "It's a horrible story. One night, Phyllis complained of being in an agony of pain. She always complained and usually recovered after brandy and sympathy. It was decided not to bother the doctor until morning. By morning her appendix had burst and it was too late."

I said how dreadful that must make Eliot feel.

"It was shocking. It's such a horrible story, like a real-life version of the boy who cries wolf. I told him, and Benjie told him, he and his mother are not to blame."

"What was his wife like?"

Gertrude thought for a moment. "One shouldn't speak ill of the dead, and I don't, and wouldn't. But she thought herself a cut above. She was a cluster of anxieties. She didn't ride for fear of being thrown. Always had an opinion on things that didn't really concern her."

"What sort of things?"

"Oh, poor people, the downtrodden, the sort of people who wouldn't help themselves if they could. It wasn't that Phyllis was a lady bountiful, we all have to do that occasionally. Where she'd got it from I don't know, but she had this obsession about justice and making the world a better place. It was all talk, all an act."

I felt a sudden sisterly warmth towards the late Phyllis Dell, with her cluster of anxieties, and her untimely, painful death.

"You know Eliot is our nearest neighbour. I would love to see him settled. He's a shy man but he'll be a good catch for someone." She lowered her voice. "His mother can be difficult, but she can't last much longer."

"Mrs. Dell seems perfectly charming to me. And I haven't come looking for a husband."

"Of course you haven't. But wouldn't it be good if we were neighbours, we could go riding. You might come to London with me and look at babies." She laughed. "I know I'm being fanciful and jumping ahead and all that, but you should see Eliot's house. His family have done very well out of the railways, just as we have. Old Mr. Dell cunningly avoided death duties by dying at the right time. You'd want for nothing. Eliot's late wife brought money into the marriage."

"Thanks for the suggestion. I'll tuck it away with the others."

Gertrude laughed. "You're a hopeless case."

She had always tried her hand at matchmaking. It came as no surprise that she was still at it. In spite of Gertrude's narrow view of the world, she had been what you might call a staunch friend over the years. When a woman is widowed, married friends often fall away. The Christmas cards continue, with the message that we must meet soon. Probably that is meant in the moment the pen moves across the card. In Gertrude's case it always was meant, and followed through.

Gertrude said, "We go to church in the morning, at Holy Trinity in Rothwell. The vicar is away and so we're obliged to support his stand-in. Would you like to come? Afterwards the stand-in will come to Eliot's for drinks."

"I thought I'd look for something a little different, perhaps attend a chapel, in the interests of research."

"Apart from Raynor and the housekeeper, most of the staff attend chapel. Milly will tell you the times of the services."

That was exactly what I intended to do. I felt sure that Gertrude knew nothing about the man on the train. Servants know everything.

The knowledge was between the words, behind the silences: Benjie knew I was here to solve the riddle of the unknown man. So did Raynor, and possibly Eliot. I must brazen it out. Let them think that they were imagining things, because perhaps that's what I was doing: imagining that because Benjie knew they all knew. Benjie had given a strong enough hint. I didn't mind the hint, but it could have been more subtle, one of those ways of letting a person know without saying.

Mrs. Dell returned from powdering her nose. The men cut short their confab in the dining room and came to join us.

Gertrude chose a record. Benjie wound the gramophone. Eliot came to sit beside me.

The curtains had not been closed. The sky was black and full of stars.

Almost recognisable music floated from the gramophone in the corner. It might have been something from Elgar.

Old Mrs. Dell sat very upright, her walking stick close by the straight-back chair. She did not take part in talk of this and that, but watched. I thought that she paid particular attention to me. This did not make me uncomfortable. I moved to sit closer to her and asked about her daughter-in-law.

She spoke very quietly and with great sadness. "I did not hear her call out." She sighed. "Times have not been good since she died."

At that moment, Raynor was beside us, offering drinks or coffee. We both declined. Raynor glanced at Benjie who was deep in conversation with Eliot and paid no attention. Gertrude got up, picked a record and gave it to Raynor. She then came to sit with me and Mrs. Dell.

"Am I butting in?"

Something was going on, and I did not know what. I wished now that I had come straight out with it when I arrived. I needn't have admitted to investigating, but I could have said that I heard a rumour.

A tongue twister came into my head: do they know that I know that they know that I know that they know?

Later, lying in bed, with the curtains open so that I could see the stars, I wondered had I imagined the silent warning signals between Benjie and Raynor, and my uncomfortable feeling that Raynor had been ordered to watch me.

As I fell asleep, it occurred to me that whoever had killed the unknown man would go to great lengths and take desperate measures to avoid discovery.

Chapter Sixteen

Gertrude had insisted I should stay in bed on Sunday morning. She would have breakfast sent up to my room.

Milly brought one of those trays, made for the lazy. I believe they come from the Gamages catalogue. I sat up in bed, propped on pillows, the sturdy tray with its fat legs in just the right position.

Milly was pouring tea. "Madam said you want to go to chapel." She spoke in a flat voice that told me this would be a terrible nuisance for her.

"Or to just know directions and times."

There was a clink of crockery and a cry. "I've spilt the milk."

"Don't worry about it."

"No, but I have." She began to cry.

Breakfast in bed on the Gamages tray began to seem less of a treat.

"It's all right, nothing is broken."

"No." She continued to cry, and was about to flee from the room.

It is not altogether easy to move that sort of tray once it has trapped the legs. "Milly, wait!"

Milly was by the door, which she opened and immediately shut. Someone must have been on the landing.

I was out of bed now and beside her. "You know what they say about spilt milk."

She mopped at it with a doyley. "It's not the milk."

"No I didn't suppose it was. Have you had a cup of tea?"

"A long time ago. We're up early."

"Then you shall have one now and a slice of toast."

After some protests, she sat down in the wicker chair. We came to the compromise, at her insistence, that she would drink from the saucer and I must have the cup.

Crumbs from our toast fell generously onto the rug. We salted the boiled eggs which had grown hard. It took a little encouragement to make her speak. I told her about a hospital where I once worked. One nurse cried an awful lot. Another never cried at all. "We're all different."

Slowly her story came out. She could not go to chapel this morning because something was going to happen afterwards. The Temperance Band intended to march to the railway station, take the train to Wakefield and from there march to the prison. They would play outside the prison walls so that their music would reach Stephen Walmsley's cell. He would know that they were there. They would play out his innocence to heaven and the authorities.

"Milly, we'll go together."

She shook her head, unable to find words. Eventually, her tears lessened. She folded her arms and rocked. Her story of why she couldn't walk with the band came out with little sighs and sucking in of breath as she tried to compose herself.

She and Stephen had been to the pictures. They had walked over the common. She liked him and was waiting for him to hold her hand but he never did because he was shy and so was she. And then he took up with Joan and it wasn't fair. Joan played the tambourine in the band and so she and Stephen were together a lot. She saw them holding hands. Joan was supposed to be her friend.

"That's not so terrible, Milly. You still like him, and you still like Joan. It might be a flash in the pan that they held hands. There's nothing to stop you walking with the band."

This brought on a fresh bout of weeping. "It was Joan's idea that we go to the prison. It should've been mine."

"Do you play in a band?"

"No."

"Well then."

There was something to stop her, she explained. It was this.

"On that Friday, I thought I'd just go see. I knew they walked back together from band practice and so I went to look. I kept out of the way, round the corner. I said to myself if Stephen walks her home, and if he holds her hand, I'd know it was hopeless. Along they came, she playing her tambourine as she walked. I watched them walk to the top of the street, and go into her house. She lives with Mr. and Mrs. Arkwright.

"I didn't know what to do. I thought, I'll just go see Mrs. Farrar. She'll tell me if there's no hope. She'll tell me if they are courting. The shop door was locked, but I knocked. There was no answer."

"What time was this?"

"I don't know but it was starting to rain."

"What else?"

"I went round the side, thinking, should I wait? Is Mrs. Farrar upstairs? There was a bit of a fire in the garden so I thought perhaps she'd been cutting back brambles and overdone it, got tired and gone to bed. It was, should I or shouldn't I? Should I go in and make a mug of myself? Should I not go in and be a fool? And then I saw him, coming back along the street from the Arkwrights, carrying his trumpet. I stepped into his view. He was right surprised, asked me what I was doing. 'Looking for you,' I said.

"He said, 'You look upset. You best come in.' I hung back, feeling stupid. He went inside, and then he screamed. I've never heard a man scream. There was Mrs. Farrar on the floor, and him kneeling beside her. I just stood in the doorway. He went to pick her up. Then he called to me. 'Get yerself home. This is right shocking. Get yerself home.' And I went to go in but he said, 'Go. You don't want to see this.' And so I went, I just went. And I said nowt."

"What happened next?"

"Joan would've known what to do. I'm useless."

"You did as he said. You weren't to know."

We were quiet for a long time. Through the window, I heard the car setting off to take Gertrude and Benjie to church.

"Did you tell anyone what you saw?"

"No. When it came out, and Stephen was taken, and people started to talk, I'd left it too late. I couldn't speak up." She stared at the crumbs on the carpet. "Who'll believe me if I say it now?"

"Go put on your Sunday frock and your warm coat. You and I are going to the chapel. We'll join the Temperance Band procession and we'll think what to do."

The chapel had emptied by the time we arrived, but the congregation did just that—congregated, in the doorway, on the steps, and on the pavement. There were no other cars in the vicinity, but I parked a few yards from the chapel, so as not to get in the way of the massing band.

It was difficult to count the bandsmen because they all wore the same dark jackets with gold braid and peaked caps with shiny nebs. They strode about, blowing the odd note. There must have been twenty of them, with their trumpets, cornets, tubas, saxophone and trombone. A lad with a drum was ushered to the front. Next to him was a dark-skinned young woman, a little older than Milly. She wore the band's fine jacket, a cap that was too big, and held a tambourine.

She waved at Milly.

Milly said, "That's Joan."

We went over.

There were no introductions.

Joan said to Milly, "I knew you'd come. Mr. Arkwright has a jacket for you."

"What am I supposed to play?"

"Mrs. Arkwright brought a triangle. You'll want to walk with me and Dennis, behind the conductor. You're Stephen's sweetheart."

"Am I though?"

"Course you bloomin' are."

The young drummer gave a slight nod. One could see at once that he was an artist, too intent on his coming performance to enter into conversation.

Milly turned and walked over to an elderly couple who stood by the wall. The man helped her into a jacket. She fumbled with the buttons and had to start again, refusing help from the old lady.

Milly now held a triangle. She struck it with the rod and seemed suddenly startled by the sound and the reverberation.

She returned and took her place between Joan Arkwright and the drummer boy. The band's conductor, a thin man whose long moustache made him seem melancholy, came to speak to Milly. "Have you played it before?"

"At school."

"Sparingly, that's the word. Sparingly. Watch mi left thumb for your signal."

The conductor called to his band to make ready. Within five minutes, they were in formation.

During the five minutes, Milly and Joan had a rather animated conversation. I guessed that Milly was repeating to Joan what she had told me.

Milly hurried over to speak to us. "I'll see you at the prison?"

Joan was close on her heels, barely able to keep still. The tambourine in her hand rattled. The fist of her other hand clenched. She glared at me. "Why didn't you tell her she has to speak to the police straight away?" To Milly she said, "If you don't stick up for him, who will?"

Mrs. Arkwright intervened. "Give over your squabbling. Here's a bob for your fare."

As they gathered, ready to march, members of the congregation fell in behind them, creating an impressive procession. I took out my camera and snapped a picture, just as the band struck up "Onward Christian Soldiers".

Men and women unfurled embroidered miners' union banners, and banners from nearby collieries.

The elderly couple stood by the wall, clapping.

I went over to them. "It's too far for you to go?"

The woman spoke. "It is, love, or we would. It's not this end getting to't station, it's t'other end, all along to't prison."

"I could drive us there, if you don't mind squeezing up."

"In a motor car?"

"In that car over there."

They looked at each other as if assessing whether there might be some unseen danger in this suggestion, and then, as one, they decided in my favour.

"We'll do it," Mr. Arkwright said, "for the lad's sake, and for the lassies. Stephen never did what they said, never in this wide world."

I set off, driving slowly behind the band, keeping a reasonable distance so as not to detract from the music. People came out of their houses. They waved, applauded, or simply watched as the band went by. Mr. and Mrs. Arkwright sat up as straight as circumstances allowed, now and then raising a hand or nodding in acknowledgement of our audience.

At the railway station, the band stopped playing and filed into the station.

Chapter Seventeen

～

I parked a little way from the prison, remembering Philip's insistence that parking close by was not allowed.

As we walked towards the prison, the Arkwrights told me that they had worked at the children's home, as superintendent and matron. "We was heartbroken when the Bluebell Home closed," Mrs. Arkwright said, turning to her husband. "Tell her, Simon."

"Heartbroken," Simon said. "We'd seen 'em grow up and we'd seen 'em into the world and would have gone on doing so with the little uns."

Mrs. Arkwright straightened her scarf. "At least we have Joan. She wasn't happy in her digs and Mrs. Brockman, give her credit, let us have free rent of the little house we're in. We was able to give Joan a home, just as Mrs. Farrar did for Stephen."

Mr. Arkwright shook his head. He spoke as if Stephen's imprisonment was a minor inconvenience, a mistake that would soon be put right. "What will the lad do now, without Mrs. Farrar behind him?"

"And what about you, Mr. and Mrs. Arkwright? Have you found work since the home closed?"

"Why Simon has a job in the mill –"

"Sweeping," Mr. Arkwright admitted.

"I knit coats for a shop in Wakefield, and we have the garden."

There was no sign of the band yet, but the police must already have been alerted.

A sergeant and a constable appeared. They stood by the prison gates.

We looked at them. They looked at us. We were a few yards apart.

Mrs. Arkwright smiled.

Mr. Arkwright nudged her. "Don't make it obvious."

"What?" I asked.

"She can lipread, from her mill days."

Mrs. Arkwright turned her head, as if suspecting that the police shared her skill. The sergeant said, "Have you ever heard of a protest march where they come by train?" She glanced at the pair again, and then said, "The constable asks if they're to turn them back. Sergeant says that wouldn't look good, not when it's the Temperance Band."

As the band rounded the corner, playing "Jerusalem", the sergeant looked over at me. Through my dad, I know many local police officers by sight. Neither of us acknowledged the other.

The band's followers had increased. They started out with fifty or so. Now there were over a hundred.

The police always need to find the organiser, so they can deal with that person. I expect it was a relief to assume that the band's conductor was the man in charge.

The officer had to wait until the last note of "Jerusalem" before the conductor would acknowledge him.

Joan called, "William Tell! That's a favourite of Stephen's."

There was a brief exchange between the sergeant and the conductor.

The band began to play "The William Tell Overture".

It was Joan who took up the chant as the music ended. "Stephen Walmsley is innocent. Stephen Walmsley is innocent." Others took up the refrain.

Mrs. Arkwright whispered, "Let's hope the lad hears them."

Mr. Arkwright said loudly, "He knows he's innocent. It's the police who need to listen."

We had come closer to the band. The sergeant walked across to the conductor. He spoke to him, but I knew that the message was also meant for me.

"Three more hymns and we have to clear the street. I know you all have homes to go to. You've made your point."

Joan kept up her chant.

I spoke quietly to Mrs. Arkwright. "The police are doing their job. We won't let this go. We'll live to fight another day. Tell your Joan."

The conductor called, "We have faith in the Lord and in justice. "Pomp and Circumstance.""

Mrs. Arkwright went to speak to Joan.

Her tambourine was not required for this. Milly decided that the triangle was not needed either. The two of them and Mrs. Arkwright fell into conversation.

I did not listen to what music came next because my attention was on Milly and Joan. Milly blew her nose. She seemed to hesitate. Joan took her arm and marched her towards the nearest constable. I went closer, feeling sure that Milly would be her normal timid self. I need not have worried. With Joan beside her, Milly seemed to draw strength from her fearless friend.

She spoke calmly. "I have a statement to make concerning Stephen Walmsley."

Joan wanted to go with her, and made loud objections when she was turned away with the explanation that she had already given a statement about walking back with Stephen from band practice.

Mr. and Mrs. Arkwright, Joan and I waited for Milly's return. The street had all but cleared by the time she appeared again. Her cheeks were flushed. She no longer looked ready to burst into tears, but angry. "They didn't believe me. And I swore it and I swore it was true."

"We'll make them believe it." Joan grabbed Milly's arm.

Milly pushed her away. "They said we're both in love with him and should know better than lie for a murderer, and we could go to prison for false testimony."

There was nothing else we could do, for the moment. "The truth will come out," I said, making a great effort to sound convincing. "Milly, you and Joan go on to the station. I'll take Mr. and Mrs. Arkwright home."

My passengers were glad of the ride. They stayed placidly in the car When I stopped outside the Goodchilds' house, having spotted Philip and his mother in the garden. If I called on my parents, it would be difficult to escape.

Mrs. Goodchild was delighted to see me. She is a kind woman, with a particular neatness that includes wearing a tight hairnet six days a week, and Sundays if she is in the garden.

"Is everything all right?" Philip asked.

"Yes, all's well."

Mrs. Goodchild beamed. "I'm so pleased Philip is helping you, Kate."

"Philip is helping me enormously, and would you mind if I use the telephone? I don't want to disturb Dad, in case he is having his nap."

She tactfully made herself scarce while I made my telephone call. Stolidly, my man-at-arms stood by me while I waited to be connected to Martin Yeats. I thanked Philip for leaving his treatise on rhubarb in the third bee bole.

Martin could not promise that he would be able to arrange a second visit for me to see Stephen Walmsley tomorrow morning, but he would do his best. "What time do you want to go?"

I thought for a moment. The sooner the better, as far as I was concerned. "If I could see Stephen first thing, say 7 a.m., I could be back in time for breakfast."

"I'll do my best, Kate."

There are some people whose best will always be good enough.

Chapter Eighteen

My car likes to be heard. Without shouting at the top of one's voice, it is impossible to have a conversation over the racket of the engine while driving.

We reached Thorpefield. Mr. Arkwright yelled directions to the top of Silver Street, end cottage, number 42. This was the street leading to Mrs. Farrar's shop. This was the house Stephen Walmsley had walked to with Joan, after band practice.

Although I needed to be back for Sunday lunch with Gertrude and Benjie, I was glad that they asked me in. There would be time for a chat.

Mrs. Arkwright was apologetic. "We're not settled, but you'll excuse our mess."

We stepped into the single downstairs room that doubled as kitchen and parlour, with a door leading to a small scullery. Mrs. Arkwright hung our coats on the back of the door. I was urged into the upholstered cane seat that must be Mr. Arkwright's. Mrs. Arkwright sat in the rocking chair.

The kettle was on the hob. He put on a couple of cobs of coal and used the poker to push the hob nearer the flames.

After I had admired the room, and assured them that it wasn't at all a mess, I gave my by now practised account of the planned photographic essay for a magazine—my passport to nosiness. "I had hoped to photograph the Bluebell Home. I'd no idea it had closed. Was that recent?"

Mrs. Arkwright nodded. "And sudden, very sudden." She took out a hanky.

"Now, now," her husband said. "Don't fret."

"What was it like there? I used to cycle out this way with my friends. We'd look through the railings and envy the children their swings and slide."

She smiled. "We were there twenty years. The couple before us, they did everything they could to make the Bluebell a proper home, the best kind of family home."

"We followed suit," Mr. Arkwright said. "It was never a heart-break house. Trustees insisted on after-school training. I taught woodwork and suchlike to the boys."

"And for the girls, I would have taught cooking but we had a lovely qualified teacher." Mrs. Arkwright set her chair rocking. "No one demonstrated bedmaking with neater hospital corners than Miss Stafford. She brought out the best in the children and so did we. Joan and Stephen are living proof. And if they don't let the lad out of prison soon, there's no justice in this wide world."

Mr. Arkwright took a short pipe from the mantelpiece, tapped tobacco in, and lit it with a taper. Under other circumstances, the sweet scent would have been soothing. "It'll all come out in the wash."

I felt gratified that so many people, besides me, believed in Stephen's innocence.

The old couple now seemed so despondent that I felt obliged to prompt them to happier memories. "And now you have Joan as your adopted daughter. Is she a dab hand at hospital corners?"

Mr. Arkwright laughed, but left his wife to answer.

"She is if she feels like it. She wanted to do what the lads did. There's more to her than her cheeky ways and the colour of her skin, but domestication is not one of her virtues."

"Tell her," he said. "Tell her how we came to have Joan. She won't mind. She likes hearing the story herself."

There followed such an odd tale that I must tell it.

One May morning, Mr. Arkwright opened the back door, to fetch the milk, as usual. He noticed a wicker shopping basket on the back doorstep but thought nothing of it. He would pick it up as he came back. People often left something towards the children's upkeep: a loaf of bread, a pie, new-laid eggs. In the autumn, they had more apples than they knew what to do with.

He walked to the gate to meet the milkman, taking his can to be filled.

He picked up the basket on the way back. Even when he took it inside, he did not look, but left it on a stool for his wife to see to. And then the sheet moved, just a small movement, like the ripple of a stream. He lifted the sheet. There lay a baby, cocooned in a crocheted blanket, face the colour of a hazelnut, dark eyes wide open, looking up at him.

Mrs. Arkwright came in at that moment and said, "Where did you come from?" She picked her up. She and the baby looked at each other, and that was that.

At first there was no thought about who she was and where she came from. It was all a matter of making sure she survived. He wanted to call her Hazel, for her colour. Mrs. Arkwright wanted to call her Joan, after her own mother. They chose May as her surname, the month she was found.

She was going on twelve when she said, "Joan May and Joan may not. I want to be called Arkwright, like you, which is a proper name." She harped on so long that they paid out the money to do it, to change her name by deed poll. It was no use telling her that she might wait until she wed, and pick a young man whose name she liked.

They could only guess at where she came from. Rumour had it that she was from the north. Oh not Durham, not Scotland, not as far as that. Somewhere in the Dales, where years ago an unchristian fellow brought back slaves from the West Indies and set them working on his farm. It was said that the daughter of the family fell in love with one of them.

When they had told me the story, Mrs. Arkwright said, "If she's from that strain, 'tis a pity there's not more like her. She's the best lass you will meet, honest and true. She has such good eyesight, and a feel for perfection, she'll be a burler and mender by the time she's twenty, if she doesn't get herself sacked for speaking out."

Mr. Arkwright frowned. "We wanted all our bairns to be fearless but she overdoes it."

"Why did the home close so suddenly?"

Mr. Arkwright re-lit his pipe. "In an area where you've had mining over the centuries, you never know what shifts and changes go on underground."

Mrs. Arkwright said, "It was the early hours, that we heard a rumble. Not that I have ever known of an earthquake, but it was something like that, and nearby. It shook the house. The next day, we told Mrs. Brockman. She had it checked right away by mining engineers. We was moved out within twenty-four hours."

"How shocking."

She nodded. "The children were so happy at being sent to the seaside, and us with them. We came back one way and they another, to another home, temporary, until a new site can be found. They couldn't make the old one safe."

"When will that be?"

Mrs. Arkwright did not trust herself to speak.

The kettle had boiled. Mr. Arkwright made tea. "You would never have thought a house that old and that sturdy could be demolished so fast. They brought an army of experts in to do the job."

"And we never said goodbye to the children."

"When was this?"

"Two weeks ago. We are still waiting for the new place."

Neither Commander Woodhead nor DC Yeats had mentioned the influx of an "army of experts" in demolition. I must find out whether Wakefield CID had looked into the appearance and disappearance of the demolition men. One of them might have murdered

Mrs. Farrar. One might have murdered one of his fellows, and put his body on the train.

The unknown man did not appear to have been a manual labourer, but demolition takes brains as well as brawn. "Have the demolition men gone now?"

Mr. Arkwright reached out and patted his wife's back. "We don't know and we don't care. All we want to know is, when will we see the children again?"

"We don't like to pester Mrs. Brockman," Mr. Arkwright explained. "You see she's been very good to us. There are just two grace and favour cottages in this row, and we're grateful that this one became available and that she let us move in."

A troubled look came into his eyes, but so fleetingly that I wondered had I imagined it. Was there a price to pay for this grace and favour occupancy? A price of silence?

It seemed callous to follow my own line of investigation when this couple were so upset at losing their flock, and with one of their former charges in prison. This moment of intimacy may never come again. Though my reason for being here was to find out about the man on the train, the instinctive sense of a connection between the two crimes had not left me.

As Mrs. Arkwright poured tea, I slipped in my remark. "You have had some shocking and upsetting events here recently. I overheard an odd story outside the post office in Rothwell."

Mr. Arkwright sat down in a straight-back chair. He watched as Mrs. Arkwright passed me a cup, and then he reached for his mug. "Oh aye?"

"Two men were talking about a body that was found when the rhubarb express arrived in London."

"Oh that," Mr. Arkwright said.

My hopes rose. "You've heard about it then?"

"One of our old boys works on the railway."

This might be my breakthrough. "Is he based at Ardsley?"

He shook his head. "Leeds Central. They was all questioned by the railway police. Nobody knew a thing."

Mrs. Arkwright handed me a cup. "The lad they ought to have asked is young Alec Taylor. He loves railways. Goes along to the stations and the junctions with his notebook, writing down the engine numbers, making a note of the sidings and what wagons go where."

"Not that he'd know about a body," Mr. Arkwright said quickly. "From a little lad, he loved motion. Cycles, cars, engines."

She smiled. "Do you remember that engine you carved for him, and painted it red?"

"Hours of fun with that! When Mr. Brockman took him out of the home and give him a job, he left it behind for the little ones."

This visit was providing some of my best information so far—my only information so far. Alec, Benjie's son, if not heir, knew all about railways. There had been a transient army of demolition men in the area. There were two grace and favour cottages in Silver Street. The Arkwrights had one, because they had lost their positions as superintendent and matron of the Bluebell Home. Such cottages were often given as a confidential thank you for services rendered. Who occupied the other cottage, and why?

I would set Sykes to tracing the demolition men. Alec, I would tackle myself.

"Which is the other grace and favour cottage, Mrs. Arkwright? Not that I'm thinking of moving in."

"Now which is it?" Mrs. Arkwright asked her husband. She knew well enough, but was asking his permission to tell me.

"Why it's the one at the bottom end, same side as ours."

She nodded. "You could be right. Tall woman, lives all on her own."

Life could be difficult for women living alone in a working-class community. I was curious. "I suppose she must have been an employee of the Brockmans, or a distant relation?"

"Women's talk." Mr. Arkwright stood. "I'll just take a look at my rhubarb." He put on his cap.

When he had gone, Mrs. Arkwright said in a whisper, though there was no one else to hear, "It's said she had a baby and went a bit funny afterwards."

"What happened to the baby?" Even as I asked, I knew.

One advantage for wealthy individuals of supporting an orphanage was that there would be a place for offspring that might otherwise be difficult to explain. She looked a little embarrassed. "I'm sorry, Mrs. Arkwright. I don't mean to pry. You have a lot on your mind."

"We do, and I wonder what the world is coming to. All of us in this street miss Mrs. Farrar."

"Were you close, you and Mrs. Farrar?"

"Always on good terms, and recently she came to talk to us, just as we were moved in here. She was the voice for the children you see."

Something told me to tread carefully, to wait and hear what Mrs. Arkwright would have to say. If I seemed too eager, too nosey, she might clam up. Yet I took the risk.

"What was Mrs. Farrar's connection to the Bluebell?"

"She was one of the trustees. When it came to closure, she was outvoted by the others, by Mr. and Mrs. Brockman and Mr. Dell. It broke her heart. She came to talk to me about it. When she started, she couldn't stop. She was here till midnight, saying the same things over and over. And my man with work in the morning."

"What did she say?"

"She said subsidence didn't make a noise. She knew this because as a girl she worked in a house where they woke up one morning and the back garden was gone, and just a big hole. They were lucky to be alive."

An unwelcome thought came into my head. As a motive for murder, robbery of Mrs. Farrar's paltry takings did not convince me. Silencing a trustee with a willingness to speak out was a different matter.

"Tell me about the terms of the trust, Mrs. Arkwright."

"Nay I can't do that 'cos I don't know. That trust was set up a lot of years ago by a man with a good head on his shoulders. He knew that fools and money are soon parted. He put his brass in safe places until it grew and grew. And there was a lot of money in that trust when they wound it up. Oh they said to Mrs. Farrar that there wasn't, but she had a head on her shoulders as well."

Mrs. Farrar had tried to stop the closure of the children's home, and failed. Any other person may have given up. She seemed unlikely to do so.

Mrs. Arkwright's hand went to her mouth. "I shouldn't be saying this. We could be out on our ear."

I rose to go. "Mrs. Arkwright, what you say won't go farther than this room. May I ask the same of you?"

"You can that, lass."

"Then we'll talk another day."

I put on my coat.

She touched my arm. "Mrs. Brockman's your friend. Might you find out about the children?"

"I'll try."

"And I won't rest until Stephen's let out of that place." She walked me to the gate. "I made sure all the Bluebell lads washed their necks. Last night I woke from a dream about Stephen. He was in his cell. I lifted his chin, and I heard myself saying, I'm glad to see you've a clean neck."

Chapter Nineteen

There is no better way of having a person on your side than to promise a flattering portrait. Alec, the railway enthusiast, was sitting on a bench by the stable door, wearing Sunday-best trousers, an old woolly, and a tweed cap.

He had been reading *Comic Cuts* but now put his comic on the bench.

He stood as I approached. "Oh, I was miles away. Wasn't listening for a car."

"Well this is your time off."

He grinned. "You went to chapel with Milly."

"I did, and I took her photograph. Now I'd like to take yours."

He stared. "Me, just me?"

"Yes."

"I've never had a picture on my own, only with the others at the Bluebell."

Once more, I went into my explanation about an article, and people and places. I could see that he had already heard the story, but listened politely.

I took out my Thornton-Pickard. "Where would you like to have your picture taken?"

"I'd like to stand next to your car."

"There are bigger cars to choose from. I won't tell."

He looked thoughtful. "If the car was too big, I would never pass it off as having once been mine. Besides, I like the Jowetts.

There's an old one for sale in the garage where I work on Thursdays, It's tip-top."

"I'm guessing you like most cars. I know you like trains, I've been hearing about the little red engine you had."

His face lit with a brilliant smile. "I hope one of the kids took it with them." He stood by the car, waiting.

"Go on, get in the driver's seat." The sky was a perfect blue, the bright sun sandwiched between a mass of white clouds with dark centres. "Let's make the most of the light."

"Should I take my cap off?"

"You're fine just as you are." I like to chat as I set up a photograph, to put my subject at ease. This time there was an ulterior motive. "So which comes tops for you, trains or cars?"

"I've given up on watching trains." He hesitated. "Mr. Raynor said best not go any more."

I made a guess at why. "Since what happened last week?"

He nodded. "You heard then?"

"A bit gruesome, eh?"

"Someone came to the house asking questions but they didn't talk to me. I thought I'd be asked about Ardsley station, but I wasn't. I suppose they asked the railwaymen."

With the light behind me, I clicked the shutter, and again.

"Stand by the car, Alec, as if you're just about to get in."

He did so. There was a sudden shaft of brightness. Alec's shadow was longer than himself. "What would you have said, if you'd been asked about that business? You see I can't think how anyone would get a body on a train without being noticed."

"I've watched the men working. There's a man to shunt the wagons into the sidings, make sure they're in the right place to be connected. The driver and firemen are seeing to the engine. There's a man stacking the boxes of rhubarb. He takes a break when he can. It would have to be when the shunting's done, when the wagons are assembled in the marshalling yard ready to go. If it'd been January or February, you wouldn't get an extra box in, never mind a body. But by March, towards the end of the season, not every wagon is full."

"Has anybody talked to you about this?"

"No, but I asked Mr. Raynor should I give the police my railway notebook. He said I best steer clear."

"Mr. Brockman and Mr. Raynor seem kind."

"Mr. Brockman is. He buys me *Comic Cuts* every week. It was his idea for me to go to the garage and learn a trade."

"One more smile for the camera!"

He smiled. I clicked the shutter.

Alec stopped smiling. "Mr. Raynor was right telling me to steer clear of the police, after what happened to Stephen Walmsley. They pick you up for nowt. They might have taken me in, for just being on the slope watching."

"Another for luck!" I clicked again. "It was a good hobby though."

"I've grown out of it now."

"Sounds really interesting." I glanced back at the bench. "We should have one more, you sitting on the bench, reading. Take no notice of me, just look at your comic."

I took one more picture.

"This notebook you kept, might I have a look at it? I don't know anything about railways and sidings and shunting."

His eyes lit. "I've got drawings and everything. Ardsley is the biggest junction around here. Serves everywhere, Leeds, Wakefield, Methley, Stanley, Bramley. It's like the centre of the world for railway sidings, or at least the centre of the West Riding."

"It must be a busy station."

"Well, not busy with people. It's the point for the goods trains because of its situation. One of the clerks told me that in all the times he'd filled in at Ardsley, he'd never sold a ticket on his middle term. I wish I could show it you, my notebook, only it's disappeared."

"When?"

"I looked for it when that business happened. I keep my stuff in a biscuit tin, up where I sleep. Everything was there except my railway notebook. Mr. Raynor said not to mention it. He said it'll turn up."

Alec suddenly grew quiet, as he glanced over my shoulder. Barely moving his lips, he said, "And he said not to tell anyone."

As if mention of his name had conjured the butler, Raynor bore down on us. "I saw you coming back, Mrs. Shackleton. Has this young scallywag been wasting your time?"

"On the contrary, Raynor. I was taking up Alec's time, insisting that he pose for me, but we're done now." I put away my camera. "Am I holding up lunch?"

"No, madam. Mrs. Brockman prefers a late Sunday dinner. The gong will be in about half an hour."

"Thank you, Raynor."

When he was out of earshot, I said, "Didn't the landowner mind that you watched the trains?"

"Nobody ever chased me off. They all know me."

"Who does own the land over there?"

"Some of it belongs to the railway, where the rails are—obviously. On this side it belongs to the Brockman estate and on the other side, that's part of the Dell estate. But Mr. Dell's a friend of the family here, so he wouldn't have me turfed off."

Chapter Twenty

Milly claimed a bad head. She sat on her bed in the room at the top of the house, biting her nails, wishing herself somewhere else. She hated this room with two old oil paintings on the wall. Stags at bay. She felt sorry for the stags. The frames were backed with brown paper that had come loose and sometimes rattled when the door opened or if the wind blew through the top part of the window that wouldn't ever shut right.

She told herself that she wasn't biting her nails. She was biting the skin around one nail. Her mam said that she would not be kept on if she bit her nails. She didn't want to be kept on. She wanted to be at home. But then she wouldn't have met Stephen. Besides, there wasn't enough food at home for everyone.

Milly felt proud of herself for speaking up today. When she arrived back at the manor, the housekeeper pointed to the clock. "What time do you call this?"

Milly answered that Mrs. Brockman's guest had asked to go to chapel, and walk with the band.

At least today she had been brave enough to do the right thing. She was trying to be a person who isn't scared all the time. She had kept her hands in her pockets when she talked to the police-man, so that he wouldn't see they were shaking. That part worked. He took her inside the prison yard, into a little house, so that she could make her statement. She was so frightened, she couldn't see. If anyone asked her now what the room was like, she wouldn't be able to describe it. Some kind of fog came between her and out there.

She made herself give the account exactly, and say why it couldn't be Stephen Walmsley who killed Mrs. Farrar.

When she had to sign her statement, her hand shook. She had to hold her right wrist with her left hand to keep it steady.

Back at Thorpefield Manor, the first person she saw was Alec Taylor. He was tinkering with a car, which he was not supposed to do on a Sunday.

He once told her that Mrs. Brockman didn't like that he went to Holy Trinity, but if Mrs. Brockman didn't like it, she could lump it. He worked for Mr. Brockman.

Even before Alec told Milly that the top floor where she slept was haunted by a maid, murdered and hidden in the eaves, she had been afraid in this room.

She had pushed the chair against the little door that opened into the eaves, but a chair would be no good. She couldn't move the chest of drawers so had taken out the three drawers, one at a time, and put them on top of each other against the little door. The top drawer toppled off and landed on her toe, making her yelp with pain.

Just her luck that the housekeeper chose that moment to do one of her inspections, walking along the corridor. She came to see what the noise was.

She told Milly it was only thanks to stout boots that she hadn't broken every bone in her foot, and not to believe a word that Alec said. He was a silly boy. Milly knew he wasn't a silly boy. He took care of the horses. He was sent once a week to a garage where he learned about looking after cars. He could drive. Nothing silly about that.

The housekeeper had put the drawers back. Milly should be grateful for a good room, all to herself and nicely done out. Look at that lovely jug and basin, decorated with such pretty tulips. It used to be in the mistress's room,

She opened the little door and showed Milly there was nothing behind it. Such a space under the roof was called the eaves. There was nothing to be afraid of. She lit a candle, made Milly take it, made her look left and right—at nothing. The candle flickered. The flame died. Milly knew that was a sign. The dead maid had blown out the candle, as a warning.

Since then, there had been more noises in the night.

Last night she woke from a dream. Stephen, blindfolded, bleeding, being led along a corridor to the gallows.

What woke her was the sounds. Someone was in the room. She had lain still, not daring to move, not daring to open her eyes. It was the dead maid, come to warn her, but a ghost could not warn you if you kept your eyes tight shut and your body stiff as a log. The ghost slipped back into the eaves.

If a person can be brave once in a day, she can be brave twice. She struck a match, watched it splutter. The wick on the candle was low and so she held the match close, watching the black wick turn blue before the flame took and burned yellow.

There is nothing there, she told herself. Open the door. Do what the housekeeper did. Make yourself look. She would look right, she would look left. There would be nothing.

The candlestick trembled in her hand. The flame flickered as she stretched her arm into that cold dark space.

And then she dropped the candlestick. Metal clattering against beams, candle falling, the flame still glowing, and then blackness.

But before the blackness, she saw that there was something there.

She did not want to go below stairs and be mocked for her foolishness.

It was not time yet to turn down the bed for Mrs. Shackleton, but she went and did it anyway. After that, she sat on the carved oak chair in Mrs. Shackleton's room, and waited.

Chapter
Twenty-One

～

We were three for Sunday dinner, Gertrude, Benjie and me. Over Yorkshire pudding and gravy, Benjie gave a brief account of the sermon at Holy Trinity. "Vicar's away still. Thought we'd have the curate but we had a stand-in from Wakefield. Sound chap, doesn't overdo it. He spoke compassionate words on the loss of poor Mrs. Farrar."

"That must have hit people so very hard."

"It was a terrible shock. Left people frightened for their lives, until an arrest was made, and even then –"

Gertrude rested her knife and fork. "Darling, you were very good at reassuring the congregation afterwards." She turned to me. "And what was your experience of the chapel, Kate?"

Knowing very well they would soon hear of the protest at the prison, I praised the music of the Temperance Band, and the peaceful vigil outside Wakefield Prison.

It was now or never. "And I heard a most odd story, of a body discovered on the rhubarb express. If it's true, that surely ought to have made the papers?"

Benjie seemed suddenly on edge. "You didn't hear it from me, Kate, because it's a sordid business, not to be repeated in polite company."

That was telling me. I waited, in case of more. There was more.

"If you want my view of that matter, it didn't happen here. That train stopped farther down the line. I could speculate, but I won't. We may never get to the bottom of it."

I had touched a raw nerve.

Gertrude spoke soothingly. "It's natural for Kate to be curious. It's one of those mysteries that eventually will become embellished and turn into folklore. Gives me the shudders to think of it."

"Then don't!" Benjie forked the last morsel of pudding.

It was my guess that having been asked to keep quiet about this shocking event, he expected everyone else to do the same.

Raynor deftly whipped away the plates, and brought roast beef. Benjie gave the carving of the joint his complete attention, while Gertrude passed the vegetables.

Later, in the music room, Gertrude said, "I'm sorry Benjie was sharp with you over that business. He is very sensitive about it. As deputy Lord Lieutenant, he takes personally crime on his door-step—a blot on his own copybook."

* * *

Milly, still as a statue, was seated in the oak chair in my bedroom. It surprised me to see her there. "Hello, Milly."

"I can't stay here."

Somehow, I knew she did not mean in the oak chair. It was ridiculous to ask if something had upset her. She had stood outside that dreadful prison, thinking of her sweetheart incarcerated for the worst of crimes, and given a statement that must have cost her dear.

"You're thinking of Stephen?"

"No. Well, yes but no."

"What then?"

She explained. It was about her bedroom. Something strange was going on.

"Let's go see."

"You won't want to."

"Yes I will. Mr. and Mrs. Brockman are resting after dinner, but I'm not tired."

* * *

The backstairs of a fine house are sometimes not just shabby but grubby. All effort and labour goes into the parts of the house that owners and guests see.

Milly led the way. The place was clean, but the narrow carpet worn to its threads. Yellowing distemper covered the walls of the corridor.

Milly's room was tidy, with two single brass bedsteads, a chest of drawers with basin and jug, table and chair and a clothes rail. On the walls were a couple of enormous old pictures, those dark oil paintings of a gloomy Scottish landscape hunting scene, banished to the attics when tastes changed.

Milly kept her eyes averted. "I try not to look, but the stags stare at me."

I tried to be encouraging. "This could be a nice cheerful room. Let me have a word with Raynor. He'll speak to the housekeeper. I'm sure she can find another place for these pictures."

Milly pointed to the little door in the wall, where the roof sloped. "There's stuff in there. There's noises. Mrs. Blanchard, the housekeeper, says it's just the old house groaning. But somebody comes. Alec said this room is haunted."

"He was having you on."

"I think he was." She folded her arms across her chest and rocked. It was cold in here. "Because I don't think a ghost would keep a pair of shoes and a box in someone else's room."

The little door to the eaves had no knob. It was made of planks, the kind where you had to put your fingers on the edge and pull it out. I opened the panel. "It's storage space, that's all." Knowing we were going to the attics, I had brought my flashlight, and shone it in the space. "You're right, but it's only a shoebox, and a man's shoes."

"There was nothing there before, when Mrs. Blanchard looked. Someone crawls round the roof and into the eaves."

I knelt down to take a closer look. The only other light came from the roof where there was a gap in the tiles. On closer inspection, I saw that the shoes were of good quality. There was a brown paper carrier bag with a string handle.

I closed the door. "How long have these things been there, Milly?"

"I don't know." Mrs. Blanchard looked last week and there was nothing."

"Have you looked at the shoes or the box, or touched anything?"

"No. I never saw them until today."

"Do you think one of the other servants might have been in here, one of the men?"

"They don't come this side of the attics. The men have their own stairs. Somebody must crawl through, all the way round the house. That's why I hear noises."

"Try not to worry, Milly. The housekeeper is right. The noises you hear could simply be the creaks and groans of an old house. But don't tell anyone what we've seen today. Let me look into it."

If I had killed a man, and had something to hide, what better place than the room of a girl who was in love with a murder suspect?

Milly pulled a battered brown suitcase from under the bed. "I'm off home. I don't care if there's too many mouths to feed. I'd rather starve."

"Don't be hasty. Either there is a simple explanation, or there is something odd going on. Be brave."

Milly decided against being brave. She began to cry. "Everything's going wrong. Mi mam'll say I've let the family down. And Stephen, poor Stephen, he'll be –"

She could not say the word "hanged".

I glanced at my watch. This was not a time to rouse suspicion through absence. "Milly, pull yourself together. If anyone asks why you're upset, say it's because of Stephen –"

"It is."

"There are other maids here, and you have two beds. Who else on this corridor could share with you?"

"They don't have as many servants as they used to. Freda, the kitchen maid, she has two beds as well. She'd let me go in with her."

"Good. And you explain that it's because you don't want to sleep on your own. You've had nightmares. No mention of any other reason, unless it's the stags in the painting. Understood?"

"Yes. But –" Milly sniffled. She wiped her nose.

"Comb your hair, blink your red eyes and go for a walk round the garden, if the housekeeper doesn't need you."

"What are you going to do?"

"I'll think of something. Meanwhile, say nothing about this, not even to Freda if you share her room."

Chapter
Twenty-Two

❧

Early on Monday morning, I approached the prison. It felt strange to be here, ringing the bell, asking to be let in. Those on the other side of the gates, perhaps including the staff, would prefer to be on this side of the wall.

After a wait of about five minutes, the wicket gate was opened by a pale man of skeletal proportions. His vividly black eyebrows met as he frowned, and I saw that they were tinged with grey and white. Variegated-eyebrows man stared through eyes of stone. If it had not been for the uniform, I would have thought him the condemned man.

"Good morning. I'm Mrs. Shackleton, and am expected."

Let that be true.

He said nothing but simply opened the gate wide enough for me to step through.

We walked across the yard and into the dimly lit entranceway. Here, it was colder than outdoors. We came to a stop by a bench, to which my escort nodded. I ignored his nod and remained standing.

The sound of footsteps heralded the appearance of the tall officer. Last time I saw him, he looked cheerful. Today, cheer had deserted him. He did not meet my glance.

"Would you come this way, Mrs. Shackleton?"

Another corridor. Footsteps echoed from the opposite end.

Stephen appeared, head bowed, his gait more shuffling than previously. There was no singing of "The Grand Old Duke of York" today. Slowly, he raised his head and gave me a look of such hopelessness that I felt a shiver.

Stephen's escort came into the room with us. My escort waited by the door.

I was offered a chair in the corner. Stephen was seated at a table, his escort behind him.

It was the kind of room where simply to speak seemed inappropriate. That did not stop me. "Stephen, I saw Milly and Joan. They were outside the prison on Sunday. Did you hear the band? Milly has given a statement about what happened."

He gave me a look that was so briefly hopeful, and then he glanced away.

Wouldn't it be wonderful, if he would be released? Now. This morning. I would have a bit of explaining to do as to how I came to be taking him home—wherever home would be now—but that would be worth it.

"Officer, I should like to speak to Mr. Walmsley alone."

He gulped. "Sorry, madam. That is not allowed."

"Why not?"

"Not today."

I soon realised why.

The police officer who entered, nodded, and with great civility wished us good morning.

The officer urged the prisoner to his feet, and then came the blow.

"Stephen Walmsley, you are charged that on Friday, the first of March, 1929, in the Corner Shop, Silver Street, Thorpefield, you did wilfully murder Helen Farrar. You do not need to say anything but anything you do say may be taken down in writing and used in evidence against you. Do you have anything to say?"

"I didn't do it. I didn't kill Mrs. Farrar."

"Take the prisoner away."

He passed so close to me that I could hear the gasp of his breath. "Don't give up, Stephen. Don't give up hope."

When he had been taken back to his cell, I stayed in the room for several moments, trying to make sense of what I had just seen and heard.

The prison officer who had escorted me simply waited for me to move.

I turned to him. "Why now? Nothing has changed since Mr. Walmsley was arrested over a week ago."

He spoke quietly. "He was being given the opportunity to plead guilty. That would have saved time, trouble, and public expense."

Trudging back through the prison yard, I had to force myself to think ahead to what must come next. One thing was for sure: Stephen must have better representation than the solicitor appointed by the police.

I sat in the car to write a note to Mrs. Sugden, asking her to contact our fiercest legal friend, stopping at the first pillar box to post it. Mr. Cohen's fees might swallow the fee we would earn from Scotland Yard, but my pristine Rolls-Royce languishes in the garage. That would fetch a pretty penny.

As I drove back towards Thorpefield, I tried to think what to do next. There is always that desire to Do Something Quickly.

Yesterday evening, when the house was quiet, I had taken two flashlights and every candle I could lay my hands on into Milly's room. Wearing gloves, I took the items from the eaves and photographed them, alongside that day's newspaper. Someone had done this deliberately, as a way of pointing an accusing finger at Stephen Walmsley. If I was right, and the pair of expensive shoes belonged to the unknown man, Milly would also be regarded as an accessory. There were coins and notes, a signet ring and a fob watch.

The brown paper bag contained a pair of socks, a tie, and a gun. By doing nothing, I was withholding evidence. To do the "right thing" might damn Stephen for two murders. He could hang only once.

Chapter
Twenty-Three

~

My visit to the prison had not taken long. I was back at Thorpefield Manor by 8 a.m.

Naturally, the ever-watchful Raynor noticed my return, but made no comment. Let him think it was my Monday habit to go out for an early drive, and come back looking as if I'd found a penny but lost a five pound note.

At about ten o'clock, Gertrude and I made our way to the stables. It had been so long since I wore jodhpurs and riding jacket that my outfit felt like a disguise, which in a way it was.

As we entered the stable, I felt warmth from the heat of the horses' bodies. The familiar scent of hay and horses swept me back to the days when I first learned to ride.

Alec was lifting down a bale of hay. "I've saddled Jasper for your guest, Mrs. Brockman. Is that all right?"

She didn't answer Alec, but said to me. "Jasper's a good-tempered creature and knows his way about."

Gertrude's piebald whinnied at her approach.

We mounted, and moments later were riding along the broad drive into the now bright morning.

Gertrude called to me. "You still have a good seat, Kate. Do you remember our old instructress? She was full of praise for your riding. "Look at Catherine! She has glue on her bum."

"I'd forgotten that."

Beyond the drive, we crossed the road and took the bridle path that led to the hamlet of Thorpefield. Our way took us through a small wood and over furrowed fields.

At the edge of the hamlet were the long rows of miners' cottages, small two-storey dwellings built of local stone and with stone roofs. Philip and I had passed them during our drive in the grocer's van on Friday. A woman in a colourful pinafore knelt on the pavement, scouring her doorstep. Gertrude slowed her horse. "Do you want to take a photograph?"

I had a small knapsack with me, containing camera, notebook and pencil. "She wouldn't appreciate being pictured on her knees."

We rode on until we were alongside the railway line, by a row of attractive brick and slate houses, rather ornate, and in groups of four, with arches between.

I stopped, and took a photograph.

"Benjie's grandfather built these," Gertrude explained. "Having the railway meant they could bring in bricks and Welsh slate instead of using local stone."

"They're grand looking, but why use bricks when there's Yorkshire stone?"

"The railway barons liked to show off, as evidence of how well they were doing. It cost more to bring in bricks. They thought they would recruit better workers."

The railway line ran behind the houses. They all knew each other, these men, these trusted superior railway workers with brick houses. Three years ago, like their fellows, they had gone on strike. And now?

Had the tenor of their lives been disturbed by a man who came to stir up trouble, among workers who had troubles of their own? A stranger murdered for his Russian gold, as Commander Woodhead suspected.

How would they have achieved the task of placing a body onto a goods train? There was a signal box not far along. Halt the train. Slide open the door of a truck, perhaps marked with chalk to show there would be room among the boxes. The dead weight of the unknown man dumped alongside boxes of rhubarb. Wipe off the chalk mark. The houses looked so perfectly neat and orderly, yet what lay behind that civilised façade?

We rode by the stream, towards the mill and mill stream. Outside the millworkers' houses, a group of little children stopped their play on the pavement and stared up at us, and at the horses. We dismounted.

A couple of mothers came to see what we were up to. I asked permission, and was soon snapping away, taking photographs of bow-legged children with rickets, sitting on the pavements and the cobblestones. They were cautious rather than excited. The mothers, self-conscious of their appearance in pinafores, turbans and slippers, refused to have pictures taken.

I took names and promised to let them have copies of their children's photographs.

We were about to re-mount when one of the women approached Gertrude. "What about the shop, Mrs. Brockman? It's awful shocking and no one wants to be disrespectful towards Mrs. Farrar. Will it stand empty now?"

"I don't know," Gertrude answered quietly.

"Only it's a trek if you're just after a couple of eggs or a teacake. Now if we could have a Co-operative Store here –"

Gertrude cut her off. "I'll look into it."

Another woman joined in. "Millworkers miss going in there. It was handy for their packets of fags. And Mrs. Farrar, God rest her soul, made decent sandwiches."

Gertrude nodded graciously. "As you say, we don't want to be disrespectful to Mrs. Farrar. It's rather soon."

We rode on, side by side. "Gertrude, that was a dreadful murder. I hope I haven't made it difficult for you, joining in that procession yesterday?"

"You're investigating again, aren't you?"

I dodged the question. "I'm tempted to investigate, but no one has asked me to." Given that we were talking about Mrs. Farrar's death, I was telling no lie.

"You must believe Stephen Walmsley is innocent or you wouldn't have joined the march."

"He has a huge amount of support from people who believe he didn't do it."

"It was utterly sickening, Kate, what he did to that poor woman. It was him all right. The police have the killer. Walmsley had blood on his hands."

Just for a moment, I let myself imagine that Stephen was guilty, that she was right and I was wrong.

Gertrude had no doubts. "We don't know what sort of wicked strain Stephen inherited. No one knows who his father was."

"What about his mother?"

"Her husband threw her out, and then took her back. They moved away, to avoid the shame. As soon as Stephen was old enough, Benjie gave him a job at the pit. He's very generous like that. And this is how we're repaid. Murder on our own doorstep."

"I hope he'll get a fair trial, Gertrude."

"Of course he will. Everyone does. This is England. We bend over backwards to be fair to rascals. I know that you thought I was being picky, not wanting a child whose history is unknown. There is such a thing as bad blood."

We rode on.

The Miners' Welfare Institute stood at a little distance from the school. I dismounted and took photographs of both buildings. It was one of those standard-built schools, put up to meet the requirements of the 1870 Education Act.

"I expect you want to see the mill, too."

I had not thought of that, having seen enough mills to know what they are like, but I said yes.

From the way Gertrude said, "Oh come on then. I suppose you might as well," I realised I had given the wrong answer.

"What's up, Gertrude?"

"I had a telephone call just before we left. It was for Benjie but of course he's off on one of his jaunts. We had to cut the workers' hours and halve pay."

"I'm sorry to hear that."

"We have no choice. The over-lookers have accepted the inevitable, but the women are objecting. With their impeccable logic, they have walked out. I didn't want to burden you with our troubles."

"Do you need to talk to them?"

She sighed. "I should. The foreman seems to think I might be able to persuade the women to listen."

The upshot was that we left the horses by the mill gates and went into the yard.

The group of women turned to look. Surprised by the sight of Gertrude, they became silent. I recognised just one: Joan Arkwright.

Gertrude took a deep breath and wished them good morning.

A few replied.

Joan spoke first. "Mrs. Brockman, we know it's your mill but it's our wages you're snatching from us. Half time means half pay and no one can live on that."

"What have you been told?" Gertrude asked.

"That we're to be on short time until further notice, well we won't have it."

"We are in this business together," Gertrude said. "You are all good workers. We make excellent cloth, the best."

Joan's short speech emboldened others.

"If we're good workers, be a good boss. Pay us properly."

"We can't pay half rent, we can't pay half the price of a loaf."

Gertrude waited. "It's not your fault and it's not mine. The trouble is, fashions have changed. There isn't the same call for our good cloth as there once was, and we have competition from overseas."

"They don't produce what we do."

Gertrude ignored this. "You must have heard about the jobs lost in Bradford. We are trying to find another way. By the end of the month, we'll have new machinery—suitable for artificial silk, crepe-de-chine and georgette. Bear with us. You are the best work-force. I know you will adapt."

By now a man in a white smock had appeared, and two men in brown smocks. They came to stand beside Gertrude.

"Talk among yourselves," she said. "Don't be hasty. But I do hope you will go back to work." She turned to the men. "Your fore-man and over-lookers will be on reduced hours too. I'm sorry to say that short time is what may keep us afloat, until the new machinery comes. We'll start to produce the material people want these days. But if we don't fulfil the present order, we'll have nothing."

The women had already begun talking to each other.

Joan called, "What if the machines don't come? What if there isn't enough work for all?"

Gertrude turned to the man in the white coat. "Mr. Monty, please give our staff your best reassurances."

"Right, Mrs. Brockman."

"Good day, ladies and gentlemen." With that, Gertrude and I left the yard.

"That was very good, Gertrude."

"One tries."

"Will there be new machinery?"

"Eliot is onto it now. He's a shareholder, and so is old Mrs. Dell."

That was not the answer Gertrude's workers would have wanted to hear. "You said it to get them back to work?"

"They have no idea what we are up against. If you saw the bal-ance sheet for this mill, you'd wonder how we keep going. And it truly is out of our hands. Some of the best mills in Bradford felt the pinch even before we did."

"Why is Eliot looking into things, and not Benjie?"

"You must have noticed a change in Benjie, he seems so detached from everything. He works up a little enthusiasm about the new mine, but not much. He pretends to be working when he goes into his study, but if you barged in, you'd see his stamp collection on the table, or his coins."

We rode in silence for a while, in single file along the lane, coming to the closed Corner Shop by the back way. It looked different when approached from the rear. The building appeared more solitary, set back from the row of houses.

It still seemed difficult to imagine this innocuous setting as the scene of a brutal crime. I put that thought from my mind and attempted to sound matter-of-fact.

"I can see why the shop is convenient for people on this side of the village."

"Yes. It was always a shop, the last house in a row that was demolished forty years ago. That's how it came to be called the Corner Shop. The then-owners wanted to keep on renting because they did good trade."

"It looks odd, standing all alone, cut off from Silver Street."

Gertrude's horse whinnied, anxious to move on.

She stroked his neck. "I don't know whether anyone will want to take it on after what has happened."

"Would you consider doing what that woman suggested earlier, and having a Co-operative Store?"

"Well it's our shop, you see. Once you let the cooperatives in, they sell for less and share dividend with their members. They swallow up all the trade. They're an anathema to owners of small shops."

The garden behind the shop was beautifully tended. Some crops had been sown, overseen by a scarecrow. Scraps of newspaper had been threaded on string to keep away the birds

"Mrs. Farrar took pride in her garden."

"I feel terrible about it, Kate. I didn't like Mrs. Farrar, not that I had much to do with her. She was a busybody. Raynor acts as estate manager. He said she never paid the rent without moaning about how difficult it was to make ends meet, but I wouldn't have wished that death on anyone."

"It was a robbery?"

"Yes, though for such a pittance. Thank God they have him behind bars."

I thought of him, in that cold whitewashed room, and saw him in my mind's eye. Defeated. Dejected. As if he had given up on himself.

"What do you know about him?" I asked.

"He had the best of care and attention in the home. And a good job at the Finney pit. There's gratitude for you."

"If he was in work, he couldn't have been so hard up that he would kill for a paltry sum, could he?"

"Some people never have enough, Kate."

If at that moment I had said what was in my mind, I would have had to pack my bags and go. Gertrude was a person who never had enough. I had forgotten what she can be like. I thought back over our friendship, and for the first time wondered how it had lasted this long.

My explanation was that we had met for lunch, in department store restaurants or select cafés. She had invited me to her version of country house weekends. Alongside her snobbish, self-satisfied guests, Gertrude seemed a saint.

She continued. "Mrs. Farrar had more money than she let on. Who knows what he stole and where he stashed it before the police picked him up?"

A tall woman from the end house opened her door, stepped outside, noticed us and retreated.

Unless I was mistaken, that was the grace and favour house, and she was the woman who lived rent-free.

"Who is she?"

"I don't know all the tenants by name." Gertrude steadied her horse that had become restless. "It won't be easy to find someone to take on the shop. There's a lot of superstition. People began to see Mrs. Farrar's ghost hours after her body was taken away." She turned and gave me a smile. "Are you ghoulish enough that you want a picture of the shop?"

"Yes, but just for my own information."

"Not that I'm asking to be a censor or anything but this is a rather sensitive time."

I took the photograph without dismounting. "It will be an aide memoire to where we've been today."

"I've told the estate agent to be sensitive about advertising—at least until things have quietened down."

I would make sure that Mrs. Sugden was the first person to come and look around. She would find out about the mysterious neighbour in the end house.

"Let's get away from here." Gertrude urged her horse into a gallop, calling, "I'll show you a sight worth photographing!"

Chapter
Twenty-Four

～

After a mile or so, Gertrude slowed her horse. "Have you ever seen a pit being sunk?"

"No."

"Neither have I. But you'll see it now. I told you Royds wasn't re-opened after the strike. Benjie had tests done, bore holes and such like. He's opening new seams at Overton. There's a company getting on with the work now."

"That sounds like a huge undertaking."

"A messy one! You'll need a bath when we get back!" She trotted ahead. The breeze carried her words to me. "You have to speculate to accumulate. Our future is pinned on this. Fortunately, we have a lot of potential investors. Eliot and I have been drumming up support. It will be so up to date. Even Raynor—and I don't quote him lightly—says it will be a gold mine of a coalmine."

We were on a hill. Now I had the lie of the land. Looking down at the wood gave me my bearings. We were at the other side of the wood. Overton Wood was its name, but it was always the Bluebell Wood, even when bluebells faded and died. Beyond it had stood the children's home.

The ground dipped, creating a miniature valley. My horse hesitated on the steep incline. A little way ahead, a cloud of dust rose. Sparse grass gave way to dirt ground. We rode on. Seen from this distance, the group of men clustered at the bottom of the valley made me think of busy ants in a basin. There was something very much like an encampment. Makeshift huts had been erected. Smoke rose from a brazier. On the hill to the left were horses and carts. As we paused to watch, one of the carts set off.

"What are they doing?"

"This will impress your editor. I don't suppose many lady photographers will send in photographs of a pit shaft being sunk."

As we dismounted, two of the men came from the group and offered to take our horses. They seemed glad to have something to do. From the number of men standing about, this must be a job where everyone is needed, but not all at the same time.

"Snap away, Kate. I'm going to talk to the engineer. Benjie will be proud of me. I'll be able to give him an up-to-the-minute report. And then I'll ask the engineer if he'll explain it to you."

I followed the man who had taken my horse. Neither of us said anything, but I recognised him as one of the people in Sunday's procession to the prison. "Will you object if I take photographs? I've never seen anything like this before."

"Nor me, missus."

"What is it that you are doing?"

"I'm a farrier, nothing to do with the job in hand but to keep the horses harnessed and the carts filled."

Rubble and soil was being loaded onto a cart.

I took photographs of the men and the horses and carts, of the brazier and a young fellow with blackened teeth. Grinning, he held up a tin mug as if making a toast.

My farrier escort seemed pleased to be in a photograph. I made a note of his address and promised to supply copies for him and his workmates.

"What exactly are the men doing?" I asked him. "How do you sink a pit?"

"You can't see it from here but there's a big timber plate, size of the shaft where the cages will take men to the bottom. There are men below, digging it out and sending up buckets of earth through the hole in the middle of the timber plate."

"Won't the sides be in danger of giving way?"

"They would, but bricklayers are building a wall around the plate. You'll see that heap of bricks—that will become the wall. When the plate descends, it takes the wall with it. That provides the surface for the shaft where lifts will take men down into the mine, eventually."

"What a hard job. You must be glad to be on the surface."

"I am that, missus. I'd hate to be in the bowels of the earth. This pit's being sunk so deep that we'll be fighting Australian miners for the coal."

"Thanks for the explanation. I'll take a look."

"Aye, you do that, and listen out for the cries of the orphans and waifs and strays."

"What do you mean?"

"The Bluebell Children's Home stood nearby for a century and more. It was a lucky place for some. They'd be sorry to see it come to this."

"What does this have to do with the home?"

Gertrude waved for me to join her.

He turned back to his horses. "Her ladyship summons."

He had not answered me. "When was the home demolished?"

"The minute the young uns left, and just in time for the contractors to gather up the stone blocks and bricks from the house to use again for the shaft wall."

"The subsidence didn't make any difference then, to the sinking of a new pit?"

"Don't know nowt about subsidence, not round here." He turned away, to talk to two men who were tipping buckets of earth and debris onto a cart.

I noticed a small, blood-red toy, a wooden engine, lying by a rock. It seemed such an incongruous juxtaposition that I took a photograph.

I wondered where it came from, and whether one of the men might want to take it home. The farrier I had spoken to earlier was now waiting with the horse and cart.

I went across. "Look, here's a little engine. Do you have a boy who might like it?"

He took it from me, holding it this way and that. "Whoever made it did a good job, and painted it too."

This might be the engine that Mr. Arkwright had made for Alec Taylor.

My guide pointed to a space between two boulders, where a small heap of items had been set aside. There was a child's shoe, a whip and top, a toy car and a doll with one arm.

The sight of these items made me feel uneasy. "What did happen to the children?"

I had heard something from Gertrude, and from Mrs. Arkwright, but this man also seemed in the know.

He glanced across at Gertrude who was speaking to the engineer. "Perhaps the Pied Piper came and led them into the slag heaps. They were gone before the demolition men came. Before you knew it, the ground was cleared."

"But where did they go, and so quickly that their toys were left behind?"

He shook his head. "Progress moves fast, missus, when there's money in t'ground."

Gertrude was still talking to the engineer. We each had saddlebags, with a bottle of water and some chocolate. I put the little wooden engine into my saddlebag, and then joined Gertrude.

"There's a pile of what the children left behind. It looks so sad and pathetic."

"Honestly, Kate, those children were given so much. If they chose not to take stuff with them to Stoneville, then it was because they didn't want it."

"Stoneville?"

"It's a very good children's home in Wakefield, on York Street."
She waved to the man who was making his way towards us. "I told
the engineer you'd like to talk to him."

Someone interrupted the engineer's progress. He stopped to
answer a question.

Gertrude looked up to where the farrier had tethered the horses.
"Do the horses and ponies look well, Kate?"

"They do."

"I'll go take a look." She smiled. "Giles is a good farrier. We
take the best care of the horses. I make sure the pit ponies have
a week a year on the surface. You must come one day when they
are brought up. That's a sight you'd love to photograph. You'd be
overjoyed to see them when they have light and air and freedom."

A man in his fifties, dressed in tweed suit, twill trousers and
wellington boots, came to join us. "Kate, this is Mr. Greenwood,
the engineer. Mr. Greenwood, my clever friend Mrs. Shackleton.
She'll understand everything and write it all up for her article." She
walked towards the hill, where the horses were standing.

Patiently, Mr. Greenwood explained how this hole in the
ground would eventually be transformed into a mine that would
provide good quality coal.

I made a few notes. It was a unique experience to be brought
here and shown how mining begins, how the earth is scarred and
opened so that its black gold can be brought to the surface to keep
us warm.

"I suppose the subsidence will help, because you won't need to
dig so far down. Nature will do it for you."

He frowned. "What subsidence?"

"Subsidence at the other side of the wood—where a building
stood." Something told me not to name that building. "It became
unsafe."

He shook his head. "Well if there had been subsidence, it would
have been unsafe, but there wasn't. We would have found that

out when we did the exploratory tests. That building would have stood for a hundred years or more, but they're shocking houses to maintain. Built in the days when there was a lot more money to be made, in mills and mines and everything else. Fancy villas were all the rage. You could pick one up for a song now."

One of the workmen called to him, and our conversation came to an end. Who should I believe? Gertrude who had told me that children had to leave the home because it was no longer safe, or the engineer who said it would last another hundred years?

After a few moments, Gertrude and I retrieved our horses and set off.

"Thank you for showing me this, Gertrude. It's an extraordinary sight. How long will it take to open the new pit?"

"Search me, Kate. I don't usually have much to do with this, but I thought you'd find it interesting—for your article."

Either she said those last three words in a way that let me know she mistrusted my story of an article, or I was imagining her distrust.

"It's a pity there hasn't been someone taking photographs from the time the building was demolished, creating a photographic record."

"I suppose so. But it doesn't do to be sentimental, or to look back. There'll be decades of work here. The miners made a mistake, going on strike. They won't do that again in a hurry—let themselves be led astray by hotheads."

"I thought they simply wanted more pay."

"They preached that the coal in the ground and the plenty of the land is there for everyone. They didn't understand how much outlay, how much investment is needed. Not that I have much to do with it."

I thought of Commander Woodhead's suspicions about a representative of a foreign power bringing money to foment unrest. Perhaps that was not a chimera, dreamed up out of desperation. If men who had suffered great hardship to the point of starvation met a man who said, "Let's do it all again," he might receive a savage welcome.

Think of something practical to ask, I told myself. Don't give yourself away.

"How will you transport coal from here?"

"It's not difficult to lay an extension to the rail line, apparently. There's nothing between here and the main line except waste ground and a few trees."

A few trees.

She meant Bluebell Wood.

Chapter Twenty-Five

❧

Back at Thorpefield Manor, Gertrude and I ate a light lunch and went to our rooms, agreeing to meet before dinner.

Feeling like a character from a girls' adventure story, I left the house and strolled about the walled garden, admiring the daffodils. From there, I slipped through the gate and along to the bee boles, holding a short note for delivery by Philip.

Mrs. Sugden, Please visit Stoneville on York Street, Wakefield. Enquire about the children from Bluebell Children's Home, Thorpefield. Also, the shop is now with an agent.

As I slid the note into the space in the wall, my fingers touched something hard and round. It was a pebble—a message from Philip that he was as good as his word and had called again.

As I turned away, ready to stroll back the way I had come, I heard a low whistle.

Philip gestured to me from the trees.

Quickly I grabbed the note and casually walked into the wood. "How long have you been here?"

"Ages."

I handed him the note. "It's a job for Mrs. Sugden, my housekeeper."

"Shall I take it to her?"

"Yes, if you want a ride to Leeds. Or you might telephone."

He frowned, and read the note. "I could say exactly what you have written."

"Yes."

He nodded.

"Philip, when you said you'd keep an eye on the bee boles, I didn't think you'd camp out in the wood."

"I'm not camping out."

"What then?"

"Mam wanted me to go see Mr. Battersby again about that garage. I told her I'm helping you."

"It won't hurt to look."

"I can't look at a garage yet. I'm helping you."

"A telephone call to Mrs. Sugden will do. You might still look at the garage."

"I told Mam I'm helping you. She'll know that's a good thing."

It was no use arguing with him. Mouth set tight, eyes full of hurt, he looked away.

I relented.

"Yes, it's a good thing that you are helping me. Perhaps you could take the message to Mrs. Sugden in person. She won't know anything about the Bluebell Home or why it is called that. She would like to know."

His mood changed in an instant. Poor Mrs. Goodchild. She tried so hard to make Philip's life the best it could be. And she had succeeded. Perhaps the Battersby Garage was a step too far.

"I'll do that now, Kate." He took a sheet of paper from his pocket. "Here is a list of two hundred rhubarb growers. Which have you seen so far?"

He was pointing out the blindingly obvious. I hadn't visited a single one. "Mr. Sykes has been visiting growers. But I do have an acquaintance at one of the farms in Rothwell. I'll talk to him."

I glanced at my watch. Hours to go before dinner.

Philip shifted his gaze. He looked over my shoulder at someone or something.

I heard the crunching footsteps before I saw Raynor, coming from the wood. He tipped his hat. Philip and I watched as Raynor walked towards the gate in the walled garden.

When he had gone, Philip said, "Was he hiding? Was he earwigging?"

"I don't know."

"Kate, I wish you would go somewhere else. I don't like this place."

He stopped to listen. More footsteps crunched through the wood.

This time it was Alec. Had we had an audience of eavesdroppers?

"Oh hello," Alec said.

He wasn't talking to me.

Philip tilted his head. "I've seen you before."

"When you came to our garage for spare parts."

"You work at Battersby's?"

"I work there on Thursdays, learning the trade. Mr. Battersby calls you the best mechanic in Wakefield."

Philip perked up. "A lot of people say that."

"He's going to live in Morecambe but I wish he wasn't."

"Why?"

"I still have things to learn." Alec looked at me, and then at Philip. "Do you know each other then?"

I got in first. "Mr. Goodchild takes care of my car."

Well, wasn't this cosy? So much for my being undercover. But credit to Philip. He turned away, saying. "I'm just out testing a van. I have to go now."

Chapter
Twenty-Six

～

Most of the time, these roads are empty of cars. I did not think much of it at the time, but on the road to Rothwell another car followed mine at a consistent distance. When I slowed down, so did that car. When I speeded up, it also increased its speed.

After that odd sensation of having been followed, it was a relief that the black car continued on its way when I turned onto the lane that led to Whitwells Farm. I left the car in the lane and walked along the muddy track.

Ahead of me were the low rhubarb sheds, each with its own chimney, and with tracks leading from shed to gate.

I first met Josh Whitwell, the family's younger son, when Rothwell Camera Club put on an exhibition. He is a good photographer. One particular image stayed in my mind. It was the interior of a forced rhubarb shed, lit by candles. He modestly said that it was trickery. Much of the rhubarb had been picked, and there was a certain amount of light from the open door. He had taken the photograph from an angle, to make the shed appear full of a regiment of rhubarb soldiers.

As I neared the first big shed, a stocky farm labourer, work trousers tucked into his boots, came over, to see what I wanted.

"Is Josh Whitwell about?"

"He's packing. We're expecting the van soon."

"I'm a friend, and I just want a quick word."

The man directed me to a large shed whose doors were wide open. The rhubarb had all been picked from the forcing sheds and brought here. It lay in heaps on a long table. At one end a woman was lining small crates with blue tissue paper, and passing them along. Another woman and three youngsters were filling the boxes with rhubarb. Josh was at the end of the table, placing them onto a cart. He waved when he saw me, and called to the man who had shown me in to come and take over.

Josh grinned. "I heard you were here, Kate."

"Who told you?"

"Half a dozen people who know I'm in the camera club. A lady photographer, they said, writing an article about the area. I'm jealous."

"Don't be. I want to include your rhubarb shed photograph."

"Really?" He leaned forward as if waiting for me to pin a medal on his chest. "I'd love that."

"I'll need the negative."

This was going too far. If I didn't interest a magazine in this article, that was becoming both real and surreal, I should have to publish it myself and bear the cost. If I didn't solve this case for Scotland Yard, I could see myself having to wave a wand over my bank balance.

"When do you want the photograph?"

"No great rush. We can meet when it's convenient. This is a busy time for you."

"Not now we're into March. Things are quietening down."

If this was quietening down, I'd hate to see the place when they were busy.

He called to the woman at the table. "Mam, are you all right without me?"

I offered to get stuck in alongside them, but his mother called back that they were nearly done.

"Mam, this is Kate Shackleton, the photographer I told you about."

"Well as long as she doesn't want to take a snap of me she's welcome."

He and I sat on stools at the side of the shed. We chatted about the photographs I had taken, and he suggested other views that I might include.

I turned the conversation.

"Josh, what's all this business about a body on the rhubarb express?"

"It's bizarre." He waved at the boxes of rhubarb. "Rhubarb is delicate, perishable. A grower wouldn't risk damaging his crop by adding a sack of potatoes, much less a body." He listened for a moment, heard the noise of an engine, and jumped up. "That's the railway van. Give me a minute."

Men wheeled the carts to the door, and when Josh saw he wasn't needed, he came back.

"What you were asking me about, that body, it just wouldn't happen. It's got to be a fairy story. Some cockney porter knocked off his worst enemy and pretended he fell out of a rhubarb truck."

He explained how the vans would now take the rhubarb to Ardsley station. The produce would be booked in and packed on railway trucks. The trucks would be shunted into the siding at Ardsley station—trucks from Ardsley, Carlton, Stanley, Morley and all the other places in the district where rhubarb was grown. The man on duty would telephone the full list of rhubarb van numbers to Leeds Central, and the Leeds rhubarb trucks would start from there, behind the engine that would continue on to Ardsley to link up with the rest. By quarter to nine, all the trucks would be marshalled and ready to be coupled to the engine.

This must be information that Alec Taylor had recorded in his missing notebook.

Josh paused. His eyes widened. "Oh, oh, don't tell me. Let me guess. You're investigating the death."

"I'm curious that's all."

He laughed. "A lady detective turns up at what might be the scene of a crime and all she's interested in is –"

"Writing and illustrating an article, with her own photographs and those of a brilliant local photographer."

"Rhubarb growers don't have time to go around murdering people. Mind you, I might make an exception for our Tom."

"Why?"

"He's gone to teach agriculture at a college near York."

"Your parents must be proud?"

"Proud? They're devastated. He's betrayed the family. There's no way I'll escape now."

"And do you want to?"

"What do you think? I was hoping you'd take me on as a private detective."

"I'm here for my article, Josh, photographer's honour! But you can't blame me for being curious. I think someone went to the sidings and put the body on the train."

"Have you seen the sidings?"

"I know what sidings look like."

"Then you'll know that there's a foot difference in height between the sidings and the platform level where the loading's done. If the killer was a big fellow, eight feet tall and with an identical twin as his accomplice, he'd be in with a chance."

"But it's possible."

"Well, yes, especially if the tall burly murderers aren't spotted by the clerk as he plods up and down the sidings swinging his paraffin lamp."

Sometimes it is useful to ask a question to which you know the answer, or part of the answer.

"Just out of curiosity, were there any strangers in the area over the last few weeks?"

"The wrecking men, demolishing the children's home, there were plenty of them. And now the men who are sinking the pit."

"Were the demolition men local?"

"They were from a company in Pontefract. They've gone now. One stayed about, looking for work, big brawny chap, nickname Giant Jack. He'd worked on a farm in Ireland and had a fancy to be on the land again."

"And could you give him work?"

"We have enough workers now. I told him to come back at harvest time." He grinned. "We don't just grow rhubarb."

"Do you think he might still be around, looking for work? I'd like some link in my article to the demolition."

"Doubt it. He'll have moved on. He wanted to earn extra money to take back to Ireland, to his family."

"What was his real name?"

"Kevin O'Donnell. I took his photograph, because of his size really. I got him to stand next to my mam."

"Can you show me?"

He stood. "Come on then, and your secret is safe with me. If there's a reward for catching this murderer, and you find him, I want my cut."

We walked across a muddy track to the farmhouse. He went to the dresser, opened a drawer full of albums and envelopes. From the topmost envelope, he took out a photograph and passed it to me. "There he is. Six feet four if he's an inch, but the most gentle and polite fellow you could meet. I sent him to the Dell Estate. Nothing came of it."

"Do you have a copy of this photograph?"

"Take this, if you'll give it me back."

I tucked the postcard size photograph in my satchel. It was an unlikely possibility that a transient worker was involved. This odd and contradictory murder appeared both totally ludicrous and carefully planned.

*   *   *

In the local post office, I penned a note to Sykes, enclosing the photograph of Kevin O'Donnell, nickname Giant Jack, an employee of a demolition firm in Pontefract, and now looking for work. I asked him to have an extra copy made.

Just as I was about to pop it in the box, the postman came and so I handed him the letter. Sykes would have my message by tomorrow's first post.

As I turned to go, I practically bumped into Raynor. He was holding several letters, which he also handed to the postman.

"I could have done that for you, Mrs. Shackleton. Mr. Brockman says if you have any post or messages, you might just give them to me."

He had come an awfully long way to post letters.

I thought of Commander Woodhead's suspicions that some agitator was murdered for his Russian gold. He was wrong, that was my overwhelming feeling. This murder was home-grown.

But Josh Whitwell was right. The killer wasn't a rhubarb grower. It was someone who didn't know how tricky it would be to put a body on the rhubarb express.

Chapter Twenty-Seven

⟡

The cold of the cellar rose to meet me as I went down the stone steps to my makeshift darkroom. Gertrude and I would meet an hour before dinner, so I had sufficient time to begin work on developing my photographs. When turning my attention to an absorbing activity, I sometimes come up with a solution to a problem. Developing and printing might help me find a way into the puzzle of why two murders occurred around the same time in this quiet spot.

I was close to something, had gathered threads. It was a matter of holding a kind of stillness inside while staying alert. Waiting for some chink of light to crack open an investigation can be difficult.

The cellar runs the length and breadth of the house, with large rooms, such as the wine cellar—which looked more sparsely stocked than I had ever seen it—and smaller rooms, cold stores, pantries and other mysterious places.

I pinned a note on the door of the little room that had been cleaned and prepared for me.

Do Not Disturb.

I do not always have time to do my own developing, but it feels like cheating to hand the film on to be done by a professional's apprentice.

As I poured in the fixer solution, I heard footsteps, and the sound of something being dragged across the floor.

"Don't come in!" I called.

No one answered.

There is always a moment of excitement when seeing a picture emerge, as if by magic.

Recently, I bought a second-hand but more up-to-date enlarging box. I can make postcard-size prints from my negatives, using the daylight method. Thanks to the cellar door that led to the garden, it should have been easy to go out into the light and time my exposure, but the day was dull and I am still getting used to it.

There was something forlorn about the picture of the small heap of toys and shoes left behind after the closure and demolition of the children's home. When my efforts were clipped to dry, I felt satisfied. That was enough for now.

After clearing up, I turned to leave the room, and made to open the door. It was stuck. Perhaps because of this room being small, the door opened outwards. Or it would open outwards if I could do it. I pushed harder. No movement. Something was stopping it. I put my shoulder against the door and pushed as hard as I could.

This was not just annoying, it felt humiliating. How could I end up fastened in a room without a lock?

Milly knew I was here. Raynor knew I had come back. Alec would have seen my car.

Someone would come.

After listening for footsteps and hearing nothing, I began to knock. I knocked until my knuckles were sore. I shouted, took off a shoe, banged with that.

And then I waited. It was hard to believe that I was trapped. I tried the door again, absurdly expecting it to move this time. Something was holding it firmly shut. Once more I banged, with the heel of my hand.

I could imagine the conversation between Gertrude and Benjie. She has become very odd. Doing nothing but snap, snap, snap, ignoring the fact that she is a guest. Refuses church, goes with a servant to chapel, marches in procession to the prison. Snap, snap and snap again, taking over the cellar, treating the place as a hotel.

And now, Benjie would know where I had been this afternoon. Raynor would have given him an account.

A cellar is a terribly silent place. This felt like a tomb. It was reassuring to hear, briefly, the groan of pipes somewhere.

There is nothing dangerous about the chemicals I use for developing my pictures. Yet the smell now seemed overpowering. I began to feel slightly dizzy, needing to sit down. The only place to sit was the floor. Once more I banged on the door, once more—no reply.

This must be what it felt like to be buried alive. As a child, I read a story about such a horrible occurrence and it gave me night-mares. I willed myself to be calm. Just sit down for a moment.

I sat down, with my back to the wall and my legs outstretched. Think. Think. This is what my cat would do. She would wait. Sit and wait. Listen for footsteps.

Perhaps it was the lack of air in the room. In spite of the cold, I began to feel drowsy. The floor was cold against the back of my legs.

After the longest time, I heard footsteps. I got to my feet, and yelled at the top of my voice while thumping again with my shoe. "Someone, open this door!"

I have never been so glad to hear a voice as at that moment. It was Milly. "Mrs. Shackleton?"

"Yes. I can't open the door!"

"Just a minute."

The minute stretched, and stretched.

And then came a sliding sound outside. The door opened a crack.

Milly spoke. "One more shove, Alec!" The sound again. "Doing it!"

The door opened. A large chest had been pushed in front of it.

Raynor appeared. "I came down for wine." He picked up a basket. "What happened?"

"That's what I'd like to know."

"That chest shouldn't be here." He turned to Alec. "Is this your doing?"

"No, sir! Milly came, asked me to help."

Raynor bared his teeth in imitation of a smile. "I'm very sorry, Mrs. Shackleton. I can't imagine who would have done such a thing."

I was not in the mood for conversation with Raynor. I could certainly imagine who had done it. The person who followed me along the road to Rothwell, going several miles out of his way to post letters.

This was a warning. Raynor and I both knew that.

"What's in it that it's so heavy?" Milly asked.

"Leave it!" Raynor said. "Mrs. Shackleton, let Milly help you upstairs. You look quite shaken."

"I'm all right now, thank you." I moved to open the chest and find the answer to Milly's question, but the chest was locked.

* * *

Back in my room, I could not stop shivering. Milly ran a bath for me.

As I lay in the warmth of the bath, coming back to life, I thought how close I might have come to suffocation. Of course it would have taken days for me to die. I was being melodramatic. No one would have risked that. A warning, that's what it was. The stables are round that side of the house. Alec, Benjie's favourite, or to be blunt, Benjie's son, must have told Benjie or Raynor about my interest in his railway notebook.

It seemed unlikely that Benjie would have instructed Raynor to terrorise me. Why? As I lay there, feeling the bathwater grow tepid, I wondered what I had said, done, or uncovered that merited such a response. It made no sense, or none that I could fathom.

I must be coming close to an answer. And the answer was here, in this house.

*   *   *

The library is at the bottom of the stairs and the door stood open. I paused, wondering if Benjie and Raynor were in there.

Benjie was talking rather excitedly with a man who spoke calmly. Although the calm voice was low, it carried sufficiently for me to catch the drift. "Undercapitalised," "overstretched," and Benjie's "It's not going to come to that."

If Benjie had set Raynor to watch me, there was good reason to mistrust him, and yet Benjie was prepared to come to the aid of someone in trouble. Given the revelation about financial difficulties at the mill, perhaps he ought to consider putting his own house in order first.

When the other man spoke again, more clearly this time, I recognised the voice. It was Eliot Dell. This put a different slant on the conversation. One of them was in trouble, but which?

Chapter Twenty-Eight

❧

Gertrude was seated at the piano, picking out a melancholy tune. Abruptly, she stopped playing and came towards me. "Oh, Kate, I'm so sorry. Milly told me. What idiot pushed a trunk in front of your darkroom door?"

I made light of it. "At least Milly had the sense to come looking for me."

"I wouldn't be surprised if it's Alec Taylor. He comes and goes through the cellar doors as if he owns the place. If I find out it's him, it'll be the last trick he plays."

"Don't worry about it, Gertrude. I'm all right now. It was just a scare, that's all. There's no reason to suppose it was Alec."

I did not add that there was every reason to suppose it might be Raynor. Alec would not act off his own bat. Raynor would instinctively know how to protect Benjie. I was coming close to something, sufficiently close that I represented a threat.

There were two glasses of sherry on a low table. We sat down and each took a glass. Gertrude sat by her embroidery frame. She loves embroidery and has produced some fine work. A lawn material was stretched across the frame, showing an unfinished garden, stitched with summer flowers.

We made a little toast to each other.

"There's something I want to show you, Kate, because I don't want you to think badly of me."

"Why would I think badly of you?"

She did not answer straight away but picked up a large silken envelope, embroidered to look like a letter. The penny stamp in the top corner must have taken some careful stitching. Perhaps the item was intended for some sale of work because across the centre, where the address would be, she had embroidered "The Lady of the House".

I thought about how many hours she must spend in this room alone.

She took a sheet of paper from her silken envelope. "There is more than one thing for you to look at, Kate, but see this first."

It was a handwritten list of children's names. Beside each name there was an age, a date and a name and address. "You see, there is a record of where the children from the home went, and they are all in good hands."

I looked at the list. "It must have taken you a long time to find places for them."

"Oh we had some help. Some childless couples are willing to take an infant. It's harder to find apprenticeships, but a few of the boys and girls of working age have been placed. We paid a teacher to come in after school hours to train the boys as shoe repairers and the girls to cook and sew. They have that under their belts now."

"Eight children have gone to the same address, 112 York Street?"

"Yes, that's Stoneville. They'll do well there. The Bluebell Home may once have been a desirable residence, but it was no longer. From the outside, it looked like a castle but there were three rooms and a kitchen downstairs and three up. The children are much better off in an urban setting. That's where the opportunities are."

She had said there was something else. I waited. Perhaps she thought better of it and did not want to show me the "something else". She refilled our sherry glasses. "We have had a lot to put up with, Kate. It is not easy having a large workforce and their families reliant on one. We have the mill, two old pits that need so much maintenance. We cannot be everything to everyone."

"I'm sure not."

"And yet since the strike, something has grown up in this area that makes me afraid. I am going to show you letters that were sent to Benjie. Vile letters."

"Will he want you to show them to me?"

"Whether he does or no, you're going to see them. He doesn't want me to go to the police but something must be done." She thrust the embroidered envelope at me. "They are in there. You look. I can't bear to, not again."

I walked across to the writing table and chair by the window. If the letters distressed her, I would look at them here. I slid them onto the table and then thought to put on the gloves from the pocket of my dress. There would be fingerprints.

The envelopes bore Benjie's name, and the address.

Taking each letter out of its envelope I set them side by side. There were six. One poison pen letter would be annoying. Six was worrying. A magnifying glass lay on the table, but the writing was large enough.

The same hand wrote the envelopes in block print.

The individual letters appeared to be written by different people. One was backhand, another neat, the third had childish writing, as if the person did not get beyond school at about age eight. Two of them were composed of cut out letters from a magazine, untidily pasted, bulging with too much glue.

Postage stamps were neatly placed. Yet there were no postmarks.

The brief messages had a unifying theme, some secular in tone, others vividly biblical.

Snatcher of bread from kids.

Unrepentant greedy thief.

A certain rich man clothed in purple and fine linen fared sumptuously and a certain beggar full of sores laid at his gate.

It be harder for a Brockman to barge into heaven than for a rhinoceros to thread itself through the eye of a needle.

Repent or die, ye who are greedy of filthy lucre

The meek shall inherit the earth.

It was understandable that Benjie wanted to ignore the missives. If these messages were from the meek, I hope never to receive messages from the bold. Strictly speaking, they were not poison pen letters, more a cry of outrage, with some help from scissors and paste.

I returned letters and envelopes to the embroidered case and put my gloves back in my pocket.

I went to sit with Gertrude. "Any ideas who might have sent them?"

"None at all."

"What do you think prompted them?"

"I thought it might be to do with resentment about the children's home, people who refused to believe it was for the best."

"They don't seem threatening, more someone's attempt to get something off his or her chest." I thought of Alec, confined to living above the stable, not allowed to enter the house. Milly taught at the Sunday school, and must be steeped in biblical language, and Joan had earned her reputation as a rebel. "They weren't posted. If someone came up the drive six times, they would have been noticed, wouldn't they?"

"I'm glad I showed you them, Kate. I'm probably making too much of it."

"Leave them with me. Let me think on this overnight."

Who would be sufficiently rash to pay for postage stamps and then hand deliver?

Most of her staff would know their Bible, but would everyone know how to spell rhinoceros? It occurred to me that she might set her staff a spelling test.

I had already discovered that the story about the children's home being blighted by subsidence was not true. Others may have uncovered the lie. In an area teeming with experienced miners, people would know about such things.

For the first time, I felt anxious for Gertrude. In spite of her faults, I felt sure she always tried to do her warped best. I had seen that this morning at the mill. Much was out of her hands, and yet she tried to do something.

Someone from this area had killed the unknown man. Perhaps the question I should be asking was, Who next?

"Gertrude, why did you have the Bluebell Home demolished?"

She took her time to answer.

"It wasn't my choice."

"There was no subsidence."

"If we don't open another seam, Benjie will end up filing for bankruptcy. The mill will close. It will be the end of Thorpefield."

"So Benjie created an explosion in Bluebell Wood, to make it seem that there had been some disturbance underground. The earth quaking, followed by 'subsidence'. The kind of thing that people are so afraid of."

"Benjie didn't light the touch paper himself, of course. The story about subsidence could have been true. And now we are being threatened."

"Do you suspect a member of staff sent these letters?"

"It's a possibility. And Kate, there's something else."

"Oh?"

"The chest that was pushed in front of the darkroom door, I asked the housekeeper to find a key and see what was in it."

"What?"

"Dynamite. We could all be blown to kingdom come. Whoever did that could be the same person who is sending the letters."

At that moment, Benjie came in. "I have some good news!"

"Benjie, darling, did you know there is a chest of dynamite in the cellar?"

"Oh yes." He placed a sheet of paper on the table. With great care, and careful use of tweezers, he produced a postage stamp from a small packet. He set the stamp down in the centre of the paper.

Raynor followed, bringing a magnifying glass.

Gertrude and I looked at the stamp. I thought she might burst into tears. She was a woman dredged of patience.

"Benjie, this is not a good time to be adding to your stamp collection."

"Don't you see the significance? I have the largest collection of Penny Blacks in Great Britain, possibly in the world."

"You are sleepwalking through our lives."

Benjie put his postage stamp back in its packet. "I said Dell could join us for supper, discuss what we're to do about the mill and so on."

"Have you forgotten we have a guest?"

Before Benjie had time to answer, I stood. "Gertrude, you're being the perfect hosts, and I'm the less than perfect guest. I'm not inclined to go in the darkroom again. If you'll forgive me, I'll drive into Wakefield and take the rest of my film in to the chap at Picture This for developing. Then you can have your discussion in peace. We'll chat when I get back."

She was about to protest, but I insisted.

As I reached the hall, I heard Gertrude say, "I suppose you've heard. This morning that wretched employee of yours was charged with murder."

My camera bag was in the hall. Gertrude's embroidered letter case, with its poison pen contents, fitted easily inside.

It was perfectly true that I would visit Picture This and leave my film to be developed.

I did not mention that I would also call at police headquarters.

Chapter Twenty-Nine

I climbed two sets of stairs and turned right. Dad, Chief Superintendent at Wakefield Police HQ, has a view of the street through permanently grimy windows, but sits with his back to the view, facing the door.

He was not surprised to see me since he is the official go-between for me and DC Yeats.

"Kate! I wondered when I'd see you."

"Hello, Dad."

He closed a thick manila folder and pushed it to one side. "Cup of tea?"

"Thanks, but this is a flying visit. It's been a strain, playing the part of a photographic journalist, but I might be getting somewhere."

"How can I help?"

"Would you see if you can get hold of Mrs. Sugden for me? We should have arranged carrier pigeons. I want to know how she and Sykes are getting on."

He picked up the phone and asked the operator to connect him to my home number. He listened. "Well as soon as you've a line then."

While we waited, I brought out the silk document case. Dad stared at the embroidered stamp. "Gertrude?"

"Yes."

"She must have a lot of time on her hands."

I put on my soft gloves. "Benjie has been receiving odd—I can't call them letters—more notes of accusation of some wrongdoing. He doesn't want to make a fuss, but it's upsetting Gertrude."

I spilled the notes onto the desk between us. Dad took a pair of gloves from his drawer and examined the letters. "Is that how you spell rhinoceros?"

"Yes."

"What do you want me to do?"

"Have them checked for fingerprints." I took the sherry glass from my bag. "Gertrude's prints are on here. I swiped it when she wasn't looking and refilled a different glass."

Dad picked up his internal phone and dialled.

"Come through, Harker. Bring a pair of gloves."

If Gertrude found out that I had brought in her letters for examination without her permission, there would be two possible outcomes. I might be promoted to best and most loyal friend, or crossed off the Christmas card list.

A stout constable limped in from the adjoining office. He tried not to smirk as he took the satin embroidered envelope. "Have the contents checked for fingerprints. Right away if it can be fitted in."

When the PC had left, Dad said, "Macintosh owes me a favour. But what is it you hope to find out?"

"Whoever is sending them knows something about Benjie and what he has been up to."

"Which is?"

"Not sure. He's sinking a new pit on the grounds on the other side of the wood from the orphanage, which he has had demolished."

"A lot of industrialists are feeling the pinch. He's fortunate to be expanding at a time like this."

"I want to know what he's really up to. He has this air of the detached country gentleman. What matters are his collections, stamps, coins, and he's so amiable."

"But?"

"He had me followed today. I'm convinced Raynor the butler does Benjie's dirty work."

Dad was prepared to agree. "Wealthy men often have loyal retainers, in the habit of doing their master's bidding. But surely you don't suspect someone you've known so long and who's a pillar of the community? Didn't he meet the King last year?"

"He did, but he and Gertrude are short of cash. He won't be able to ask His Majesty to invest in his schemes."

"All the same, it sounds like a bold enterprise. This might be the moment to do it, when everyone else is cutting back."

"The words bold enterprise and Benjie Brockman don't fit together somehow. And I'm wondering who has a grudge against him, and why. I would like to know who is writing to him."

"Of course, if there are prints on these missives, they might be a person or persons unknown to us."

"I realise that, but with so little to go on I need all the help I can get."

"It seems an oblique way of investigating, but if you think it helps –"

"I'm not sure what will help. It's a blow that Stephen Walmsley has been charged. You see if I'm right, and the crimes are somehow linked –"

"CID know what they're doing, love."

"If CID and Scotland Yard knew what they were doing, I wouldn't be here."

He gave one of his chuckles. "Be a feather in your cap if you come out ahead of Scotland Yard."

I decided not to tell Dad everything. At present he did not need to be alarmed by my having been fastened in the dark room. Certainly, I would not mention the incriminating items in the eaves of the house. He'd pass that on to CID, and swing the noose closer to Stephen.

"Stephen Walmsley is convinced that Mrs. Farrar was expecting a visitor. If he was right and we could find out who, there might be more to go on."

"But don't forget, Mrs. Farrar's murder isn't your case. Best not to try and ride two horses at once."

"Dad, I'm not planning to join the circus. I'm thinking there may be someone or something we haven't thought of yet. Do you know when Mrs. Farrar's body will be released for burial? It might be enlightening to see who turns up for her funeral."

Although he showed no great interest in my theory, Dad obligingly picked up the telephone. "I'll find out."

While he made the call, I went to look through the window at the street below. A police van drove into the yard. A delivery boy went by on his bicycle. I listened to Dad's end of the conversation, the pause, and his thanks.

I went back and sat down.

He put his hand over the mouthpiece. "The vicar of Holy Trinity, Rothwell is back at his post. He has arranged for the local undertaker to collect Mrs. Farrar's body. They'll let me know when a funeral is arranged, though you'll probably hear that before I do. Anything else you want?"

"Please check that they will send information to DC Yeats at Scotland Yard."

He asked for that to be done, and then put down the telephone. "All settled."

"Why is Mrs. Farrar being buried in Rothwell when she lived in Thorpefield? Ardsley church is nearer."

"Is that important?"

"Probably not."

The telephone rang. Dad picked it up. "CS Hood." He listened. "Put her through." Dad placed his hand over the mouthpiece. "Mrs. Sugden."

"Hello, Mrs. Sugden. I'll pass you over to Mrs. Shackleton." He handed me the receiver.

Mrs. Sugden sounded a little perturbed, and excited. "I said they should get a telephone."

"What is it?"

"A call just came through from the steward at Moortown Golf Club for Jim Sykes."

"What did he say?"

"An American golfer by the name of Espinosa claims to recognise the man from the train."

"How do you spell that name?"

"E-s-p-i-n-o-s-a."

My hopes rose. I tried to flatten them, just in case. "Where does Mr. Espinosa know him from?"

"France. Says they met at a golf course in Paris."

"Thank you, Mrs. Sugden."

Dad interrupted, "Tell her to ring the steward back and ask her to keep the man on the premises."

I ignored this instruction. The golfer had come all the way from America. He would be unlikely to leave before the Ryder Cup was played.

"Mrs. Sugden, did you tell the steward that Mr. Sykes would come as soon as possible?"

"I did, but Jim's out and about on his investigations. He's in Wakefield. He said he would make contact with Mr. Hood."

"Thanks. This is our best possibility so far. And did Philip give you a message?"

"He did. I'll be onto that business tomorrow."

We ended the call.

"We have our first good lead, Dad. An American golfer claims to have met our unknown man."

"You deserve some luck, Kate. This might be the breakthrough."

Of course we both knew it might also be a dead end.

"Dad, when were you going to tell me that Mr. Sykes is in Wakefield?"

"Just as soon as you stopped giving me orders and let me get a word in. Since Sykes can't keep in touch with you, he's kept in touch with me."

"Where is he?"

Dad took out a sheet of paper and began to write. "He's based himself at the White Swan. I'll send a note."

The White Swan is a pub near the railway station, better known as the Mucky Duck.

I could imagine Sykes's relief at having something definite to do. I envied him. By comparison, I was a woman chasing shadows.

As Dad reached for an envelope, there was a tap on the door.

It was the constable who had taken the poison pen letters, returning empty-handed. "Something a bit odd, sir."

"Oh?"

"Only one set of prints, the same on the letters as on the wine glass. You'd think with letters there'd be the prints of the writer and the prints of the receiver, not to mention someone who picked up the envelope."

"Are you sure?"

"Wasn't me, sir. It was Macintosh tested them."

Chris Macintosh was Wakefield's fingerprint expert, a man with a reputation for accuracy.

"Macintosh asks can he keep the letters, sir. He wants to check them against his records."

At the same time as I said no, Dad said yes.

"Right-o, sir. I'll tell him." With that he was gone.

Naturally, it was Dad the constable had listened to, not me.

"Dad! They're Gertrude's letters. She doesn't even know I brought them out of the house."

"Gertrude's letters in every sense of the word, written by her, sent by her, opened and read by her."

"But they were to Benjie."

"Did you see Benjie with them?"

"No."

"Your friend Gertrude, is she all right? Might there be something the matter with her?"

"I know you all treat Macintosh as the oracle, but he could be having a bad day."

"You'll think of something to tell Gertrude."

"Oh yes, that'll be easy. Gertrude, your confidential poison pen letters, that you probably wrote yourself to get my sympathy, are now in police files."

"Why would she want your sympathy?"

I stood. "It's a long story."

Something told me that the highly regarded fingerprint man was right. Why had she done it, and why shown me? Perhaps she wanted me to understand that she and Benjie were more sinned against than sinning, or that she felt under siege in her own community. "Dad, I have to return them. I don't know what game she's playing but it's her game not mine."

"If I don't let Macintosh do his little check, he'll cotton on that it's not a legitimate job and that would not look good."

He was right, and what harm could it do? If Gertrude asked me, I'd find some excuse to prevaricate.

"Don't let him keep them too long." I picked up the note Dad had made of the golfer's name. "I'll take this to Mr. Sykes."

Dad gave one of his small groans. "You don't want to go in the Mucky Duck."

"But I'm going to."

"They won't let you in, unaccompanied female."

"Then I'll just have to stand in the doorway and shout Sykes's name."

Chapter Thirty

I parked just beyond White Swan Yard. This is where my birth mother lives. Thanks to that fact, I had no difficulty in entering the Mucky Duck. The landlord recognised me as the woman who occasionally came to the out-sales counter to fetch her mam a jug of stout.

Sykes was seated in the corner, with a group of railwaymen. He gave a wave and came over. "Slumming it, Mrs. Shackleton?"

"All in a good cause."

We found a seat by the window. Pale sunshine gleamed on the beaten copper of the table top. He set down his pint glass. "Do you want a drink?"

"No thanks. I need to get back, but I have news. An American visitor to the golf tournament, Mr. Espinosa, claims to recognise our man." I handed him Dad's note of the name.

He tried to conceal his excitement, but failed. "Let's hope this takes us somewhere." He lowered his voice. "I'm beginning to think whoever put that body on the train was paid handsomely, or met with an accident afterwards."

"No luck with the rhubarb growers?"

"None whatsoever. They're so taciturn, they ought to be employed by the secret service, only they'd never report to their own side or any other. Oh and I'm losing count of how many pints bought for railwaymen who know nothing."

"Be sure to keep a note of expenses." I stood. "I'm parked next to you. Wait with me while I order something at the bar."

"Let me do it for you."

It was tempting to let him, because I was already causing something of a stir simply by being there. But I would do this myself.

"Jug of stout please, Fred."

"Right you are, Kate. Deposit on the jug."

"I know."

Sykes stared as the landlord pulled the drink.

I took it and paid.

Outside, we stopped by the entrance to the dingy yard. "Good luck, Mr. Sykes. It will be such a relief if this American golfer really does know our man."

"Do you want me to wait with you?"

"No. It's just a quick call. I'll tell you another day."

"Mrs. Shackleton, you never cease to surprise me."

* * *

A stone's throw from the Mucky Duck and my birth mother's house, a framer of pictures scratches a living, working from a narrow shop called Picture This.

It was time to give him some business.

The clapper sounded as I opened the creaking door.

After a moment, Maurice Lewis shuffled in from the backroom. He wears carpet slippers, due to some unspecified problem with his feet.

He cheered up at the sight of me, which cheered me too. We exchanged pleasantries and then I asked, "Mr. Lewis, might you do some framing for me quite quickly? I'm a house guest at a friend's and would like to leave something for them, photographic portraits."

I took the pictures from my bag. He duly admired Gertrude and Benjie, and Gertrude with her horse.

Raynor the butler looked exceedingly smart and, on paper, less like Dracula than in real life.

A sign read that Mr. Lewis now developed and printed photographs. He saw me reading it. "I don't suppose you'll need that
service, Mrs. Shackleton."

After my experience in the cellar, I decided that such a service
was exactly what I needed. I wound on the film in my camera. "I'll
leave this with you, Mr. Lewis. Develop and print everything in a
decent size, and frame the best."

He worries about money, not just his own lack of it but other
people's. "Are you sure? All of them?"

"Yes." This would be courtesy of Scotland Yard after all. "And
have them sent to me at Thorpefield Manor, so include a delivery
charge." I took out my purse. "Here's something on account."

Chapter
Thirty-One

~

After emptying his wallet buying drinks for thirsty railwaymen who had nothing much to say, Sykes cheered inwardly at the news that someone at Moortown Golf Club might have information for him.

He had come to only one conclusion during his stint investigating the intricacies of northern railways, while trying to solve the mystery of the body on the train. He took his hat off to the chaps who drew up timetables. It was no mean feat, ensuring trains didn't bump into each other and that signals worked all the way along the line.

Other than that, it had been a waste of time. He felt like a man trapped in a carriage, pushed onto a sidings and left to wait for a coupling that would never materialise.

In spite of raised hopes and suppressed excitement, he drove back to Leeds at his usual cautious speed, rehearsing questions, imagining a successful outcome, warning himself against expecting too much.

A name, that was all he needed. Not too much to ask.

Once more, he drove into the golf club car park. This time he paid no attention to the other motors but went straight to the clubhouse. Of course, Mr. Espinosa may be on the course, or back at his hotel. Sykes hoped not. He had waited long enough.

He liked this bar, this clubroom. It might even be worth learning to play golf in order to come in here for a pint.

A young steward took his coat.

"I'm Jim Sykes, here to see Mr. Braithwaite."

"He's expecting you, sir." He signalled to the steward who was seated at a table with an attractive woman, dark-haired and vibrant. She could be a film star.

Jack Braithwaite rose and came across.

Sykes offered his hand. "Thank you for coming back to me, Mr. Braithwaite. You have some information. A Mr. Espinosa?"

"Yes, Mr. Sykes. Mrs. Espinosa is the person who has information for you. Mr. Espinosa is on the course. Come and meet his lady wife."

The steward introduced them. "And what will you have to drink, Mr. Sykes?"

"Pint of bitter please. May I get you something, Mrs. Espinosa?"

The steward intervened. "Leave that to me, Mr. Sykes. This is on the house."

As Sykes sat down, he began to think that he had the best job in the world. The woman was smiling at him. "It is so nice to meet a British policeman. I think you are wonderful."

"Thank you." Sykes did not trouble to correct her. "Are you enjoying your stay, Mrs. Espinosa?"

"We are having the most interesting time. You see, we decided to make a real vacation of this. We started in Spain, came all the way up through France, visiting courses, and then to Paris. Don't ask me the name of the course, I've forgotten."

Sykes spoke quietly. "And where did you meet the gentleman whose sketch you saw?"

She was quick on the uptake. This was a public place and she was talking confidentially to a policeman. She lowered her voice. "Why at the course in Paris. Mr. Sykes, would it be impertinent if I gave you a tip?"

Usually quick on the uptake, Sykes did not quite follow her meaning.

She laughed and made a "money" gesture with thumb and fingers. "Not that kind of tip."

Sykes smiled. "Then yes, by all means please do."

"If you are looking to find a gentleman and you have a picture—not that this happens very often, I'm sure. This is such a law-abiding country. Not a single person in this golf club feels the need to carry a gun."

"No I don't suppose they do."

"Well then, here is my tip. Show the picture to a lady. If the case is reversed and you are looking for a lady, show the picture to a gentleman."

"I'll remember that."

"You see my husband, he thought I might be right but he could not be sure. We were with our friends, the Diegels. Mrs. Diegel is of the same mind as I. She is back at the hotel now, but she would say just as I do that this is the man we met in Paris. He gave my husband his card."

A cocktail glass was placed before Mrs. Espinosa. Sykes's beer was carefully set on a small beermat.

"Cheers!" Mrs. Espinosa raised her glass.

"Cheers!" Sykes said, "And do you have the gentleman's card?"

"I do, and I shall be sorry to part with it but I will remember his name. When you find him, please give him our warm regards. He has done nothing wrong, I hope."

"We have no reason to believe that, Mrs. Espinosa." He looked at the business card, expensive, embossed and, most importantly, with a name: Harry Aspinall. Under the name was an address of a chateau in Bordeaux.

"He said if we ever came to France, we must look him up. He would show us over his vineyard. I don't suppose we shall ever see his vineyard. Of course he might arrive here, and then I could introduce you."

"He expects to be at the tournament?"

"Yes, we're looking out for him."

Sykes took out his notebook. "It would be helpful if you could tell me everything you remember, Mrs. Espinosa."

Mrs. Espinosa began.

"He is originally from England, as I expect you know, but has been living in France for a long time. He had to come back here. Truth to tell, he was a little agitated about it but he gave no details. He said that it would not be such a hardship because he would come and see the Ryder Cup and we would be sure to bump into each other. If the Brits won, the champagne would be on him, and vice versa."

"Did he say why he was coming back to England?"

"He did not. We talked golf, not business. But there was a gentleman from Panama and I know that Harry Aspinall and he got to talking. The Panamanian gentleman had something to do with a mining company and the two of them seemed to have a lot of knowledge in common."

Here was what Sykes called a reliable witness. Her story made sense. She had noticed the man's agitation, and discovered something of his plans. Where she did not remember something, the name of the golf club and the Panamanian with an interest in mining, she did not invent.

"Mrs. Espinosa, you have been extremely helpful. Thank you very much. May I ask where you are staying?"

"We have rented a house here in Moortown." She gave him the address. "We shall be here until the end of the tournament, and then we go back to Southampton." She sighed. "I wouldn't have missed this trip for the world."

She and Sykes had continued speaking quietly. Two men and a woman sat down at the next table. One of the men was talking in a loud voice, that upper-class-everyone-listen-to-me voice that made Sykes want to charge him with gross showing off and extreme poshness.

"Just one more thing, Mrs. Espinosa."

"Sure."

"How did Mr. Aspinall speak?"

"Well, like you. English."

"Really like me?" Sykes tried to think of a sentence that might give an indication of regional origins. Nothing came immediately to mind. He tilted his head towards the nearby table. "Like me, or like the man with the big mouth?"

"Oh like you, certainly like you. I am only just beginning to get the hang of this accents business. Of course we have accents in the States but I am not sure they carry quite the same connotations as they do here."

"Mr. Aspinall was a northerner?"

"I have my ear in now, since arriving in Moortown, and I would say he was a northerner. I would also say, just so you know, that he was what I call one of life's good guys."

And in that moment, Sykes lost a little bit of his heart to her. Of course, being a true Yorkshireman, he could think of nothing more expansive to say except, "Thank you, Mrs. Espinosa." After a pause, he added, "It has been a pleasure to meet you."

She would never know just how big a compliment that was.

He set off back to Headingley, feeling like a man driving a car fitted with eagle's wings.

Chapter
Thirty-Two

❧

Sykes was never sure just what Mrs. Shackleton's arrangement was with certain people. She carried sway with librarians, including Mr. Duffield at the local paper and the entire staff of the Leeds Library. He had at first wondered whether bottles of Scotch changed hands at Christmas, or the occasional crisp new five pound note. Recently, he had come to realise it was neither of those things. It was Mrs. Shackleton's natural charm and grace.

Without her, Sykes would simply have to do his best.

The Leeds Library would be closed. Mrs. Sugden, was on good terms with Miss Merton, the true glue of that place. If anyone could open doors after hours, or rustle up a person with a key, it would be Miss Merton.

Mr. Duffield, newspaper librarian, would have gone home by now. Sykes knew where he lived. Newspaper buildings buzzed with life the whole night long. Mr. Duffield would, for Mrs. Shackleton, willingly return to his many files and index cards to search out a man called Harry Aspinall.

With a library linchpin and a newspaper archivist on his side, Sykes hoped for good results.

* * *

Sykes and Miss Merton sat at a large polished table in the new room of the Leeds Library. A light from this room would not be seen from the street because the windows were in the roof. All the same, they took no chances. An old oil lamp stood on a raffia mat in the centre of the table, casting a soft light over the membership cards from the index box.

Several cards were fastened together for members with the name Aspinall.

Miss Merton carried two pairs of spectacles. When she looked at the cards, she wished for a magnifying glass. "How good is your eyesight, Mr. Sykes?"

"Perfect in a good light, but I can squint well enough."

He drew the lamp nearer. "It appears that Harry Aspinall is the third generation to have library membership."

"I knew his father," Miss Merton informed him. "They lived somewhere south of the city as I recall. Am I right?"

"You are." Sykes had the card. He made a note of the family address. Rothwell Manor, Rothwell.

Miss Merton sat in the warm glow of knowledge that she was not yet losing her marbles. Strange how certain things came back to you. "The father died, the elder brother died before he had time to take up membership. It passed to Mr. Harry Aspinall. Now that we have his name, I remember the treasurer complaining that she had to write to France for the annual contribution, and that when she explained the inconvenience, he paid ten years in advance."

"Do you happen to know whether anyone kept the house open in his absence? Were there younger siblings?"

"If there were, I know nothing of them." Miss Merton was already putting the index cards back in the box.

Sykes would have liked to telephone to the newspaper office to tell Mr. Duffield he was on his way, but the date, time and number would appear on the library's telephone bill and that might lead to trouble.

As they descended the marble staircase, the light from Sykes's torch cast long shadows across the stairs and the ground floor hallway.

He walked Miss Merton to the tram stop, waiting with her until the tram came. "Thank you for your help, Miss Merton. I could not have done it without you. Mrs. Shackleton will be very grateful."

She gave a gracious nod and took a couple of coppers from a small purse, ready to pay her tram fare. "Always happy to assist. Good luck, Mr. Sykes."

He waited until the tram pulled away. They waved to each other.

She is a good old soul, Sykes thought as he walked to Albion Street, and not the fusspot that some make out.

He strode on, walking quickly, hoping that Mr. Duffield at the newspaper offices would be able to confirm whether Rothwell Manor was still in the hands of the Aspinall family.

It had surprised Jim Sykes when he learned Mr. Duffield's Christian name was Niall. He'd had him down as a Septimius or a Theodore. The lank elderly gentleman was waiting at the entrance. Sykes felt a surge of gratitude that Mr. Duffield had come from home after being ready to put his feet up for the night and listen to his newly acquired wireless set.

Mr. Duffield had a good firm handshake. "Do you want me to tell you what I've found out as I walk you to your motor? You said it was urgent."

"That would be grand. Is there much to tell? I'm parked just round the corner."

Mr. Duffield was precise, as might be expected of a man who all of his life had worked at cataloguing and storing information that may or may not, now or in some distant future, be of interest to reporters or the vast local readership.

"Harry Aspinall has lived abroad for years. As far as I can gather, the family home has been locked up since the elder brother died fifteen years ago. And before you ask, it was natural causes—a heart attack. The Ordnance Survey map shows Rothwell Manor as quarter of a mile east of the church. Family money comes from interests in the railways, mines and land. He is a major shareholder in several local mines and the Northern Railway."

"Any other local connections, distant relations, friendships?"

"He hasn't been back to England for years, or not that I know of. One suspects a rift of some kind but not the kind of thing that finds its way into the papers. Oh, he is a trustee of a children's home. I came across an account of a meeting from a few years ago. He had sent apologies for non-attendance."

"Had he put down roots in France?"

"I'm sure he had, after all those years. He left England thirty years ago. I suppose as a second son he had to make his way in the world. I don't know what he did during the war. Perhaps he passed as French. Here's a note of sources." He handed Sykes a quarto sheet. "That's as much as I could find in the time available, Jim."

So they were now on first name terms. Sykes was glad. As they passed under a street lamp, he glanced at the tiny writing. "Thank you very much, Niall." They had reached the car. Sykes felt suddenly awkward. "I should offer you a lift but I'm going to drive straight to Rothwell."

"I don't need a lift. I took the tram and I could do with the walk back. But is it a good idea to go tonight? It's getting dark."

"I'll take that chance. I know my way to Rothwell."

That was not entirely true. Sykes knew the general direction: south and east.

He drove along unfamiliar streets, on the eastern outskirts of the city. At a crossroads, he took out the road map and shone his torch. Yes, he was on the right track.

Street lamps became less frequent. By the light of the moon, he found his way to the village. It occurred to Sykes that it would have been extraordinary if Aspinall hadn't let one single person know he was coming. But perhaps someone did know he was coming, and that someone had been waiting for him.

He knew he must have a story ready and thought of possibilities. Pass himself off as a fellow golfer who met Mr. Aspinall at a course outside Paris. He could do that. He had seen pictures of the Eiffel Tower and the Arc de Triomphe. He knew how many golfers make a team.

Now that he thought about it, he didn't know how many golfers made a team. If he knocked on a door and started spouting about birdies and holes in one, he'd be unmasked as a fraud in two minutes.

He saw the church first, a fine building framed against a darkening sky. But he wasn't here to admire the church. The clock struck nine as he glanced at the churchyard and wondered where the vicar lived and how he would find his way to Rothwell Manor House.

He asked a man walking a dog. Rothwell Manor was nearest. He was directed up some stone steps on the opposite side of the road.

The iron gates to the Manor House were padlocked. Someone had made attempts at keeping the grass to ankle length and the bushes and trees from turning into a petrified forest. Whatever happened here in some murky past to turn this house into something so unloved that its younger son escaped across the channel and its elder son died here?

Sykes walked the perimeter. Someone had bent the railings at a point where an apple tree and blackberry bushes grew. Nature must be having a field day. The dark shapes of nests added to the sculpted impression of the beech trees. A feral cat stopped long enough in its patrolling to stare and snarl. Sykes guessed that only the forbidding aspect of the place prevented it from being burgled of whatever dusty possessions lay within. The height of the building would deter strippers of lead or roof tiles. Perhaps this was the kind of place where a legend grew up that kept local people at bay. At the back of the house, only a broken fence separated the kitchen garden from the land beyond.

Sykes entered the grounds. He walked round, looking through dirty windows at empty rooms, half expecting to see a body or to hear a cry of distress. A feeling of emptiness and absence prevailed. Even a tomb might be filled with busy spiders.

He turned and walked back the way he had come, feeling a cold place in his lower back, as if something malign and damp had attached itself to him.

"No wonder you didn't come back here."

On his way back to the car, Sykes shone his torch over the ruins of Rothwell Castle. Perhaps the ghosts of long ago kings and their knights had returned to distress and usurp the newcomers who had the temerity to take over their manor.

His informant with the dog had advised him to drive straight on to the vicarage, all along the lane to the edge of the village, passing the last houses, looking out for a high wall on his right. This surprised Sykes. He had expected the vicar to be housed near the church.

As he drove, Sykes wondered what it was about the parishioners of Rothwell that prompted the vicar to put such a distance between himself and his flock.

He pulled up near the gate in the high wall.

The gate was locked. A dog began to bark. Short of scaling the wall, there would be no way to gain entry. He looked through a gap between gate and gatepost and made out the shape of a house, in total darkness

A cloud slid away from the moon, outlining the dark and somewhat forbidding building, much larger than he had expected. Rothwell was turning out to be full of surprises. First an ancient house abandoned, and now a vicar who lived like a bishop.

The church clock struck one.

Sykes consoled himself that he at least knew his destination. The Vicar of Rothwell would not be going anywhere. Sykes would come back tomorrow.

Chapter Thirty-Three

⸙

Gertrude and I were having breakfast. Benjie had gone from the house, leaving his newspaper and a magnifying glass on the table.

Gertrude cracked her boiled egg. "Don't even think of going yet. All that 'in three days guests are stale' nonsense simply doesn't apply to you. It's such a pleasure having you here, and I love the idea of your article. Stay as long as you like."

"I've imposed long enough. I'll pick up my photographs this morning—some for you, and after that I'll be making tracks. I'm sure you have lots to do."

"Eliot is arranging dates for us to see potential investors in Manchester and London. While I'm in London, I'll go to the Adoption Society. There's an infant who sounds just the sort of little fellow I'm looking for."

"What good news! You must want to scoop him up and bring him home."

"He has some minor ailment and so I can't fetch him yet." She was looking through the latest copy of *The Lady* and slid it across the table to me. "Third one down in the employment wanted. She looks a likely candidate for nursemaid. I wouldn't know what to do with a sick child."

I read the woman's advertisement. "She is experienced and has references."

"I shall write today. She could meet me in London and bring the child back."

"I can't wait to meet him."

Raynor came in to call Gertrude to the telephone.

She stood. "Excuse me, Kate. That'll be Eliot."

"It's all right. I'll pop into Wakefield and pick up my pictures."

* * *

At Picture This, Maurice Lewis set out my framed photographs on the table. He placed the palms of his hands on the counter and looked for my approval. His work made a fine display. Gertrude alone, and Gertrude and Benjie together, were framed in hallmark silver. A finest French gilt frame set off Milly in her Sunday hat. Raynor looked out from a frame of best quality crushed Morocco.

"You've done a grand job, Mr. Lewis."

"I'll send over the rest tomorrow." He angled the portrait of Raynor. "I like your composition, and the black of his outfit against the wood of the hand-made seat. He is every inch the proud butler."

"He's a good subject."

"You caught the shadow pattern of the leaves. Very fine!" He held the portrait at arm's length. "He puts me in mind of someone I saw on the stage, but I can't think who. It will come to me."

I smiled, knowing very well who it was. I took out my purse. "Thank you for doing them so quickly.

He wrapped the photographs and brought them out to my car, placing them carefully in the dicky seat, packing them round with newspaper. "Ah now it comes to me. He played Count Dracula at the Wakefield Opera House."

"I'm sure he would be flattered to be compared to an actor, Mr. Lewis, but perhaps not the character."

We parted, with his assurances that he would send on the rest of the photographs.

* * *

Alec must have heard my car. He appeared from the direction of the stables, looking hopeful.

"You'll have your photographs tomorrow. I think you'll be pleased." The poor boy blushed. I was glad that as an afterthought, I had asked Mr. Lewis to make several postcards so that Alec could give some to his admirers. "Will you give me a hand with these framed pictures?"

He picked up the pictures, carried them as far as the door and then came to an abrupt halt. The noise of my car engine had also alerted Raynor, who opened the door before we reached it. He took the parcels from Alec.

There was an odd moment of understanding between the three of us. Alec turned back and looked at me. I smiled. As stable boy and minder of cars, he was not allowed through the front door. Had he been born on the other side of the blanket, he would be heir to the Brockman fortune, or its debts.

Gertrude would insist that her newly adopted baby would be the Brockman heir. Alec, Benjie's by-blow, would remain just that. It crossed my mind that her animosity towards Alec was so great that she would go to any lengths to exclude him.

Raynor and I stood in the hall. I would not let him know that he had rattled me by following me to Rothwell, and by his constant observation. "One of these pictures is for you, Raynor."

He is a proper butler who has trained himself to suppress expressions of surprise, delight or dismay. Yet he glowed with pleasure as he looked at his portrait. "Oh, Mrs. Shackleton. I don't know what to say."

"Do you like it?"

"Like it? I have never had such a portrait, never one of myself at all."

"It's a fine likeness. You look noble."

He nodded in agreement. "You have captured my better self. You have captured my soul."

The thought of that was disconcerting. "Then it's lucky I didn't suffocate in the darkroom. Your better self might have died with me."

He looked suddenly shocked, and opened his mouth to speak but I got in first. "Mrs. Brockman will think I got lost."

"She will be relieved to see you, madam. It has been a trying morning for her."

With that intriguing remark, he carried his portrait away, but he turned back. "In return for this gift, I want to do something for you, Mrs. Shackleton. You see I have an interest in casting astrological charts. If you would be willing to divulge your date, time and place of birth, I should be happy to undertake a chart for you."

Some sort of warlock, ready to cast a deadly curse if I fathomed his and Benjie's secrets.

I gave him the date and place. If he was surprised to hear that the place was White Swan Yard, he made no sign. As it happened, I knew the time: six o'clock in the morning. My adoptive mother, Virginia Hood, had given me every detail as soon as she thought I was old enough to understand.

* * *

Gertrude lay on the chaise longue staring at the ceiling, a wet flannel on her brow. The air smelled of vinegar.

"Gertrude?"

She peered from under the flannel. "Oh Kate, I wondered where you'd got to."

"Can I get you anything?"

She lifted the flannel. "This helps."

"Let me." I took the flannel from her, refreshed it in the basin of cold water and vinegar, and squeezed it. "Lie still a little longer. Is it a headache?" She let me place the cloth across her forehead and temples.

"More than a headache, but talk to me. Tell me what you've been up to, and don't talk about going yet."

"Well I have all the photographs I need for my assignment, so the time is ours. And I've brought you your portrait, but you can see it later."

"I'll look now!" She raised herself up and lifted the flannel.

I held out the portrait of her and Benjie. "Oh Kate, that is lovely. How did you make such a big photograph?"

"By magic. And here's another of you with your bonny piebald."

"Isn't he gorgeous?" The flannel dropped to the floor as she held the picture at arms' length. "We've been shocking hosts, only it's been a difficult time. And now we have a funeral tomorrow."

"Ah, poor Mrs. Farrar."

"How did you know?"

"I saw my dad. He told me that the vicar is back and that the coroner gave permission for the body to be released."

"It should be a solemn time, but it's become a farce."

"What do you mean?"

"Word spread that the murderer has been charged. Your Milly and that girl they call Joan of Arc have stirred up women and girls from the mill. They're off to Wakefield, to make mischief."

I almost said "Again?" but stopped myself just in time.

"Do sit down, Kate, you're making me nervous." She sighed. "The aspirins are beginning to work. Perhaps a cup of coffee."

I crossed to the fireplace and rang the bell. "What brought on your headache? If you were cutting the workers' hours, does it matter that the women and girls will take time off to go to Wakefield?"

"There's an order arrived at the mill for blankets. It's exactly what we needed to keep afloat. Benjie has done one of his disappearing tricks, so the manager comes to me. If the women walk out, we'll miss the delivery date."

"No wonder you have a headache."

"What on earth good do they think they can do? One of the girls has a bicycle chain and said she would chain herself to the railings." She sat up. "You rode a bicycle, Kate. Is that something it's possible to do? Those chains always look so horribly oily."

"That wouldn't work."

"Our reputation will be in the dust if this gets into the papers."

Raynor came into the room. He hovered discreetly.

"Gertrude, you know that my dad is a senior police officer in Wakefield?"

"I knew he was something."

"Why don't I telephone him?"

"Will he be there? Don't they go out keeping us all safe?"

"Men of rank are usually at their desk. He is very good at calming situations."

Raynor's clearing of the throat indicated an intervention. "I'm told there's been a whip-round among the men. They have fare for the train."

Gertrude groaned.

I put my idea to her. "Dad would see the women are spoken to in a reasonable way. He might even do it himself, promise to look into things."

My idea would also keep Dad in the picture, and through him Mr. Sykes.

Gertrude asked, quite reasonably, "What is there to look into?"

Raynor leaned forward. "If I may, madam?"

"What is it, Raynor?"

Solomon himself could not have spoken better. "When a party who considers himself or herself injured believes someone is looking into a grievance, they might be soothed."

Gertrude sighed. "Then Kate, do try it, please."

"I will." Now was my moment to take a giant step. "I can look into the murder and see whether there is any cause to suspect a miscarriage of justice, starting from the presumption that Stephen Walmsley is innocent."

From her lounging position, Gertrude suddenly sat bolt upright. "Have you gone completely mad? Stephen Walmsley is guilty."

Raynor, who must by now have forgotten why he came into the room, spoke up. "Oh but madam, presumption of innocence is a cornerstone of British justice."

Gertrude stared at him, suddenly speechless. It crossed my mind that seeing himself look so noble in a portrait had turned him into a reincarnation of a fair-minded Roman senator. She opened her mouth to speak.

At that moment, Eliot Dell arrived unannounced. He went over to Gertrude. "I've heard what's happened. Leave this to me."

Raynor and I exchanged a look. He gave the slightest of moves that in another man would signify nothing. Coming from Raynor, it indicated alarm.

Gertrude allowed Eliot to place a soothing hand on her brow, creating a tableau for a sentimental painting. "We'll sort this out, Gertie. I'll put the fear of God into them."

Gertrude, who had her legs outstretched on the chaise longue, swung round. "Kate has come up with an idea of having her father do something. I told you he's a high-ranking police officer."

It was my turn. "Let me telephone Dad. This might buy you some time, enough to complete your order at least. Dad can be very persuasive."

Gertrude sighed. "Kate, you are a wonder woman."

"I'll do it now."

Gertrude turned to Eliot. "I told you. I said we should have Kate on our side."

The one good thing about the morning's events was that Gertrude had forgotten the poison pen letters.

Dad listened. As expected, he pointed out the murder enquiry was not his investigation. He would be trespassing on CID territory. I was ready for that. "This is a civil matter, Dad, preventing unrest. No one wants another march to the prison, especially by workers in the employ of the Lord Lieutenant's deputy. If the mill-workers know something is being done –"

His sigh came over the wires. "As it happens, some anonymous seeker after justice has engaged a fast-talking legal representative for the accused."

He paused, letting it sink in that he knew very well I was that person.

"I'll ask the local constable to go there now and pass that on. It might do the trick. Tell your friends I will do what I can."

Chapter Thirty-Four

~

Mrs. Sugden and Sergeant Dog busied themselves in the front garden, Mrs. Sugden doing a bit of pruning and weeding, Sergeant Dog sniffing his little heart out.

The furniture van drew up outside. Sergeant Dog immediately took an interest. "Not for us," Mrs. Sugden said to him. "We've all the furniture we need."

Someone climbed from the driver's seat. He must need directions.

Mrs. Sugden straightened up.

The van had a Wakefield address. The fellow opening the gate seemed familiar, and yet she had never seen him before.

He took off his cap. "Mrs. Sugden?"

"Aye."

"I'm Philip Goodchild, next door neighbour to the Hoods, Kate's friend from when we were little."

"Ah, hello, Mr. Goodchild. You're the one who looks after cars." She understood why he was familiar. Mrs. Shackleton had sung his praises. She called him the professor of motorcars.

"I'm come to take you to Wakefield on a job."

"Oh?"

"Kate said you'd catch a train, but I can take you there."

191

"That's kind."

"I don't need to be home just yet. I don't need to look at Mr. Battersby's garage. I've seen it."

"Do you want a cup of tea?"

"No thank you."

"Well just come in and tell me what this job is, and I'll get my coat."

Philip stroked the dog. "He can come with us."

* * *

During the several miles between Leeds and Wakefield, Mrs. Sugden worked out what she would do first.

A building, Stoneville, on York Street, would not be going anywhere. An estate agent might be shutting up shop early for his midday meal. She would try the estate agents first.

Philip knew where to take her. He stopped on Kirkgate. Sergeant Dog whined to come out of the van with her but Mrs. Sugden told him to stay with Philip.

The first agent had very little on his books just now. There was a butcher's shop.

Mrs. Sugden didn't want a butcher's shop.

The estate agent had a garage, fully equipped, to rent or buy, put up by a Mr. Battersby who was retiring to Morecambe. It would be a grand investment.

Mrs. Sugden thought this might not be right for her.

The agent explained that she could put in a mechanic and the money would roll in. There was serious interest in this business. She should not waste time. He also had a big house that would make a corner shop. He showed her a photograph.

Mrs. Sugden noticed that the big house was not on a corner. She thanked him for his time and would call another day.

Philip kindly drove her to Westgate, to a second agent.

Mr. Gopnik of Gopnik and Company quickly put a small bottle back into his desk drawer as Mrs. Sugden entered.

He listened carefully to her requirements, and then praised a tobacconist's shop in a prime location. Mrs. Sugden knew this was not the ticket, but it didn't do to appear uninterested in what the agent described as a proper little gold mine.

When she asked about something more general, such as a corner shop in a village, his eyes lit up.

"I can show you just the thing, in Thorpefield."

That was the place. Mrs. Sugden hid her interest. "If you give me the address, and trust me with the keys, I can take a look. Will the shopkeeper be there to answer my questions?"

"Sadly no. She died."

"Oh dear. When?"

"I'm not sure exactly when, but I know she'll be buried this week."

Mrs. Sugden stepped back. There were limits. "I won't look at the poor woman's shop before she's in the ground."

"She wouldn't mind."

"Well I mind. It's not proper." She gave him her telephone number. "Ring me when it's decent to visit the place."

She felt sure that Mrs. Shackleton would agree. It would be no way of going on to pick over the woman's life before she was respectably buried.

It then occurred to her that the estate agent might think she was wasting his time, and not come back to her. "I think that corner shop will be right up my street, but I'll take a look at the tobacconist, as well. If it's all the same to you."

As she came out of the estate agent's office, Philip looked at his watch. He explained that the furniture van, which he was testing after a repair, was overdue for return.

Mrs. Sugden didn't want to inconvenience him any more than she had already.

"Point me in the right direction and I'll walk. Sergeant Dog likes the exercise. And don't worry about taking us back. We'll find our own way to the train."

It would be good for the dog to know how to board a train, and how to conduct himself in the carriage.

Philip seemed relieved. Mrs. Sugden remembered Mrs. Shackleton telling her that he liked people who talked straight, said what they meant, meant what they said.

She walked to the tobacconist's shop. Sergeant did that dog-thing of acting as if he knew exactly where he was going.

They were there in a little under ten minutes.

Everything about the shop was brown, brown painted wood, brown oilcloth, yellowing ceiling turning to brown. The tobacconist, Mr. Swarbrick, wore a brown overall. His fingers and sad moustache were stained from nicotine.

His brightened considerably when Mrs. Sugden told him she had come to enquire about the lease.

"I never expected a lady, I've had men, and some men with their wives, but I never had a lady on her own."

"Well you have now," said Mrs. Sugden. "If you had so many enquiries, how is it you have no one signed up?"

"Because I'm not sure, I'm not right sure."

"Of what?"

"I'm dithering, that's the truth. I want to leave this place and I don't. I want to leave because I'm on mi own now, but I don't know where I'd go or what do."

"Well that's a rum state of affairs."

"I know. I've had two fellows here, both interested. Last one told me I was wasting his time, but I never expected a lady to call. Would you like to come here for nothing, share the shop with me?"

"What are you suggesting?"

"Marriage. I'm useless on mi own."

Mrs. Sugden could see that very well. What this man needed was a good talking to. She gave him advice on how to find a wife. "You'd best try the chapels first. Don't go for some soppy flower arranger. Choose a woman who turns her hand to mopping the floor and polishing pews. Many a good widow would be glad of a fresh start. Smarten yourself up. Try not to look pathetic."

"You're very kind. Are you sure you won't marry me?"

"Quite sure. But I'll come to your wedding. Now you can do something for me."

"What's that?"

"Show me and this dog to a building called Stone something or other on York Street."

He picked up his coat and locked the shop door.

* * *

Number 112 York Street did not look like a children's home, more like offices. Mrs. Sugden considered trying to lose her escort, but he came in useful for standing by the lamppost, holding Sergeant Dog's lead.

Within seconds of stepping inside the building, Mrs. Sugden wished she had worn her Sunday hat. The woman at the desk gave her a snooty look and said nothing.

Mrs. Sugden put on her best voice. "I'm Mrs. Sugden. I need to trace a child who was brought here."

The woman sniffed. "We've no children here. When was this?"

"When the Bluebell Children's Home closed, not so long ago."

"I can't divulge the whereabouts except to a close relative. Are you a close relative?"

Without knowing a child's name, this was difficult. Play the woman at her own game. "I can't divulge a name, particularly since this child may be due a legacy from a great aunt who died in Australia. I'm acting for the solicitor."

Mrs. Sugden's best voice did the trick.

A certain amount of snootiness evaporated.

"I would have to have the name, madam. You see, children are brought here. We have frequent arrivals of pauper children. They are sent out to different addresses across the city."

"Then I'll see that a letter comes to you. Have you a letter heading by you? I can give that to my employer and he will write."

The letter heading was produced.

Mrs. Sugden studied it. Her hand trembled as the penny dropped. "You're the workhouse." It came out as an accusation.

The woman across the counter found a sudden itch by her ear, and scratched. She spoke sharply. "We don't go by that name now, not for a long time. Everything is done good and proper. The children chosen for a new life in Canada are all properly certificated."

Something funny happened to Mrs. Sugden's breath. She couldn't remember how a person breathed. Someone had taken kiddies from a home in the country near a bluebell wood and fetched them to a place with no heart, no soul, and passed them on, elsewhere in the city, or else across an ocean.

She hardly trusted herself to speak. The words came out in a gulp. "Where are the kiddies from the Bluebell, and who are you packing off to Canada?"

The woman gripped the counter. "You're not acting for a solicitor are you?"

"Oh but I am. And if I wasn't, I am now. And you're acting for the devil."

Chapter
Thirty-Five

～

On Tuesday morning, a bright clear day, Jim Sykes fitted in a call to a client whose security he dealt with. He then drove on to Rothwell.

The vicarage, that last night had looked forbiddingly Gothic in the moonlight, now took on the aspect of a bright villa. A gardener was tending the shrubbery. He looked up and exchanged a nod. As Sykes approached the front door, he took a sideways glance into a window. A man sat writing at a desk.

Sykes rang the bell, and then stood a little way back so as not to appear threatening. After a few moments, a key turned in the lock. The door opened. A pleasant-looking housekeeper, almost as broad as she was high, said hello.

She was the sort of person whose cheerful manner demanded a smile. Sykes introduced himself, handing the housekeeper his card. "I should be much obliged if the Reverend Mr. Branscombe would spare me a few moments of his time."

He had read the name last night, on the board outside the church.

She asked him in, and left him waiting in the hall. The oak floor was highly polished. A cut glass vase of daffodils sat on an octagonal table inlaid with brass. The vicar's study was a few feet away, and so Sykes listened to the exchange. No, the housekeeper did not know what he wanted, but he seemed a respectable gentleman. What a perfectly wonderful housekeeper. This was much better than hearing that he looked like a plain-clothes policeman.

Moments later, he was seated by the vicar's large roll top desk. "What can I do for you, Mr. Sykes?"

"It's about Mr. Harry Aspinall. I called at the Manor House, hoping to make enquiries there but found it shut up."

"Mr. Aspinall lives abroad."

"Were you expecting him back?"

"What makes you say so?"

The suspicion in the vicar's voice alerted Sykes that he must give some detail, to convince this clergyman to cooperate. He explained about the American he had met at Moortown Golf Club, and the arrangement they had made to meet Mr. Aspinall during the Ryder Cup tournament.

"Oh yes. I saw an article in the paper about the tournament."

"From what my acquaintance said, I thought the house would be ready for Mr. Aspinall's return."

The vicar seemed to cheer up a little. "I wish that could be true. The house has stood empty for years. Mr. Aspinall never comes back, but perhaps something has changed. A parishioner did write to him." He sighed. "Though if he has returned, it would be too late."

As the vicar spoke, he glanced at the paper he had been writing on. Sykes quickly followed his glance. A name was block printed, and below it the dates of birth and death. The name was Helen Farrar. He knew now that he must come straight to the point, and was glad to have a small interruption as the housekeeper brought coffee.

"I usually have coffee at this time. Will you join me?"

"Thank you."

The vicar poured. "So what news did the American golfer have of Mr. Aspinall?"

Sykes explained the story of the Americans having been given Mr. Aspinall's card, and the plan to break open a bottle of champagne, whoever won the tournament.

The vicar smiled. "You are genuine. That's Aspinall for you."

"And vineyards trump mining and railways."

"That's about the size of it."

"He has connections here still?"

"No family here. He married a French woman. They have grown-up children, two sons and a daughter." The vicar took a sip of coffee. "But what is this about, Mr. Sykes?"

It was time for Sykes to come clean. "I'm sorry to say, I have reason to believe that Mr. Aspinall has met with harm." Sykes took the artist's drawing from his pocket. "Would you be able to identify him from a sketch?"

"I should think so. I saw him in Lille last year."

Sykes set the portrait on the desk.

The vicar's mouth tightened. "That's Aspinall." He stared a moment longer. "He's dead."

"What makes you say that?"

"The eyes. This was by a halfway good artist. The colour is right, but the eyes are wrong. He had such life in his eyes."

There was no point in lying, or evading. "Yes, he is dead."

"When did he die, and under what circumstances?"

"I regret I am not at liberty to say at present."

"This was nothing to do with golf and Americans was it?"

"Oh yes, that part was true."

"Are you with the police?"

"I am helping Scotland Yard with the investigation."

"Why the secrecy?"

"Not secrecy, sir. Mr. Aspinall was found without identification. Now that you and his American acquaintance have identified him, there is something to go on. It would be helpful to know the purpose of his visit, and the details of his next of kin."

The vicar lowered his head. He ran his hands through his hair. "Mr. Sykes, this has come as a shock. I need to ask you more questions, just as you may wish to ask me. I came home late last night from burying my father. Tomorrow I will be conducting a funeral. Please allow me time to check your credentials before I say more."

"Of course. The most direct way to check on my credentials would be to call Chief Superintendent Hood at Wakefield Police Headquarters. His number is on the back of my card. I am very sorry to have brought bad news at a difficult time."

"Drink your coffee, Mr. Sykes. Such niceties matter to housekeepers." The vicar looked again at the portrait. He turned over the business card where Sykes had written Mr. Hood's name, title and number. For a moment, Sykes thought Mr. Branscombe would pick up the telephone but he did not.

"The parishioner who wrote to Mr. Aspinall was Helen Farrar, a shopkeeper. You may have heard what happened to her?"

"Thank you for telling me. I do know about the death."

"You may wish to know what she wrote to him about." He reached for the sheet of paper. "Helen Farrar spoke to me on the day I was going to Morley to be with my father. She was distressed about some matters being discussed by the trustees of the orphanage, the Bluebell Home. I'm sorry to say that though Mr. Aspinall was a trustee, and he gave Mrs. Farrar his proxy vote, he had long since given up responsibility or interest in what went on here."

"I see."

"There can surely be no connection?"

Sykes fell back on one of his usual lines. "I have no reason to suppose any such connection."

The vicar walked him to the door. Sykes somehow missed asking him the time of tomorrow's funeral, and so he asked the gardener instead.

He wished he had a way of contacting Mrs. Shackleton directly. But if he failed to reach her today, through her father, he felt sure that she would be at the funeral tomorrow.

Chapter
Thirty-Six

Mrs. Sugden took the telephone call from the estate agent. She could view the Corner Shop in Thorpefield today. Every instinct told her that it was too soon to be poking about that poor woman's premises. He was cagey when she asked him whether Mrs. Farrar was decently buried, but gave the impression that she was. The fellow must be anxious to have the Corner Shop off his hands quickly because he offered to be at the station and give her a lift.

Mrs. Shackleton said it was important. And Jim Sykes had called round, telling her they now knew who the man was, and things were moving. "Stand by the telephone," he had said.

She could hardly stand by the telephone while haring off to Wakefield to meet an estate agent. She didn't like this whole business. It was too spread out and too far from home. You didn't know what people would be like when all their born days they'd lived nowhere but the back of beyond, and that back of beyond was the place where a poor woman was done in. A back of beyond where helpless bairns were packed off to the workhouse.

At school she learned a poem, *The Charge of the Light Brigade*. One line came back to her: "Someone had blundered". There was a never a time when someone high up didn't blunder. It was always them at the top of the heap who blundered and them near the bottom of the heap who paid the price.

Not that Mrs. Sugden thought of herself as at the bottom of the heap, nor Mrs. Farrar neither. From what she gleaned of Mrs. Farrar, Mrs. Sugden regarded her as a sensible woman and a hard worker.

Mrs. Shackleton must be feeling desperate, feeling the strain of living in a wilderness of mines and farms and fields of rhubarb. If Mrs. Shackleton could face it, so could she.

She would take her big shopping bag. What's more, she would straight away make a list of questions a person might ask neighbours about the shop. She would draw up a plan of campaign. There might be a need to stay overnight. Anything was possible when Mrs. Shackleton was on a case.

This was a matter of what the military would call reconnoitring.

Picking up her pencil, she wrote the word Questions. A person would want to know the rent, what stock was included, what the takings might be. Some trusting shopkeepers allowed their customers to put items on the slate. If customers did that, would they, in times of hardship, have the wherewithal to pay up?

None of that would help track down a killer. Unless there existed some customer unable to pay up and sufficiently fiendish that he or she would be willing to put an end to the obliging shopkeeper, and thereby wipe their own slate clean, risking hell and damnation in the process.

A person would want to know who lived nearby, and whether a woman taking over the business would be safe from thieves and murderers.

It made her jump when Harriet and Sergeant Dog came bounding into the kitchen. She quickly pushed a few items into her bag. She had been so absorbed as to not hear the pair come in. Having lately experienced an annoying earache, Mrs. Sugden worried a little. Could this be too much wax, or the onset of deafness?

"Did you come in right quiet just now?"

"No, just the usual."

"You'll be on your own for a while, Harriet. I've a bit of business to attend to."

"Business for Auntie Kate you mean?"

"Something like that."

"That's all right. We don't mind, do we, Sergeant Dog?"

The dog wagged his tail.

Mrs. Sugden frowned. "Sometimes little bits of business take longer than you think. If you need anything while I'm away, or if I'm delayed overnight, you've got Miss Merton close by."

"I won't need anything."

"No, but if you do, you've got Mrs. Sykes nearby and you know where Mr. Duffield lives. Mrs. Duffield is a friend."

"Yes I know all that."

"Take any messages that come. If you have to go out, ask Mrs. Sykes to come and stand by the telephone."

"Where are you going?"

"Just near Wakefield. I'm only being cautious in case something crops up."

"What are you going to do?"

"I've to look at a shop." She didn't want Harriet traipsing along.

"You're nervous aren't you?"

"I'm not nervous. I leave nerves to other people. I'm just thinking about you and Sergeant Dog managing on your own."

"Well tell me where you're going."

"I'm being met at Wakefield station."

"What about Sookie?"

"She's all right. She's asleep on my bed. She can get in and out the window and everything she needs is there."

"Have a nice time."

Mrs. Sugden gave a bit of a snort, as if to say that nice times were for other people. Nice times were for softies and soppy articles.

Harriet saw that Mrs. Sugden had been making notes, and had covered them with blotting paper. "Before you go, I'll just go get myself a bar of chocolate."

Harriet thought Mrs. Sugden might be suspicious about her taking a second wander with the dog so soon after the first, but Mrs. Sugden was preoccupied.

Harriet walked along the street. Sergeant Dog, sensing some urgency, trotted smartly beside her, foregoing his usual great interest in the smells of Headingley. He looked up at her in listening mode, waiting for some important instruction.

"Sergeant, do you get the feeling that we're being kept in the dark? I don't think we need trouble Miss Merton or Mrs. Duffield. We'll visit Rosie Sykes. We won't tell any lies, just think of a way of getting a little bit of information. Do you agree?"

Sergeant Dog wagged his tail.

Rosie was sitting with her feet up, reading yesterday's *Yorkshire Evening News*. She was glad to see Harriet, and to be made a fuss of by that sloppy dog.

"Mrs. Sugden's packing her shopping bag, Rosie."

"She doesn't waste time."

"Only she's forgotten the address where she's going, some shop."

"She's being taken there isn't she?"

"Yes, being met at the station."

"Well then the person who's taking her ought to know. It's some general store in Thorpefield, sort of place that sells necessaries and sweets and such like."

Harriet chatted a bit. She asked Rosie was there anything interesting in the paper. There were all sorts of interesting things. Harriet thought she'd never shut up.

"Right then, I'd better be off. Oh and Mrs. Sugden says would you mind standing by the telephone because she might be a few hours and I have to be at work."

"You don't take that dog to the pictures do you?"

"He's no trouble. He sits in the manager's office."

None of them ever remembered Harriet's shifts or her hours. That was sometimes an advantage.

*   *   *

The stationmaster blew his whistle. Mrs. Sugden seated herself on the far side of the carriage so as to look out of the window for the short while it would take to get to Wakefield. The carriage door opened. She looked up to see who would join her. "Harriet! What are you doing here?"

"I just thought me and Sergeant Dog would come with you."

"You little monkey! How did you get here?"

"We caught the tram to the station and then –"

"Well what I'm doing isn't for a child and a dog."

"I'm not a child, and Sergeant Dog missed qualifying as a police dog only through his extreme good nature. We won't be in the way."

"I'm being met." Mrs. Sugden groaned. "It's all arranged, and no mention of an entourage."

"Well, you can say that you had to bring your daughter and the dog."

Mrs. Sugden opened her mouth to object that Harriet would not pass as her daughter, but Harriet did not give her time.

"It will be more natural to have me with you. No one would suspect a person of investigating a crime if that person had a young relative with her. And a villain would think twice about having a go at us with Sergeant Dog at our side."

Harriet decided against saying that in case of an emergency she would be able to run for help. Mrs. Sugden couldn't run for toffee.

"The telephone –"

"Rosie Sykes was very keen to practise answering it."

Chapter
Thirty-Seven

❧

Old Mrs. Dell had fallen into step with me when we entered the church of Holy Trinity. Benjie, Gertrude and Eliot Dell made their way to the front of the church. Mrs. Dell wanted to be closer to the centre, and on the end of an aisle. "I hate to hear my stick clicking on the tiles," she had said, "and to slow everyone down."

Given that this was a funeral, I thought people would not mind being slowed down, but did not say so.

The vicar, whom everybody knew had only recently returned from burying his father, looked tired and drawn. He seemed to be going through the motions, like a man with only half his mind on the task.

This changed when he began to speak about Mrs. Farrar. He glanced down at a sheet of paper where he must have had notes of what to say. He forgot it was there, looking at the congregation, with a glance of approval, as if he had only at that moment realised that the church was packed.

"We are here today to pray for the soul of Helen Farrar, whose blameless and virtuous life was brought to an untimely end. We will pray for the repose of her soul, and remember her as we knew her.

"Mrs. Farrar married late in life but even so was a widow far longer than she was a wife."

That gave me pause for thought. Someone who married late would have to lose her husband very quickly in order to be a widow for such a length of time. Perhaps there was a story there.

The vicar continued. "Helen Farrar had no children of her own, but when she was young, and for many years, she was nursemaid to the Aspinall family. She was well loved by that family, and particularly by the boys, Oliver and Harry. Their mother died when Harry was born. Helen was young, not much more than a child herself, but she became a mother to the boys. That is why there is a place for her in the Aspinall family plot, here in Holy Trinity Church churchyard, the plot she tended after Oliver died.

"She was a good Christian woman who loved her neighbour as herself. There are those of you here today who will remember her kindness when she was a friend to the Bluebell Children's Home."

The vicar led prayers. Hymns were sung. But all this was now happening at a distance for me, because an idea began to take shape.

The vicar had said that Helen Farrar took care of young Oliver and Harry Aspinall. She became a mother to them. She was so close to the family that she would share their resting place in this churchyard.

The Arkwrights were on good terms with Mrs. Farrar. They witnessed her despondency about the children's home. But on the day she died, that changed. She was expecting someone. According to Stephen Walmsley, everything that would polish was polished. She set daffodils in a jar. Full of cheer, she sang. Not just any song, but a nursery rhyme she would have sung to her little boys. The Grand Old Duke of York, he had ten thousand men. He marched them up to the top of the hill and he marched them down again.

What if she was expecting someone with the influence she lacked—the boy she mothered? Harry Aspinall. Like the grand old duke, her expected visitor would ride to the rescue. Like the grand old duke, his marching would be in vain.

I was groping in the dark.

Perhaps we would never know the identity of her expected visitor.

When the service ended, bearers carried the coffin into the churchyard. Mrs. Dell took my arm for support as we followed the other mourners. Sykes was standing to the side of the door. He caught my eye and moved closer, touching my hand. I took the note from him and slipped it in my pocket.

As we stood by the grave, I glanced at the mourners. Sykes was standing on the opposite side, behind a young man in a well-cut dark coat, and white silk scarf. Something about him seemed out of place, yet there was sorrow in his eyes.

Until the moment that Mrs. Farrar's coffin was gently lowered into the ground, a respectful silence held at the graveside. Then came sobbing. It came from Milly, crying for the day's sorrow, for Mrs. Farrar's passing, life's pitfalls, and most especially for Stephen Walmsley.

Joan of Arc put an arm around Milly's shoulders, and passed her a crumpled hanky.

The sad commotion did not give me time to glance at Sykes's note. I was standing between Gertrude and Mrs. Dell. "Who is the girl?" Mrs. Dell whispered. She watched my lips.

"Milly. Stephen Walmsley's sweetheart."

I recognised the bandmaster from Sunday. He nudged the man beside him, who produced a trumpet and began to play an air so melancholy that on the last note, the heavens opened and the rains came.

Raynor stood behind us. He unfurled an umbrella over me and Mrs. Dell, who clung to my arm.

Eliot held a huge umbrella over himself, Gertrude and Benjie.

Gertrude gave the vicar a meaningful nod, which he may or may not have noticed.

He wiped his glasses with the edge of his stole before saying a final prayer, and then addressed the mourners.

"Mr. and Mrs. Brockman extend an invitation to mourners to come back to Thorpefield Manor for a funeral repast. All are welcome." He cleared his throat. "With agreement from the churchwardens, I have arranged a charabanc to take those without transport to Thorpefield Manor."

Gertrude's mouth opened. Perhaps she had not intended to extend the invitation to the whole congregation.

Rain sped departure from the cemetery onto the cobbled lane. Mrs. Dell still held my arm. I noticed that it was Benjie who took Gertrude's arm, and not the other way round. He seemed to hesitate, and I suddenly realised what had passed me by. Benjie was losing his sight. That is why Raynor helped him with his stamp collection. That is why there was a magnifying glass at his place on the breakfast table.

Joan, walking beside Milly, saw me with Mrs. Dell. I had given the girls a lift. Now she signalled that she and Joan would go back in the charabanc.

Mrs. Dell still clung to my arm. "Mrs. Shackleton, I know Eliot will want to go back to the Manor. Would you be so good as to take me home?"

Before I had time to hesitate—for I was wondering whether to follow Sykes—her grip on my arm tightened. She lowered her voice to a whisper. "There is something I must tell you, before it is too late."

"Yes, then of course I'll drive you, if you'll give me directions." This would not take long, I hoped.

In the crush of mourners, we had become separated from Raynor and his umbrella, but he once more appeared, seeming determined to keep me in his sights.

My car was parked on the roadside. "Raynor, would you tell Mrs. Brockman that I am taking Mrs. Dell home?"

"Of course, madam." He opened the passenger door and helped Mrs. Dell.

As soon as I got into the car, I read Sykes's note.

Identity discovered: Harry Aspinall, recognised by golfers and Vicar. Resident of France. Owner of Rothwell Manor. Absentee trustee of Bluebell Children's Home. His son here. Meet at White Swan?

The message stopped my breath. My wild guess turned out to be near the mark.

If ever a summons struck a note of urgency, this was it.

And there was Sykes's motor now. He was offering a lift to the stranger—Harry Aspinall's son? I caught Sykes's eye, and nodded agreement to his suggestion. He could spot that I had a passenger so would be unable to follow.

Fortunately, the rainstorm ended, as quickly as it had begun.

Chapter Thirty-Eight

❦

Mrs. Sugden walked smartly out of the station, looking out for Mr. Gopnik the estate agent. Harriet hung back, because Sergeant Dog insisted on sniffing his new surroundings. She would not deprive him of that small joy. When they did emerge, Harriet saw Mrs. Sugden talking to a florid-faced man with a bulbous nose. He stood with his back to a black saloon car. As she drew nearer, Harriet saw that the side of the car had been lettered in gold:

GOPNIK ESTATE AGENT

Mrs. Sugden turned and looked towards Harriet and the dog. Mr. Gopnik followed her gaze. He then leaned back against his car, with a look that said he was ready to go home now.

Sergeant Dog, the instant it was polite to do so, put his leg up on the car's rear wheel.

Mrs. Sugden temporarily adopted Harriet. "This my grand-daughter who'll help in the shop."

Already in possession of grandmothers, Harriet was intrigued at the thought of adding to the collection.

"Harriet, meet Mr. Gopnik who will kindly show us round the shop in Thorpefield."

"How do you do, sir." Harriet spoke in her most polite voice, not wanting there to be any objections. "Granny and I would have our dog with us in the shop."

"Well then you'd better climb in." He opened the front passenger door for Mrs. Sugden and the rear door for Harriet. "Try and keep him off the seats."

They set off, passing White Swan Yard where one of Harriet's real grannies lived.

Sergeant Dog, who must in his own mind imagine himself small and dainty, decided that the best place for him to sit would be on Harriet's lap. Harriet was behind Mr. Gopnik, meaning that Sergeant Dog was ideally situated to sniff the back of the driver's neck.

Mr. Gopnik leaned forward. So did Sergeant Dog. He dribbled on Mr. Gopnik's collar. Harriet put her arms around Sergeant and tried to hold him back.

The smell of dog mingled with the existing odours of petrol, upholstery, whisky and cigarettes.

Mrs. Sugden looked out of the window, assessing Wakefield.

Once he had negotiated the traffic near the station, and reached a less busy road, Mr. Gopnik began to tell Mrs. Sugden about the shop's advantages. It was near the miners' cottages and the mill. There wasn't another grocery shop for three miles. Trade was brisk. She and her granddaughter would like the accommodation, and so on. He asked what she did now, and what interested her in taking on a shop.

Mrs. Sugden once told Harriet that it was better to tell as much truth as you could, because lies are forgettable. "I'm a housekeeper, but I want my independence."

Harriet put her face against Sergeant's neck so she could smother her laughter. No one was more independent than Mrs. Sugden. If Mrs. Sugden left, Harriet and her auntie wouldn't know what to do. There would be no one there to tell them.

After a longish drive, they reached Silver Street. They passed a row of cottages with well-tended gardens. The driver stopped the car beyond the last cottage, outside an odd-looking building that stood all on its own. "It was allus a shop, being the end house in a row what was demolished," Mr. Gopnik explained. "It's spacious. It's airy. It's a little gold mine."

"So you said."

"It has a garden at the back as would make a town allotment shrivel in shame. You could grow your own veg. Rhubarb puts in an appearance of its own accord and so do spuds."

Harriet looked through the shop window at rows of shelves with tins and jars. He unlocked the door. "I won't stand in the way of you taking your own good look round. How long do you need?"

"As long as you like," Mrs. Sugden said. "Give us an hour or more. We've brought us lunch. I want to stroll about, get the lie of the land and the feel of the place."

He seemed pleased at this. "That suits me very well, Mrs. Sugden. I have another call to make." He looked at his watch. "I'll come back for you. If you think of any questions whatsoever, stock, turnover, anything at all, you only have to ask."

Harriet watched the car drive away. Sergeant Dog gave a little whimper. He liked to travel with a herd and was sorry to see a person leave.

"Where is Mr. Gopnik going?" Harriet asked.

Mrs. Sugden shook her head sadly. "Where do you think?"

"I don't know."

"He hasn't had a drink since he woke this morning. He's desperate."

"I thought he must be a drinker by his face and his nose."

"Come on then, let's look inside."

They went in the shop entrance. Harriet was impressed by the array of sweet jars. The pear drops jar was almost full. The liquorice allsorts and dolly mixtures would need filling soon. She had seen bigger shops that didn't have as many varieties. "There's nothing but sweets and tins."

"Aye well there wouldn't be any perishables, not since it's stood empty."

There was a good rag hearthrug for sale, bright colours, six shillings. There was a cheese slicer, a butter platter and a bacon slicer. Harriet sniffed. You could still smell bacon and cheese. "Why did the person leave?"

"Ah." Mrs. Sugden walked through to the back room.

Harriet followed.

"People get old," Mrs. Sugden explained. "There's a time when a person is past it."

"Oh." Harriet believed her until Mrs. Sugden added, "Everything comes to an end."

The shopkeeper died, Harriet thought. Why doesn't she just say that?

They looked round the back room, the cellar, and the upstairs. Mrs. Sugden was paying so much attention to everything that Harriet began to think she was serious, and would leave them.

"I don't want you to take over a shop, Mrs. Sugden. I'd miss you. Auntie Kate wouldn't want you to go."

"I'm going nowhere, love."

"Is it to do with a case?"

"In a manner of speaking, it's to do with a case as you say."

"The shopkeeper died."

"She did."

"She was murdered."

"That's putting it very harshly."

"But true."

"Some nasty so-and-so took her life. I wasn't going to tell you. You should have stopped at home. Now I'm going to speak to a few neighbours." She took Harriet's arm. "Come on, outside into the fresh air."

Harriet watched Mrs. Sugden walk towards the miners' cottages.

Sergeant Dog did not like his people to separate. He looked at Harriet, gave a little whimper, and tugged on the lead, wanting to follow. "She's coming back," Harriet explained. "We're looking round. Keep to the edge of this allotment." For that's what the long garden was. Drills and trenches had been prepared. There was a seedbed and a cold frame. Harriet wondered whether seeds had been planted. One bed was covered with sacking against the frost.

Inspecting the shopkeeper's vegetable garden gave Harriet a strange feeling. When she was little, she helped her dad in their allotment. He always explained everything to her. He followed his own father's tradition and planted potatoes on Good Friday. She would trot alongside him when he went to consult a gnarled old man who was renowned for predicting the weather. She remembered this old man's words: "Don't venture to plant out until May comes in."

Frost was the danger. Yet Harriet liked frost. She used to look out of her bedroom window and see the furrowed ground sparkling white. What she loved most of all was the intricate frosty webs on hedges and privets all along the walk to school. That was then. That was before. That was the life she thought would never end.

When she was with her dad, she loved to pick up a stick, pretend it was a walking stick and she was going to walk a very long way, somewhere beyond the horizon.

She led Sergeant Dog to the end of the garden. Soft fruit bushes were cut back. One was a strawberry plant. Destructive little creatures sat on its leaves. There would be no strawberries if aphids had their way. You could get rid of them with soapy water, but she had none. Leaning down, she picked up a little fly and squashed it between finger and thumb.

When she dropped his lead, Sergeant Dog sloped away through the hedge, following a scent.

She wondered what people did round here for enjoyment, and where was the nearest picture house.

She picked up a stick, a perfect walking stick. Someone had cleared old branches. A bonfire had been started but was only half burned. She poked it with the stick. Sergeant Dog came to look. He took a good sniff.

He then turned his attention to the scarecrow. He began to whine. He stood on his hind legs and put his paws on the scarecrow's shoulder.

Harriet pulled at his collar. "You'll get us in trouble, Sergeant."

Chapter Thirty-Nine

Mrs. Sugden knew that she looked respectable. That was what counted among working people. She wore a serge coat, a felt hat and brown gloves. It would help that she clearly had nothing to sell.

Four doors up Silver Street, a woman had just brought out a pail of slops and thrown it onto the compost heap. Mrs. Sugden called to her before she went back in and closed the door. "Excuse me!"

The woman held the pail like a shield against evil, and waited.

"Hello, I'm Mrs. Sugden, brought by the estate agent to look at yonder shop. He's left me a wee while to get the feel of the place. There's no better way of learning than to ask someone nearby."

"What do you want to know?"

"I'm sorry to ask this and no ill reflection on you and your neighbours, but is this a place where ruffians are likely to murder a body for a shilling?"

"It is not, by no means. This is a respectable place. We pay our way and look out for each other. Our men are in the pit. When they come up they've a mind to look to their pigeons and the garden and have a drink."

"So there'd be no violence from this direction?"

"I'm not saying there's no fights. I'm not saying there isn't them that knock their wives about, but it's all among each other. If Mrs. Farrar's death is going to put a person off taking on the shop it'll be a poor do."

"That's just what I would have thought. No insult intended."

"None taken. You won't find so many people to talk to today. They're at the funeral. I would've been there myself but I have an invalid indoors."

Mrs. Sugden knew she shouldn't have come until Mrs. Farrar was decently laid to rest, and a passage of days. But now she was here, she must get on with it. Mention of the murder had not gone down well. She would keep her questions as to whether the shop was well patronised and whether a woman who charged fair prices might make a living. That would open a conversation.

A tall thin woman, wearing dark clothes and black felt hat, alighted from a heavy bicycle at the gate of the end house in the row. As she walked along the path she picked up a carpet beater and walloped a rag rug that hung on the line, as if its dust had tried to choke her as she passed by, and she must exact revenge.

Mrs. Sugden approached. "I'm sorry to interrupt you. Nice rug."

The praise of her rug drew a more friendly response than Mrs. Sugden had expected.

"Made by my great gran and it'll see me out."

In an instant, Mrs. Sugden put the woman's philosophy of life into words. "Waste not, want not."

This pleased the woman. She paused in her beating. "That's what I say. Young uns today, they want everything new." She pointed to a stool by the door. "I stuck the leg back. It'd been thrown out for last year's bonfire."

"Good for you." Mrs. Sugden's admiration was genuine.

Mrs. Sugden noticed that the woman wore no wedding ring, but a signet ring on her right hand. Now that they had reached agreement that thrift mattered, the woman commented that she had seen the estate agent's car. "They wasted no time putting Mrs. Farrar's shop out for rent. I'm just back from her funeral."

"I wouldn't have come if I'd known the funeral was today."

Mrs. Sugden would have a word with Mrs. Shackleton, and Jim Sykes, too. They must have known.

"Well she had a good funeral. The vicar gave a fine service. I saw her lowered into her resting place and I came straight back. I'm not one for funeral breakfasts and long faces."

"You'll have known Mrs. Farrar well?"

"We got on. You'll see a bonny rag rug for sale in her window and one inside, both made by me. She'd take my pies, apple, blackberry, plum. I go out picking when some'd leave fruit to rot."

Mrs. Sugden doubted many round here would leave fruit to rot. She pigeon-holed this rug beater as someone who would get there first, strip trees and bushes bare.

"Is there anything else you can tell me about what happened that dreadful night? Only I wouldn't want to put myself in harm's way. History has a habit of repeating itself."

"Nothing ever happens here. It was Friday night. All Fridays are the same. Women clear their slate at the shop. Lads go to Rothwell to hang about on street corners. Fellers go to the pub or the club as takes their fancy. Lassies stop at home and wash their hair."

"And what about the lad they got for the murder?"

"I saw him going to his band practice, and I saw him coming back."

"And after that?"

"Nay, I've stuff to get on with. I don't sit watching other folks all day and all night."

"So nothing at all unusual?"

"Only that –"

"What?"

"Oh summat and nowt. She didn't usually light a garden fire on a Friday."

"Did you tell the police?"

"They didn't ask so I didn't tell."

Chapter Forty

❧

Sergeant Dog sniffed at the scarecrow's sacking coat with such enthusiasm that he almost toppled the figure. Harriet saw that under the sacking coat was another coat. Like the sacking, it was damp from rain. It was charred, too. Scorch marks. Threads of hemp attached themselves to the wool of the second coat. She examined it more closely, knowing a bit of good cloth when she saw it, fingering the wool. This must be the most thoroughly dressed scarecrow in Yorkshire. Under the jacket, it wore a shirt. It wore a pair of trousers.

She put Sergeant on his lead. "You best leave this alone. It's a puzzle."

His interest in the scarecrow waned.

He had been trained not to pull, not to drag, not to be a blooming nuisance. Now he pulled. He dragged. He became a blooming nuisance. She let him have his way, to see where he would lead. He led her back into the shop. He sniffed all about, making small whining noises.

Harriet decided she did not like it in here, not one little bit.

Sergeant led her all around, sniff-sniffing. He led her to the back door. When he put his snout to the mat, he let out a whine.

The mat was none too clean. Harriet felt suddenly cold. This wasn't a good place to be. "Come on. We're off outside."

She forgot that today Mrs. Sugden was supposed to be her grandmother. She walked to the row of houses, where Mrs. Sugden was chatting over the fence with the woman in the end house.

Mrs. Sugden was so engrossed that Harriet went back to the garden bench and sat down. Holding Sergeant Dog by the collar, she patted his head. Still whining, he licked her face.

When Mrs. Sugden joined them, Harriet took her to see the scarecrow in its damaged finery.

They both stared at the hole with a burn mark around it. It was Mrs. Sugden who recognised a bullet hole. "This scarecrow was shot through the tummy."

Mrs. Sugden examined the jacket and shirt more closely. "Harriet, have you got that little camera with you?"

"Yes."

"Take pictures of this scarecrow. Get a picture of that Jermyn Street tailor's label, get a picture of that bullet hole."

While Harriet took pictures, Mrs. Sugden allowed Sergeant Dog to lead her to the back door of the house. Sniffing and whining, he proudly drew her attention to a doormat.

Normally, Mrs. Sugden would report back to Mrs. Shackleton. But Mrs. Shackleton was otherwise engaged.

She knew that photographs or no photographs, all Missus Waste-Not-Want-Not would have to do was deny all knowledge of the scarecrow and its outfit. Better tackle the woman now.

"Harriet, walk up and down the street with Sergeant Dog. I'm going in to talk to that neighbour. You can let people see you."

"You've already talked to her."

"So I have, and while she's in talkative mood I'm going to take her statement."

Mrs. Sugden had never taken an official statement before, but there was always a first time.

The neighbour's name was Valerie Pennington. She admitted taking some items of men's clothing from the fire. God intended her to or He wouldn't have sent a downpour to douse the flames. She slipped the shirt and jacket onto the scarecrow so as not to be seen making off with them. The shirt might make something. The jacket would go towards a quality rag rug.

When all that business blew up about a murder and stories of a body on a train, she thought she best leave it alone. She'd done nothing wrong. A woman had to live. Mrs. Sugden sympathised. It was hard when you were on your own, trying to make ends meet, paying your rent.

Mrs. Waste-Not-Want-Not Valerie Pennington admitted that it helped being granted a grace and favour cottage, but a woman had to eat, and buy coal.

They parted on good terms. Mrs. Sugden agreed that if she took the shop, she would be happy to sell Miss Pennington's pies and cakes. She did not mention a good quality Jermyn Street jacket that was intended to have a second life as a rag rug.

Even as she spoke to Miss Pennington, there was another voice in Mrs. Sugden's head. This voice told her that the shopkeeper might not have been murdered for her paltry takings. She might have been murdered because she knew something.

Did she and Harriet now know that very same thing?

A man in expensive clothes had been shot.

Chapter
Forty-One

～

Mrs. Dell's house would not have been out of place on the Rhine, or in a child's picture book. The storeys on either end were topped with turrets that came to a point like witches' hats. The imposing front door might have led to a Parisian courtyard.

I admired the design as I helped Mrs. Dell from the car, which I had parked close to the front door.

"We planned it ourselves, my late husband and I. He was an engineer but had a fancy to be an architect. You will come in?"

We entered a baroque hall, large enough to stage a concert. A broad staircase with barley sugar rails led to a gallery. Mrs. Dell's walking stick tap-tapped as I followed her along the hall and through a door. "I live entirely downstairs now." A corridor led to a comfortable sitting room. Beyond the bay windows were three tall poplar trees. A low fire burned in the grate.

"Do sit down, Mrs. Shackleton. I suppose we ought to take off our coats but I feel the cold these days."

I had not meant to come in, but it would have been churlish to refuse.

She rang a bell. Sykes's note was burning a hole in my pocket. I pictured him waiting in the White Swan, ordering another pint, looking at his watch. Would the stranger, Mr. Aspinall's son, be with him?

Mrs. Dell wanted to talk. "If the rains had not turned tropical, I should have visited my daughter-in-law's grave. We thought a lot of each other, Phyllis and I. She was more of a daughter to me than Eliot has ever been a son."

"Then I'm sorry for your loss. Perhaps you will visit the grave another day."

"That may not be possible. Thank you for your condolences. You see, she ought to have been alive."

"Gertrude told me of the circumstances."

"You mean that she repeated Eliot's story?"

The maid came at that moment. She wheeled a trolley with tea things, sandwiches and plates. A stout, motherly sort of woman, she made sure that Mrs. Dell's cushions were in place and her spectacles handy. She spoke to her mistress in a friendly familiar way. "I didn't know if you'd go back to the Brockmans for the funeral breakfast."

"I can't be doing with it, Maggie. And I didn't want to delay."

Neither did I want to delay, but here I was. Sykes would know that parting company after a funeral would not be easy.

"Well everything's ready," Maggie said as she poured tea. "And he shouldn't be long."

"Are we waiting for Eliot?" I asked.

"Oh no," Maggie said. "He'll be at the Brockmans' until late. Good timing, eh, madam?"

When she had gone, Mrs. Dell said, "Maggie is more than a servant. She is my rock and my friend. I have Maggie as Benjamin Brockman has Raynor."

I wondered whether there was a deeper meaning attached to this remark, but simply agreed that Raynor did indeed seem loyal. I did not say that he had kept me in his sights in such a way that led me to believe he knew why I had come.

"I like you, Mrs. Shackleton. The son of one of our tenants told me about your interest in photography, as well as your other exploits."

Something told me that it was the other exploits that aroused her curiosity. Perhaps now I would hear why she had chosen me as the person to bring her home.

"When my daughter-in-law died, I was in my bedroom." She indicated an adjoining door. "Maggie's room is also in this wing. Phyllis was too far away for us to hear. There was no need for her to die. I cannot say that Eliot murdered her, but I can say that he let her die, and die alone. That is one of the reasons I shall be leaving."

"Where are you going?"

"My younger son is coming to collect me and Maggie. Our bags are packed. I thought he might be here by now."

That seemed such a drastic measure that for a moment I did not know what to say. "Does Eliot know?"

"I may have mentioned it, but I don't believe he took me seriously."

"And have you confronted him, about your reason?"

"Oh yes. But he has no fears of me. Quite the reverse. And you see, I might be next."

"Surely not?"

"He wishes to move to a grander place. He will shed anything and anyone that holds him back: Phyllis, the orphanage and the children, this house, me. I cannot prevent his inheritance, but I mean to live a little longer."

"This is so shocking. Have you told anyone?"

"My younger son. Even he believes I am imagining things, but all the same he is coming for me."

I was about to speak again, but she interrupted. "Whatever breach there is between Eliot and me, how could I say more than that he has always had great plans? I would be seen as a dozy old woman, best confined to quarters."

We had both forgotten the dainty sandwiches. She picked one up and began to eat. I did the same. It had been a long time since breakfast. It saved me from thinking how on earth to respond. I did not need to. She continued.

"I noticed on Saturday that Gertrude was pretending to be in a matchmaking frame of mind, for you and Eliot. Be careful. She is rather playful. His heart is occupied."

I knew immediately what she was hinting, but felt sure she was wrong on that count at least. Had there been a rift between Benjie and Gertrude, I should have noticed.

Maggie came in without knocking. "Mr. Alfred is here madam. He has taken our suitcases." She helped Mrs. Dell to her feet.

Something came to mind, a question. If I did not ask now there may not be another opportunity. "Maggie, I'll walk Mrs. Dell to the door. I need just another moment."

Maggie looked at Mrs. Dell who nodded assent.

"Mrs. Dell, you said your daughter-in-law's death was one of the reasons you must leave. What was the other?"

She hesitated. "I'm sorry to cut short our chat, Mrs. Shackleton. Do stay and have more sandwiches."

"Please, Mrs. Dell."

She hesitated, and then spoke as if to herself. "The night Mrs. Farrar was murdered, Eliot came back here with Gertrude Brockman, in her car. It was quite late. I didn't want to see them, and went into the library to find a particular book. They came into the library, not knowing I was there. In the one room where you might expect silence, the acoustics are very good. My husband explained it, but I don't remember how it works. They were talking about Mrs. Farrar, and how stubborn she was, and that she had left them no choice. And then Eliot told Gertrude that there was blood on the cuff of her coat."

"Did they know you were there?"

"Yes, because I dropped a book, but they know I am hard of hearing. I am not as deaf as they think." She had begun to tremble, almost as if she was back on that night, in the library. "When I dropped the book, I came out, saying that I didn't know they were there, and would Eliot pick up my book because I go dizzy if I bend. I could see that they were in this odd state, excited and a little afraid. And I knew, even before Mrs. Farrar's death was announced."

"Thank you for telling me."

"I won't say this to anyone else. Don't let it be known."

I took her arm. "Come on, Maggie is waiting."

As we walked back to the hall, I hardly knew what to say. "I trust you will have a good journey, and wish you well."

"Thank you."

I walked with them to the front door. Maggie was carrying a bag, so Mrs. Dell continued to rely on me. In the hall she turned and looked about her, as if taking in the house for the last time.

There were so many other questions I wanted to ask. I gave Maggie my card. "Please let me know how you get on."

She nodded. "Don't tell Mr. Eliot we are gone. He'll find out soon enough."

"All anyone need know is that I brought Mrs. Dell to her front door."

Naturally, I was introduced to Alfred, the amiable younger son, but he was in a hurry to be off. He helped his mother into the back seat and smothered her with rugs. Maggie climbed in the other side.

Mrs. Dell beckoned to me. I leaned in to listen, because she spoke so quietly. "Gertrude went to stay with an aunt in Surrey last year, for several months. After she came back, she spoke of a sudden desire to adopt a baby boy."

As Alfred went round to the driver's side, she mouthed, "Be careful," and "Go home."

The car set off.

She raised her hand in a royal wave.

Chapter Forty-Two

~

In answer to Sykes's question, the young Frenchman had to shout above the noise of the car engine.

"My mother sent me to the funeral of Mrs. Farrar. Now I go back to her."

"How did she know about Mrs. Farrar?"

"From her enquiries with the Embassy. We came to search for my father."

Sykes wished he hadn't asked. He did not want this conversation, and especially not in the noisy motor.

Charles did not mind shouting. "The vicar, he says nothing. He is sympathetic in a way I do not like. He says talk to you."

Sykes tugged at his left ear, to indicate he was having difficulty hearing. He needed time to think. The bad news would have come better from the vicar, but the vicar didn't know the circumstances surrounding the death. The Reverend Mr. Branscombe might at least have hinted, Sykes thought. But perhaps he had hinted and Charles did not take it in, and the bad news failed to penetrate through a barrier of misunderstanding.

"We'll talk when we get there," Sykes shouted.

Sykes took him to the White Swan and bought him a pint.

Charles showed his return rail ticket. He intended to go back to London. His mother expected him.

"How long will you stay in London?"

Sykes glanced at the window, wishing Mrs. Shackleton would tear herself away from her posh friends. She would know what to say.

He took a drink of bitter, wiped the froth from his lips with the back of his hand. He wondered whether he had chosen wrongly. Had he asked Mrs. Shackleton to meet him at police headquarters, they would have been able to get word to Commander Woodhead straight away, and tell him the man's identity.

Being in police headquarters would have allowed young Charles Aspinall to know that something was seriously wrong. He was looking at Sykes, waiting, waiting for an answer. He looked at his watch. "I must go for my train. I must know about my father."

"Where are you staying in London?"

"The Savoy."

"We will get word to you."

"What word?"

"Please tell your mother to prepare herself for bad news. I am sorry."

"My father is dead?"

"I believe so."

"That is all you can say?"

"That is all I can say for now." Sykes, usually so glued to facts, so prepared to swear by them, felt this bizarre welling of hope—hope that they were wrong. Nothing was confirmed yet. Nothing would be confirmed until the next of kin had identified the body. Identifying a portrait taken from a dead man did not seem sufficient.

Sykes walked the young man to the railway station and saw him onto the next train.

It rankled with him that a top man at Scotland Yard had given those below him instructions that tied their hands behind their backs, put them in blinkers and wasted precious time by being secretive.

He went back to the White Swan, ordered another pint and a whisky chaser.

An estate agent's car stopped by the kerb on the opposite side of the road. The driver stayed put. Someone being dropped off at the railway station. The front passenger door opened. He saw a familiar hat above the top of the car door. The wearer moved towards the rear of the car. The rear door opened.

With a full view, he saw that the wearer of the hat was Mrs. Sugden. She was joined by Harriet and the dog. Knowing the dog had a soft spot for him and might dash across the road, dragging Harriet with him, Sykes stayed inside the pub.

What were they doing here? Then he remembered. Mrs. Sugden had been assigned to look at the Corner Shop where Mrs. Farrar was murdered, and talk to the neighbours.

The car drove off.

Mrs. Sugden, Harriet and the dog crossed the road.

Sykes put his drink on the counter, in view of the landlord, and went to the door.

Sergeant Dog gave a yelp of delight at the sight of him.

They stepped up to the pub doorway. "I'm here to meet Mrs. Shackleton," Sykes said. "What are you doing here?"

Mrs. Sugden opened her mouth to answer, but Harriet got there first. "We left a note in the bee bole, to say we'd go to my gran's, here in the yard."

Sykes glanced at the yard, White Swan Yard. That explained why Mrs. Shackleton had taken someone a jug of stout, or did it? If his thoughts hadn't been so focused on the unknown man turning into Harry Aspinall of Rothwell Manor, and his son turning up at the funeral, looking for answers, Sykes might have put two and two together. As it was, he just stared.

"I don't suppose you've met my gran," Harriet said. "Come and say hello, Mr. Sykes. She likes company."

Harriet went ahead down the yard, knocked on a door on the right and let herself in.

Sykes turned to Mrs. Sugden. "What's going on now?"

"All sorts of things are coming together. Like when you bake a cake and you think you have all the ingredients and you look for sugar. You go to the tin. Open the tin, and tin't in't tin, and then you find you'd put sugar in a jar."

Sykes never had this kind of conversation when he was on the force. "So Harriet's grandmother –"

"You knew Mrs. Shackleton was adopted by Mr. and Mrs. Hood, and that she was born in this here yard."

"No."

"Well you know now."

"I do."

"You and I need to bring each other up to date on the case, Jim. And it doesn't suit me to sit in the window of a public house."

"We can go in the snug at the back, unless you'd like to go to Harriet's grandmother's house."

Mrs. Sugden shook her head. "Best not. She lives on her own and likes to talk. The snug will do nicely."

They walked back to the pub.

"Will you have a port and lemon?"

"That will be acceptable."

"Don't force yourself."

Over Jim Sykes's pint of bitter and Mrs. Sugden's port and lemon, they exchanged information. Mr. Sykes knew the identity of the mysterious man, and his son. Mrs. Sugden claimed to know the name of Mr. Aspinall's tailor, and that his clothes now dressed a scarecrow in the garden of Mrs. Farrar's shop.

She was being fanciful, he thought, until she told him about the bullet hole, and Sergeant Dog smelling blood.

"We need to get moving on this." Sykes looked at his watch. "Where's she got to?"

Mrs. Sugden saw that he had begun to worry. "You can't always get away easily after a funeral. She'll be here if she said she would."

Sykes knew she was right. Even polite Mrs. Shackleton ought to know there were more important things than offering condolences over slices of pork pie.

There was no point in worrying. "So this scarecrow, do you have any inkling of who dressed it? The rational action would have been to destroy the clothing."

"Not only do I know who dressed it, but I took her statement. When I made her understand the severity of the situation, she preferred to talk to me than explain to the police."

As he read the statement given by Miss Valerie Pennington, Sykes got a sick feeling in the pit of his stomach. Mrs. Shackleton might, for once, be out of her depth. She would hate it if he went barging in to the rescue and jeopardised some delicate investigation. But what more could there be to investigate?

Chapter Forty-Three

❧

After leaving Mrs. Dell's house, I came to a fork in the road. Turn left for the White Swan and Sykes. Turn right for Thorpefield Manor.

My business there was not over. I turned right.

The dining hall at the manor was thronged with people. Mr. and Mrs. Arkwright had the vicar cornered. Gertrude was surrounded by several ladies I recognised from the Holy Trinity service.

Eliot Dell stood by the window, talking earnestly to two men. He acknowledged me as I passed by. "Good investment," I heard him say. "The deepest mine in the country."

Milly circulated with a tray of sandwiches, Raynor with a tray of drinks. "My rock and friend," Mrs. Dell had said. "I have Maggie. Benjamin Brockman has Raynor."

Had Raynor been beside Benjie when he was shown the drawing of the unfortunate Harry Aspinall?

"Drink, Mrs. Shackleton?"

"No thank you. I'm hoping for a word with Mr. Brockman."

"He has paid his respects and retired to his study, madam, asking not to be disturbed."

"Thank you." I went into the hall, and along to Benjie's study. He did not answer my knock. Knowing he was there, I opened the door.

He was at his desk, and looked up as I entered. "Benjie, excuse the interruption but I shall be going soon."

"Ah Kate, come in, come in. I'm just puzzling over my coins. You know when you have to count twice, and then count again." He scratched his head. "Is everything all right?"

I took the seat opposite the desk. This room had an air of calm, oak desk with baize top, brass lamp, and row upon row of bookshelves.

"Benjie, something's come up that I want to ask you about."

"To do with coins? Stamps?"

"To do with Harry Aspinall."

"Aspinall?"

"Your fellow trustee for the Bluebell Home."

"Ah, that Aspinall. I'm not well today, Kate, not well at all. Dislike funerals. And she was a good old soul, Mrs. Farrar."

I placed the drawing of Harry Aspinall on the table. "You were shown this and asked if you recognised him. You said no."

Benjie picked up his magnifying glass and looked at the drawing. "And I'd say no again. I've no great memory for faces, unless it's someone I know well, like you."

"If there's anything you know about his disappearance, please tell me now."

"Disappearance? Chap never appeared so he couldn't very well disappear—unless you're talking about long ago, when he took up with a French woman."

"More recently than that."

He shook his head. So that was how he intended to be, slightly dotty, forgetful, unaware that he knew the murdered man. As deputy to the Lord Lieutenant of the County, he might just get away with it.

"I'll leave you to your counting."

I went back into the hall, just in time to see Eliot saying goodbye to Gertrude. He gave me a wave, and left.

"Where did you get to, Kate?"

"I took Mrs. Dell home."

"That was such an imposition. Some aged people do rather take liberties. Give them a walking stick or a speaking trumpet and they consider the rest of humanity to be at their beck and call."

"I was happy to do it."

She took my arm. "The vicar wants to say hello, and I've hardly spoken to you today."

"Sorry but I have to leave in about five minutes. I have an appointment."

"Ah, your essay?"

"That's finished. Something has come up—a case. I'm meeting my assistant."

"Goodness, that sounds important. You will come back?"

"Either that or I'll send someone. It's been really kind of you to put me up."

It was likely, once I reported what I knew, she would never want to see me again. I hated the thought that it would be mutual. The sooner I left the better. I felt such a surge of regret and I had a sudden hope that Mrs. Dell was wrong.

"Well if you must go." She stepped outside with me. "Before you go, is my embroidery pouch with those dreadful letters in your room?"

"Sorry, no, but I will return it."

"What do you mean?"

"I thought to help solve the riddle of who wrote the letters, but you'll know that already."

"Why should I?"

"Because you wrote them. What I don't understand is why."

"You're wrong."

"There was one set of fingerprints, Gertrude."

"Yours then."

"Why did you do it?"

She gave a small smile. "I thought you'd hear things. I wanted you to know there are vicious people about. People are blaming us for closing the Bluebell Home. God knows why. It was good all the time we had it, and after we'd found placements there were only eight children left. No one blames the authorities about the home in Rothwell where the children are known to be cowed and miserable. It couldn't go on. It's as simple as that."

"So you blew up a few trees one night, caused a commotion, said the site was dangerous and must be demolished."

She was silent, her face stony, and then she gave a bitter laugh. "Holier than thou. You've never had to provide a living for a whole community. You don't know what it's like when everybody looks to you for a livelihood. Miners, tenant farmers, shopkeepers, railwaymen, all on your land, all wanting a living whether they can earn it or not. What about me? What kind of life do you think I have?"

"You have –"

"Benjie, that's what you're going to say. Of course I have. You were there. You witnessed the vows. I've kept my part of the bargain, and more. Old houses suck you dry, they make demands, and you cannot leave because there is an obligation. It's not even my house. If Benjie dies, it would have gone to a cousin, but I hope to soon have a son and heir."

It would be foolish to challenge her here and now about what Mrs. Dell saw and heard. Such hearsay would not stand up in court, and Mrs. Dell would rather die than damn her son in public. They must have had help. Raynor would have done Benjie's bidding. Benjie stayed in the background covered with his cloak of respectability.

"It must have worried you that Benjie might have acknowledged Alec Taylor and made him his heir."

"I thought you saw the family resemblance. Every day I look at a stable boy, who is very bright, good-looking, turning into a clever mechanic, and that's all he will ever be."

"At least Alec Taylor looks like Michael, not Benjie."

"You mean no one will know. But I know. Raynor knows. He pities me. I can't bear pity, and I loathe that boy."

"That boy" was outside the window, talking to a man with a pushbike. An advertisement board on the cycle basket proclaimed a shop name: Picture This. When the man turned his head, I saw that he was Maurice Lewis, here in person to deliver my remaining photographs. But there was one secret I wanted to crack.

"Gertrude, how did you know that Mrs. Farrar had written to Harry Aspinall about the closure of the Bluebell Home?"

"Who told you that she had done so?"

"It doesn't matter who told me."

"Everything was done properly. Mrs. Farrar was outvoted. It was too late. Harry Aspinall had notice of that meeting and every other meeting. He took no responsibility. I wish he had come. He might have shared the blame for closing the home, instead of it all being directed at me. Though of course men are allowed to be prudent and consider the balance sheet. A woman is simply hard-hearted. Believe me, I've done nothing wrong."

And I wanted to believe her. Perhaps Mrs. Dell was mistaken.

She took my arm. "I'll walk you to your car. And don't leave it so long next time. If you've had enough of this place, let's meet for one of our lunches."

Raynor was beside us. "Shall I escort Mrs. Shackleton? I do believe you and Mr. Brockman are missed, madam."

Gertrude sighed. "Hasn't he come out yet?" She leaned to kiss me. "Must go, Kate."

"Goodbye, Gertrude."

Raynor remained obtrusively attentive. "I will have Milly gather your belongings. Shall we send them on?"

"Yes that would do."

He missed nothing. I expected he would soon be in confab with Benjie, rejoicing in my departure.

Our way to the garage took us by the side door.

It was there that I saw Maurice Lewis, hovering near his bicycle with its Picture This sign on the basket. He smiled broadly and came towards me. Knowing of his foot problems, I couldn't help but glance at his feet, shod in old army boots. He carried a slim parcel, wrapped in brown paper and tied with string.

We exchanged a greeting. "I framed the picture of the lad reading his comic, because that was the best. I mounted the one of him by your car, and did a couple of postcards, as you asked. Do you want to look now?"

"I'm sure they'll be fine. He'll be delighted."

He cleared his throat, before producing a small brown envelope. "My invoice, to settle entirely at your convenience."

"Then I'll call at the shop in the next day or so." I glanced at the envelope. The handwriting was not Mr. Lewis's careful copperplate but my dad's scrawl. How annoying that he was sending me a note, as if I couldn't look after myself. I would read the note when away from the watchful eye of Raynor.

Mr. Lewis presented the package.

I handed it to Alec. "Here you are—instant nostalgia. Something for your mantelpiece, to look back on when you reach ripe old age."

Alec Taylor slid off the string without untying it and tore open the package. "Oh. Oh." He looked at each photograph. "Thank you. Thank you, Mrs. Shackleton."

"It's a pleasure, Alec."

I put on my motoring coat, hat and gloves and got into the car. "Consider it a thank you for looking after my car."

"There's petrol in it, and I've filled the can."

"Good."

Raynor gave a small bow. "Safe journey, Mrs. Shackleton."

"Thank you, Raynor."

I waved as I drove off. The gates stood open. I turned onto the lane and set off at a good speed, wanting to leave Thorpefield House well behind me. I had forgotten that the lane bends so sharply and tried to brake, but even when I braked, something was wrong. The car wasn't responding. As I turned the steering wheel, nothing happened. By the time I braked again, it was too late. The wood was coming to meet me. I heard the crash, as if it was someone else's car, and then everything went black.

Chapter Forty-Four

✎

For what seemed an age, I stayed still, my head against the windscreen, trying to work out what part of me hurt.

When I opened my eyes, I saw the sky, spinning, blue and white and grey, swirling down to my guts. Something was hurting. It was me.

"Are you all right?"

Hands on my shoulders. The voice again, nearer now. "Can you move?"

A different voice. "Mrs. Shackleton, you have to get out of the car.

I had to get out of the car because the car was going nowhere. It had let me down. I had let it down. If I sat still, they would go away, they would leave me alone.

The sky slowly righted itself, but it was too bright.

"Alec can't open this. We'll get you out the other side."

They dragged me and pulled me, one on either side. "Hurry!" "No!"

But they would not slow down. I knew them now, Milly and Alec. Alec was saying, "I think someone did it on purpose."

And whether he was right or wrong, the fear in his voice touched something inside me. We were in the wood, dizzily moving through the trees. Blasts of light and shade, sun and shadow, patterns of leaves and flowers danced around us, snowdrops and daffodils. A voice that sounded like mine said, "Keep off the flowers."

"Never mind the flowers," Alec said.

We veered, onto a path, and another. Milly was breathing heavily. And then I had to stop. They kept running so that I was pulled along, my toes scraping the ground. Suddenly they paused, and it was because I was being sick.

Milly said, "She'll choke."

He said, "Keep going."

I could see the sky revolving, and the tops of the trees and we were hurrying and I knew this must be the end.

They were walking quickly now. I wanted to sit down, to rest, even to just lean against a tree.

"We have to keep going," Milly said.

It was the urgency in her voice as much as the words. It came back to me now. We knew too much. I knew too much.

Just me and Milly now. From a long way off the echo of what Alec said. Words were slow to go from my ear to my brain.

Milly kept talking to me, catching her breath in between. "We heard the crash. Alec saw it was going to happen."

He would. Alec. Benjie's son. Had he led us into the wood deliberately? What the car crash didn't achieve, an "accident" might.

"We ran," Milly said. "We were faster than the others."

The others. The others would come for me.

The wood was so beautiful. Might this be the last thing I see? Now I felt steadier. My head hurt, I was dizzy, but my legs did as I wanted, one before the other.

Milly still held my arm. "I thought you'd had it."

"Where are we going?"

"Away from the house. We've come through the clearing with the chair the old gardener made. We're looking for his hut."

The clearing with the chair was where I had taken Raynor's photograph. It was he. He would be waiting, with a gun? Alec had led us into a trap. "How do we get out of the wood?"

"We're not lost." Milly was squeezing my arm so tightly, that I felt sure we were lost. I tried to break free.

She put her hand on my arm. "I'm not letting you go. You hit your head. You scared me."

"I scared myself." And then I smelled smoke. I stopped and sniffed. "Follow the smoke."

"I suppose you were a girl scout, Mrs. Shackleton."

"You suppose right, and this could be a trap."

"Oh no, Alec likes you. You took his photograph. You were nice to him."

Mrs. Farrar was nice to people, but someone killed her.

The old soldier was sitting on a little stool made from a log. His fire and his black pot looked like an illustration from a storybook about gypsies.

He stopped stirring the pot. "Hey up, what's all this?"

I felt too tired to explain, not that I could have explained. On the third day, guests smell stale. This was the fifth day. Was it? The fourth, the sixth, I no longer knew.

It was a relief to me to see that Milly had my brief case. My brief case, my talisman. There was something in there that would be useful. I tried to remember what.

The old soldier handed me a tin cup. "Mind, it's hot."

"Do you good," Milly said.

I took a drink, set the cup down and closed my eyes, seeing no one, feeling so alone.

It was the pong that told me he was there. "Best not shut your eyes if you've taken a bump."

"I'm a nurse. I know that."

"Then open yer flippin' peepers."

I felt sick again. "Milly, there's brandy in my bag. Pass it round. I think we all need a drop."

The old soldier grunted. "Not me. I've tekken the pledge."

"Me as well," Milly said. "What with Stephen playing in the Temperance Band. Not that alcohol has ever passed my lips."

"Good lass," the old man said.

I took the battered silver flask that had been my husband's. Just for a moment, I forgot he was gone from the world. I pictured myself telling him how after a brush with death, I found myself in a darkening wood with judgemental teetotallers. I imagined his smile, and somehow felt better as I took a drink.

I introduced myself to the old soldier. "What's your name?"

"I'm Herbert Wesley, and you're safe here."

"How do I get out of this wood, avoiding the road?"

"That depends on where you want to go."

"I'd like to be in Wakefield, as quickly as possible. My car crashed."

"Alec thinks someone tinkered with the steering linkages," Milly said obligingly.

Herbert Wesley gulped. "That puts a different slant on the show."

Part of me must have known. Even in my slightly concussed state, I had felt a sense of danger.

Herbert Wesley picked up a shotgun.

Was this the end, were we delivered to our final destination?

"I normally shoot rabbits, and game birds." He took out a knife. "And I do a bit of this and that. But I'll make an exception if necessary."

So here was not our executioner, but our protector.

Pellets might be deadly against game, but not against a determined killer.

Now would be a good moment for someone to walk Sergeant Dog in this wood. He would find me.

It is against my usual habits to sit and wait for something to happen.

Given that Alec wasn't allowed in the house, the possibility of telephoning for help evaporated. "Milly, do you know what Alec intends to do?"

"I'm not sure. We just dashed over and he said we had to be quick."

"Why did you have to be quick?"

She shook her head. "He didn't say."

From his black cooking pot, Herbert Wesley filled the tin mug and now offered it to Milly.

"That's all right. I had something earlier, after the funeral."

He nodded. "Mrs. Farrar. God rest her soul. I'll pay my respects when the crowds have lessened."

It seemed neither the time nor the place, but I asked anyway. "Do you know anything about the circumstances of her death?"

"I do not. I wish I did. If she'd accepted my proposal of marriage all them years ago, it might not have come to this. But she's with the Lord."

Milly said, "I've remembered. Alec is going to see if he can take one of the cars, telling them he's going to look for you. We should meet him on the track by the copse with the three poplar trees."

"And if he can't take a car?"

"I don't know. And I don't know where he meant. I've seen too many poplar trees and too many tracks."

Herbert stood. "Come on then."

There was a rustling sound nearby.

He raised his gun.

Chapter
Forty-Five

～

Sykes looked once more through the window of the White Swan. An old man turned up his collar against the wind. A woman wearing a shawl on her head and another around her shoulders picked up a little child who had tripped over a paving stone and started bawling.

He took a page from his notebook. He scribbled a message, for when Mrs. Shackleton arrived. She should have been here by now. He gave the note to the landlord.

Leaving the pub, he turned into Swan Yard. He knew which door. It was the house with the cream curtains. He knocked. Sergeant Dog barked.

It was Harriet who came to the door and asked him in. "I won't, thanks. Just give a message to your Auntie Kate when she comes. I've left a note at the Mucky Duck to say the same. I'm calling in to see Mr. Hood at headquarters. Perhaps she'll come round there when she's said hello to you and your gran and Mrs. Sugden."

He looked at Harriet's face, sure then that he had kept anxiety from his voice. Sergeant Dog pushed forward, waiting his turn for attention. Sykes patted his head and told him he was a good dog, and to look after everyone. He nodded to the woman in the rocking chair. "How do!"

That would have been it, but Mrs. Sugden came out into the yard. Of course she would, Sykes thought, nothing slips past her.

She shut the door behind her. "What's worrying you?"

"Mrs. Shackleton should have been here by now."

"She'll be here." If she shared his anxiety, she did not show it. "It's not easy to tear yourself away from a funeral do."

"You said that three hours ago. I'm going to see Mr. Hood."

"Oh that'll be just grand, a grown woman on an assignment being reported to her dad as a damsel in distress. She'll love that."

Sykes felt himself tense. That was the trouble with Mrs. Sugden. She thought Mrs. Shackleton invincible. He tried another tack. "Mr. Hood's stopping at his desk until he hears from her. It's only polite to keep him in touch."

A cat, tail held high, crossed the yard. It sniffed at the doorstep, and then jumped on Harriet's gran's windowsill and stared at the lace curtains. "Even a cat goes look-about," Sykes said. "We can't do nothing."

Mrs. Sugden hated to admit he was right. While sitting chatting by the fire with Harriet and her gran, she had let the time go by, telling herself everything would be all right.

"I have an idea. What about if I telephone? The Brockmans know she has a housekeeper, and they know my name. I've answered the phone to them before."

"Then they'll know you're calling from a different town."

"What does that matter? I don't have to explain why I'm at a different number. For all anyone knows, the landlord of the Mucky Duck might be my brother." Watched by the cat that was still sitting on the windowsill, she opened the door a fraction and spoke to Harriet and her gran. "I won't be long. I'll get us some fish and chips."

Sergeant Dog tried to break out. Harriet was there in an instant, putting on his lead. "I'll go for the fish and chips."

"Right." Mrs. Sugden took out her purse. "You do that then. Just get yours and your gran's for now, in case mine and Mr. Sykes's go cold."

Harriet pocketed the money. "You're worried aren't you?"

"Not a bit, there's just something we need to do."

Harriet strode up the yard. "Auntie Kate is fine. Gran said if anything was wrong, she'd feel it in her waters." Harriet turned off for the fish and chip shop.

The pub telephone was on the wall in the back room. Sykes watched Mrs. Sugden's jaw tighten as she waited to be connected to Thorpefield Manor. So she was anxious, in spite of her pretence. He listened as she made her request to speak to Mrs. Shackleton.

After a moment, she put one hand on the wall to steady herself. "Is she all right?"

She listened again. "What do you mean, can't find her?" And, "Have you called the police?"

After a few more words, she put the receiver back, preventing Sykes from snatching it. "Her car hit a tree. Two of the young servants went to look for her, and she wasn't there. Now they're searching. They haven't called the police!"

Sykes made to move. "I'll go out there now."

"I'm coming with you."

"She'll be all right," Sykes said, trying to convince himself. "If she's not there it's because she got out." He picked up his hat.

"And began to walk?"

"I wouldn't put it past her."

Mrs. Sugden hated to picture the scene, but picture it she did, seeing the crash in her mind's eye. Hearing the bang, feeling the jolt. "If they couldn't find her, it's because she didn't want them to." She put a hand on Sykes's arm. "I think it's time for your earlier idea. We go to Mr. Hood."

"You go. I'm setting off for Thorpefield. I don't trust those so-called friends of hers." He went to his car.

"Mr. Sykes!" A uniformed constable hurried across the road. "I just saw you were about to drive off, sir. It is Mr. Sykes?"

"Yes." Sykes felt the breath leave him. Something had happened. Something bad.

"Mr. Hood sent me. He's had a report from a local shopkeeper, Maurice Lewis. Seems Mr. Lewis cycled out to Thorpefield to deliver some photographs to Mrs. Shackleton. He was cycling back and heard a crash."

Sykes willed the man to speak faster, jump to the point.

"It was Mrs. Shackleton's car, hit a tree. He saw her being helped out of the car, and thought it best to go straight to the nearest police station, and report what he'd seen."

"And so what's happening now?" Sykes felt impatient with people who told you the prologue and not the outcome.

Chapter
Forty-Six

❦

Herbert Wesley's dog came running through the wood, carrying something that stank. Herbert shooed him away and so he came to me, generously dropping a long-dead rabbit at my feet.

It was the parting of the ways for Milly and me. I felt anxious for her. "Milly, do you want to come with me and Mr. Wesley, and take our chance that there'll be someone by the three poplars to give us a lift into Wakefield?"

She shook her head. "I'll just say I looked for you in the wood, which is true, and then I got lost. The housekeeper will tell me off, that's all. I'll cry if I have to."

"Thank you, Milly. I won't forget this."

Herbert Wesley reminded her of the way out of the wood, and she left.

There was no knowing whether Alec had managed to commandeer a vehicle, but I had a feeling my companion would be willing to walk me to Wakefield if necessary. Though that might mean sliding into a ditch each time a car came along the road, in case someone was looking for us.

We walked along a broad path, the trees so close on either side that I could feel darkness falling.

"Nearly there," Herbert said.

Somewhere in the wood behind us, I heard a police whistle. "Keep going," I said. Having illegal possession of just such a whistle myself I would not take the chance on the sound we heard coming from a legitimate source. In any case, I preferred that Benjie Brockman and Raynor not find out where I was from anyone. Benjie or Raynor would be capable of persuading a bobby that I was to be taken back to Thorpefield for my own good.

We reached a clearing, where three tall poplars stood. Just beyond the clearing was a laundry van. "Where did that come from?"

Herbert Wesley was no wiser than I on the matter.

"Let's just make sure it's the right driver at the wheel, before you go hopping in."

The driver at the wheel was Philip Goodchild. He got out.

"Hello, Kate."

"Hello, PH."

I shook hands with Herbert. "Thank you, Mr. Wesley. I won't forget your kindness."

Philip opened the back door. "If you get in there, no one'll see you."

I climbed into the back of the van. It was full of laundry bags. A face peered out through the bags. Alec Taylor.

"Alec's coming with us," Philip said. "This van has to go back to the laundry. It broke down and I fixed it and now I'm testing it as I take it back."

"Right." I climbed in before the explanation lengthened.

It would have been comfortable sitting among laundry bags, except that it was bag wash, that comes back to its customers damp and ready for hanging, and there was a lot of it.

I made no attempt to talk because the van was even noisier than my car. But Alec shouted above it. "I got into bother. Mr. Raynor didn't believe me. He shook me till my teeth rattled and said he'd tell where I got the pound note, but I didn't tell him."

"What pound note?"

"I was given it for driving a van, and I wish I hadn't." He took a note from his pocket. "Here. You take it."

"Why?"

"Don't tell."

"You better tell me, or I won't be able to not-tell."

Chapter
Forty-Seven

～

Sykes and I sat with Dad in his office, along with the CID chief inspector. We had been supplied with sweet tea. For the shock, Dad said. He and Sykes might be shocked. I was angry. My beautiful car, wrapped around a tree.

As calmly as I could, I set out everything we knew. Not that I expected another attempt on my life so soon, but I had no intention of taking hard-won knowledge to the grave.

The CID officer must have been on a Trappist Monk Total Silence retreat, for he said not a word.

"Mr. Sykes discovered the man's identity. He was Harry Aspinall, expatriate, originally of Rothwell, a trustee of the Bluebell Children's Home. Mrs. Farrar wrote to him when she knew the children's home was at risk."

Sykes added more information. "I've found out what I could about the trust. It was wound up. Remaining moneys—a substantial amount—have been deposited in the Morley Bank under a new account, name Brock-Dell Limited. There is a charitable purpose to the account, to cover obligations that may arise under the trust. I suppose that's to avoid accusations of sharp practice. Two percent of future profits from the new pit, after tax, will be donated towards maintaining respectable orphans."

I refrained from saying that if you believed that you would believe anything. Profits would slide into personal accounts. High moral standards would ensure that suitably respectable orphans were few and far between.

Dad leaned forward. "As far as I can see, what Mr. Brockman and Mr. Dell did is not illegal. Trustees have a great deal of leeway." He massaged his scalp with his fingertips. "They're powerful men, Kate."

"Look at Mrs. Sugden's notebook. Mr. Aspinall was murdered at the shop. I don't know why or how but his body was taken to the railway sidings from there."

Dad opened the notebook. "It won't be easy to prove collusion in murder. It's cack-handed. It's amateur, and the men you are accusing –"

"Powerful, I know, but amateurs at murder."

"Most civilians are."

"They are also arrogant and think themselves above the common herd. There's evidence—the remains of his clothing. Mrs. Farrar was expecting him."

"She didn't tell anyone."

"Because she was too canny to show her hand."

Dad spoke patiently. "The man's identity is no longer in doubt. Nothing else is certain."

From my point of view something was certain. "If Scotland Yard—if Commander Woodhead—hadn't been so intent on keeping this murder a state secret, it would have been solved by now."

The CID inspector perked up. Perhaps he shared my view. He said nothing. I took advantage of his smidgen of interest. "Chief Inspector, I can't conduct a full search of the shop, but you can. Perhaps there's another bullet that can be traced to a particular gun, or an unexpected set of fingerprints."

It was Sykes's turn. He had been making notes. "Sir, the anonymous letters that Mrs. Brockman wrote herself. You have the fingerprints."

"Yes."

"There might just be a possibility that the box under the eaves, or the shoes, have those same prints. As long as no one gets to them first, that might provide some evidence."

Dad nodded agreement. "Not strong evidence. It's Mrs. Brockman's house, why wouldn't her fingerprints be on property in her own home? And there's nothing on the statute book forbidding the penning of imaginative letters, especially those that are not posted."

I began to see Dad's point of view. A good solicitor would pick a dozen holes, find a dozen alternative explanations. "We have only touched the surface. There's motive: gain, greed, desperation. Gertrude admitted that she and her husband are doing badly. They were hit by death duties, are still recovering from the General Strike. I know from what Gertrude once told me before that rents due from their tenant farmers were set a hundred years ago. They're paying an accountant and a solicitor to find a legal way of putting up rents. Part of me would feel sorry for them, if I were not convinced of their guilt."

I did not tell them of my conversation with Mrs. Dell. That would be hearsay, something to follow up later if needed. Gertrude must know what had been happening, but I found it hard to believe that she took an active part. That would be the job of Benjie, and his trusty butler.

Dad can be so annoying, and now he excelled himself. "Kate, I think you need a good night's sleep."

"I've only just begun!"

"There'll be other lines of enquiry for CID or Scotland Yard to pursue now that you've gathered information. Someone must have helped move the body. We need to find him."

They didn't need to find him. I did. Eliot Dell had cleverly involved Alec Taylor. That would ensure, if needed, that Benjie would not break ranks. I kept to myself that I had an idea who might have been engaged for the heavy lifting: Kevin O'Donnell,

Giant Jack, from the demolition gang, who went to the Dell estate looking for work.

"You've done a good job." Dad pushed back his chair. "Speak to Commander Woodhead tomorrow."

The CID officer looked from one to the other of us. He had clearly decided to play the observer, not to break his vow of silence. He, too, made ready to move.

"Now, are you coming back with me, let your mother take care of you, or will Mr. Sykes give you a lift home?"

I stood. "Neither. I'm going to London."

Sykes opened his mouth to speak, and shut it.

Dad said, "There are no trains to London at this time of night."

The CID Chief Inspector finally spoke. "The last train is 10.45 p.m., arrives King's Cross at 2.35 a.m."

This rattled Dad. "Have you swallowed a timetable?"

"There's no restaurant car," the chief inspector said.

"Thank you. Dad, would you please leave a message for Commander Woodhead that I'll be there at eleven tomorrow morning?"

The CID officer tactfully moved to leave. "Oh and we've brought in your car, Mrs. Shackleton. Preliminary investigation shows that the steering linkages have been tampered with. We'll be taking fingerprints from everyone who had access to the vehicle."

So Alec Taylor was right. I hoped that the pound burning a hole in his pocket did not also include payment for sabotage, and that his race to the wreck of my car was not simply belated remorse.

Would CID also obtain search warrants, I wondered.

As if anticipating that question, the CID officer hastily shook my hand. "Thank you, Mrs. Shackleton. We will be liaising with Scotland Yard. Goodnight, all."

That left me with little hope. A deputy Lord Lieutenant of the County would not be someone easily taken into custody.

When the chief inspector had gone, I turned to Dad. "Dad, would you please put in a call to cousin James and say it's imperative that he meet me at King's Cross? If I talk to him, he'll argue."

James was in at the beginning of this. He would be able to tell me who skewed the investigation by dreaming up a story of Bolshevik gold.

"Who will go with you?"

Before Sykes could open his mouth, I said, "I'll do this alone."

Dad said, "You could be kidnapped."

"White slavers and the yellow peril are the product of writers with a feverish imagination."

"I know what I'm talking about, Kate."

"All the more reason James had better be there to meet me." I looked at my watch. "I hope there's a seat on that train."

Sykes chipped in. "You won't be fighting anyone for a seat at this time of night. There'll be no first class carriage, much less a ladies' carriage."

Neither Dad nor Sykes thought to mention that I looked a sight and hadn't as much as a toothbrush with me.

For once, I didn't care.

Dad said little after that. I could see he was disappointed that I would not go home with him. He showed Sykes and me into the station canteen, and tried once more. "Sometimes, when you have a good night's sleep, you see things differently the next day. Everything looks clearer."

"I'm seeing things very clearly, Dad. Thanks all the same."

"I'll leave you to order some supper then." I felt sad to see him walk away, but then he turned back. "I'll book your train ticket, and I'll be in the office until you leave."

Over egg and chips, tea and bread and butter, I told Sykes about Kevin O'Donnell.

"He was part of the demolition gang. He stayed in the area looking for work after they'd finished the job on the orphanage. The demolition company is in Pontefract. See if they know where he is." I handed Sykes the man's photograph. "This was given to me by Josh at the rhubarb farm. Oh and check hotels in Leeds and Wakefield. Did someone book a room and not arrive, or sign in and then not come back?"

"I've already checked the hotels. No results." He dipped a chip in his egg yolk. "The information I gave you about the bank accounts, I've no reason to doubt it but I didn't go through formal channels."

Of course he didn't, but Scotland Yard would have access to those formal channels. They could also check the telephone exchanges for overseas calls to Thorpefield. Somebody knew what time to expect Harry Aspinall.

What troubled me most was that CID would authorise a search warrant for Thorpefield Manor. Gertrude and Benjie had put themselves beyond the pale. What concerned me was the sudden fear that the incriminating items in the eaves might turn out to bear the fingerprints of Stephen Walmsley.

"The chips are good," Sykes said.

"They are."

"Then what's up? There's something else."

There was, but even from Sykes I held back what Mrs. Dell had told me.

Chapter
Forty-Eight

~

When Mrs. Sugden knew that Mrs. Shackleton was safe, and that
Sykes was there too, she thought it time to take her charges home.
They were in the waiting area at police headquarters, a nervous
lad called Alec, and Philip Goodchild—who explained that he had
returned a laundry van, but insisted that he must see them home
on the train.

Mrs. Sugden had taken a liking to Philip. He was both a man and
a boy, a funny combination but it suited him, as did his tufty hair.

"Are you sure you want to come back with us, Philip? You've a
home to go to."

He did not mind being asked again, and he repeated word for
word what he had said before. "My mother talked to Kate's mother.
They agreed I should come back with you on the train and that I
should see you home. I will stay the night."

"Well then," Mrs. Sugden said, "that sorts that out." She wondered where she would put him, and the other young fellow. She
didn't know what to make of that one, Alec. He was twitchy, looking over his shoulder as if expecting one of the bobbies to arrest
him. But he'd come to Mrs. Shackleton's aid, and that was good
enough for her. "We'll collect Harriet and the dog, and then we'll
all catch the train to Leeds. It's been a long day."

"My mother said you will all be tired and upset and I must look after you. I said I would."

Mrs. Sugden said, "That is very kind, Philip."

* * *

Rosie Sykes was glad to be relieved of telephone duties at Batswing Cottage. She saw that Mrs. Sugden was not up to her usual energetic doings and so made a supper of what was to hand, as well as pots of cocoa with insufficient milk, but nobody minded.

Leaving Harriet, Philip and Alec in the kitchen, Rosie drew Mrs. Sugden into the front room. "Last week, I baked more scones than anyone could eat."

"Oh aye?"

"Yesterday, I was dusting the picture rail."

Mrs. Sugden could not quite see where this was leading. She waited.

"And so I'm going back into tailoring. I have a start at Montague Burton's."

"That's a long way."

"Two trams."

"That'll be a surprise for Jim."

"It will. I'm not one who's able to sit still all day, any more than you are, so I won't be sitting in waiting for a telephone to ring. Just so you know. I want a bit of company. I want some brass in a wage packet, like I used to. I'll tell Jim in my own way in my own time."

Mrs. Sugden felt honoured by the confidence.

The telephone rang.

"I'll do it this one last time," Rosie said.

Mrs. Sugden waited.

Rosie came back. "Mr. Hood, to say that Mrs. Shackleton won't be home tonight. Nothing to worry about, but she says would you take care of Harriet and the guests."

Mrs. Sugden thought for a minute. "I'm not putting those fellows in Mrs. Shackleton's bed. Harriet can have that. They can have Harriet's room. I'll tell them."

"Do you want me to do anything?"

"You get yourself home, Rosie, and thank you for answering the telephone today."

"Oh I didn't. I sat here the day long and it didn't ring."

*   *   *

Later, Mrs. Sugden felt a stab of alarm. She knew that Philip was a trusted friend and neighbour of Mrs. Shackleton's parents, but there was no telling about the other one. He was too good-looking and too nervy for her liking.

She went up to check.

Harriet was sound asleep.

She could hear them talking, Mr. Tufty Hair and Mr. Bonnie Boy. They were talking about motor car engines.

Chapter Forty-Nine

～

Cousin James was waiting on the platform, hat pulled down, scarf wound around his throat and mouth. He strode towards me, a startled expression on his face. Who else had he expected? Then I realised that it was my appearance that shocked him.

He grabbed both my hands in his. "You're freezing. You're shivering. What on earth is it that couldn't wait until tomorrow?"

"Murder most foul, and it's already tomorrow."

"Let's get you home."

He looked about for a porter. "Where's your luggage?"

I had Sykes's motoring blanket over my arm, a flask in my hand and the satchel on my shoulder. "This is it."

He took the flask and blanket. We began walking towards the exit.

"There's a warm bed waiting for you."

"We have to talk."

"You need a good night's sleep."

"I dozed on the train."

"Don't believe you. You look whacked."

"I need to have certain things clear before I see Commander Woodhead tomorrow, and don't worry, I won't say it came from you."

"He'll know."

"But he won't have been told. That's how it works, isn't it?"

*   *   *

Dad or Mother must have spoken to James's wife. Prudence had set out night clothes, toiletries and a choice of dresses for morning. We don't have the same size feet so I would be wearing my funeral shoes tomorrow. That seemed appropriate.

Perhaps what I told James was true, and that I had napped on the train, because by the time I was in bed, sitting up with a cup of cocoa, I felt alert again.

James sat in the chair beside the bed, still in his suit, one leg crossing the other. "There's nothing I can tell you."

"You mean there's nothing you can tell me unless I ask the right questions and swear secrecy."

"You get me up in the middle of the night, drag me out into the cold and now –"

"What piece of information led you to believe that a Bolshevik with Russian gold was coming to Yorkshire?"

One has to phrase questions carefully with James. If I had asked what piece of information led Commander Woodhead to believe such a story, he would quite rightly have said that he did not know. He was not privy to Mr. Woodhead's thinking. I also needed to curb my annoyance, or I would have asked what the Bolshevik was expected to do with this gold. Buy up the rhubarb supply? Steal agricultural secrets so as to set up sheds for forced rhubarb on the Siberian plains? That all seemed more likely than the ability to start another national strike and begin the revolution.

James scratched his cheek. "We received a letter, containing reliable information from a trusted contact in Riga."

"We?"

"Not I, at least not initially. It landed on the desk of an SIS officer."

"It's the wrong time of day for me to fathom your sets of initials."

"Secret Intelligence Service."

"So you saw a copy? And did Scotland Yard?"

"Yes."

"Because it's SIS's task to keep Britain safe from the Bolshevik threat?"

He brightened at my understanding. "Of course."

"And so lots of people would have been sent a copy, just tell me who."

"You know I can't do that."

"Then nod your head if I hit the right ones: MI5, the War Office, the Admiralty, Scotland Yard Have I missed anyone?"

"Yes."

"MI5."

"You said that."

"How detailed was it? Did you have dates, time of arrival, a name?"

"We didn't have a name. Naturally the person in question would have an alias and false papers. There was no specific date, just a broad timescale."

"So this could have been a low-level informant trying to earn his keep by inventing a fanciful tale that SIS would swallow. He was testing gullibility and laughing at his own cleverness."

"Any suggestion of a threat has to be taken seriously."

"Or, perhaps the person from Riga was correct and at this moment a Bolshevik stalks the realm, distributing money to malcontents. Because the man on the train was not a spy. Harry Aspinall was a British subject from a good family who just happens to have made his life in France. He was here at the behest of his old nanny. You can't get more British than that. He was here to right a wrong, and hoping that while here he might see the Ryder Cup and toast the winners with a glass of champagne."

"If you are right, that would be unfortunate and embarrassing."

"And we hate embarrassment."

"Kate, there is no way of knowing whether this upright golf-loving Briton had been turned. Traitors do not go about announcing the fact. If he stayed abroad for years, he didn't love his country that much."

"Choosing to live abroad isn't a sign of treachery."

"You're tired, and emotional."

"And you are stubborn and your establishment-issue blinkers are too big."

"You've changed."

"Haven't we all?"

"I suppose so, though one expects less change in—well, in some people."

"Women?"

"Possibly. Sensible women at least."

"A young man might hang for a murder he didn't commit. Helen Farrar and Harry Aspinall were murdered because those who stood to benefit from appropriating trust funds feared exposure."

"I'm sure you'll tell Commander Woodhead all this."

"He, all of you, created a bogeyman. I was sent chasing shadows. Will you make it clear that Harry Aspinall was no traitor?"

"I can't promise."

"Yes you can. And while you're thinking about it, would you please bring me a typewriter, paper and carbons. I have a report to write."

"It's the middle of the night."

"Then I'll type quietly. Help me push that little table nearer the fire."

Chapter Fifty

~

In my borrowed clothes, I entered the portals of New Scotland Yard.

DC Yeats met me in the lobby. Our first-name telephone conversations had been cordial to the point of chumminess. This morning I was back to Mrs. Shackleton.

"Did you have a good journey, Mrs. Shackleton?"

"What do you think!"

"Like that was it?"

"I'd recommend that journey only to someone I heartily dislike."

"I can't imagine you heartily disliking anyone."

It was a light-hearted remark, and yet it struck a chord. In spite of everything, I was finding it hard to see Gertrude differently. If Mrs. Dell was right, she was a killer. If not, she must have had at least an inkling of what Benjie, Raynor and Eliot had done. She was responsible for tossing orphans to the winds. Yet I felt a well of pity for her. To do such deeds, she must have felt desperate beyond my imagining, or have always had a streak of evil. In my mind's eye, she was still twelve years old, riding her pony, with such a look of mischief, and laughter.

We stepped into the lift with a uniformed sergeant and three plainclothes men, and made our silent way up the building.

Mr. Woodhead stood to greet me in his usual courteous fashion, and yet with an edginess in his manner. He was moving too much, rubbing his thumbs along his fingers, leaning forward, and then sitting back. Something had happened.

"Thank you so much for coming all this way, almost on an impulse I think?"

"Not an impulse, Commander." I put my report on his desk. "This isn't complete. Mr. Sykes is tying up loose ends but I believe you will have corroborated Harry Aspinall's identity?"

"Yes." He glanced at my report. "And I have had information telegraphed to me from Wakefield CID." He could barely hide his annoyance. "You have been very busy, Mrs. Shackleton. Caused quite a stir."

That was my mistake. He wanted me to report to him so that he could choose who and what to tell. Now that Wakefield CID had more details, the investigation might take a different turn.

The three of us resumed the places we had taken a few days earlier, the commander behind his desk, I facing him, DC Yeats a little off to the side, near the filing cabinet, leaning forward, all alert anticipation. He cleared his throat. "Sir?"

"Yes?"

"More information came through just a few minutes ago There is a record of closure of the Bluebell Children's Home Trust account and a transfer of monies into the Brock-Dell Mining account."

"Was it legal?" Woodhead asked.

"Yes, sir."

Woodhead slid on his spectacles and looked at my report. "You believe Mr. Aspinall met his end at the Corner Shop?"

"I have no doubt of that." Perhaps I should have had doubts. Sergeant Dog is such an eager hound that had he smelled jam roly-poly on the doormat he would be as wildly enthusiastic as Mrs. Sugden had described.

With some reluctance, Yeats spoke again, this time without clearing his throat. "Sir, in the message that's on your desk from Wakefield, you'll see CID are conducting an intensive search of the Corner Shop this morning. It will be sealed, a little belatedly perhaps, and also –"

Mr. Woodhead turned scarlet. "Who authorised this?"

"I don't believe authorisation is necessary, sir, in the case of a crime scene, and –" He hesitated.

"And what?"

"The inspector has applied for search warrants, just a formality I suppose, for the properties of Mr. Brockman and Mr. Dell."

Mr. Woodhead brought down his fist on his desk, and the pain registered ever so slightly in a tightening of his lips. "I will not have it. Brockman and Dell have been written up in *The Times*. They are sinking the deepest pit in Great Britain, perhaps the deepest mine in Europe. They will be saviours of the nation." He glared at me. "Mr. Brockman may be the next Lord Lieutenant of your county, madam. Then where will you be?"

Had it been written on his forehead in coal dust, it could not have been more certain. Mr. Woodhead was an investor in the Bluebell Mine. What good company I had avoided by my reluctance to participate in that golden opportunity.

Mr. Woodhead rose. He pushed back his chair. "I'll be back shortly. Talk among yourselves if you wish, but not about the case."

He left the room. I listened to the receding thud of his heavy footsteps.

Martin Yeats spoke first. "One of the things I have learned is how easy it is to build a plausible case."

"You think I'm wrong to have my suspicions?"

"I don't have an opinion."

Clearly, Mr. Woodhead did have an opinion, and a strong one. My misgivings flooded back. In certain quarters, it would be convenient for Stephen Walmsley to have one more charge laid against him. "I haven't yet built a case. We're still gathering information."

He raised his eyebrows. "And none of it about a revolutionary and Russian gold?"

"Sadly, no. Cloak upon decorative cloak of secrecy is not required on this occasion, except perhaps to save embarrassment."

He gave a surprising chuckle.

"What?"

"Where I come from, embarrassment was when you made a terrible idiot of yourself at the Saturday night dance."

"Martin, I'll be sorry to meet you again in a few years' time, and to find that you are as solidly discreet as everyone else."

"But, Kate, what I don't understand is why there were gold coins in the sack."

"Neither do I, yet. Don't forget there were also two Arran Victory potatoes."

The footsteps along the corridor silenced us.

Mr. Woodhead entered with a false smile plastered on his face. He went to his desk, sat down and placed a brown envelope on his blotter.

"Mrs. Shackleton, on behalf of the investigation division, thank you for establishing Mr. Aspinall's identity. Here is a payment towards expenses, and a note of where to send your final account."

Having banged my head against a brick wall until I soaked the bricks in blood, I was disinclined to leave a job half done. One advantage of not being an employee was that although my contract may be terminated, I could not be sacked from doing the job.

I stood, ignoring his brown envelope. "An interim payment is not necessary, Mr. Woodhead. I will, as on previous occasions, send in my account on completion of the investigation." I picked up my satchel.

While he was considering how to reply, I wished him good day. If he was about to attempt any prohibition on what I would do next, he would have to put it in writing.

It was left to DC Yeats to escort me downstairs, but probably only to be sure that I left the building.

Yeats did not speak until we were at the door. He gave a sympathetic smile. "I hope you don't believe I've overstepped the mark, but you did say that you would lunch with Mrs. Kerner another time?"

That London lady detective had been far from my thoughts but a convivial lunch seemed just the ticket.

"Yes."

"I've taken the liberty of booking a table at The Savoy."

"Was this your idea, Mr. Yeats?"

His reply was ambiguous. "I could hardly do such a thing without the commander's approval, unless it was a personal matter between you and Mrs. Kerner, what with you having so much in common." He smiled. "And I'm still Martin."

He walked me to the gate, and waved at a taxi. "Is there anything else I can do?"

Certain matters involving red tape can be very difficult for a civilian to unravel. There was something Yeats might do that would save an awful lot of time. "Eight orphans from the Bluebell Home were transferred to Stoneville, York Street, Wakefield. They have been certificated for emigration to Canada, sailing from Liverpool. Please find out how the certifications can be revoked and they can stay under the care of friends."

"It's not the kind of thing I've ever dealt with, but I'll see what I can do."

Chapter Fifty-One

~

Annette Kerner has the bosom of an opera singer, which she once was, and moves with the grace of a dancer. Combs adorned her crimped hair. Her dress shimmered.

I joined her at a small table near the bar. She ordered cocktails.

"I know you've been involved with a tricky case, Kate. I thought you might be in need of moral support and a little cheer."

I smiled. "That's very sporting of you." We raised our glasses.

"The truth is, I have an undisclosed interest in your case, and now I must come clean."

"What?" I expected her to say that Commander Woodhead had offered her the job first, but it was not that.

"A good friend of mine, Bernard Campaner, attached to the French Embassy, is here, with someone who'd like to meet you, before you and I have lunch."

I felt a sense of dread, remembering the day of Helen Farrar's funeral, and the young man at the graveside. "Harry Aspinall's son?"

"Yes. You don't have to. Now I feel I've brought you here under false pretences."

I stared at the glazed cherry in my cocktail. "I'm not sure what I could say to him."

"And to her. Harry Aspinall's widow is also here."

It was one of those moments when my mind went completely blank. Suddenly I felt the strain of the last few days, and my sleepless night on the train and at cousin James's. How could I say I didn't feel up to this?

"We have a private room, Kate. They will be going back soon, taking Mr. Aspinall's body to France."

It was the kind of situation where there was only one possible answer. "Yes of course I'll meet them."

She glanced across the room. "Oh look! What good timing, there's Bernard now." She waved to an elegantly dressed man who approached us from the other end of the bar."

On cue, I thought.

"Kate, may I introduce Bernard Campaner. Bernard, Mrs. Kate Shackleton."

"*Enchanté*!" He kissed my hand, causing me slight unease. He was about thirty-five, not handsome but with an attractive vitality about him.

It was up to me to make the next move. "How do you do, Monsieur Campaner. Do draw up a chair."

"I am grateful that you have agreed to meet me, Mrs. Shackleton."

"Yes, though I am not sure –"

He shook his head and shrugged. "Who of us is sure, especially at such a time? I commiserate with you for undertaking a distressing case."

"I'm sorry that it has turned out so tragically."

He waved away my apology. "No one could have imagined such an end. I believe that Mr. Aspinall's fate was sealed when he left the country. Certain people knew that he was arriving."

"His former nanny was expecting him, Mrs. Farrar."

Bernard crossed himself. "May she rest in peace. He was devoted to her."

"But devoted from such a distance." It was not tactful of me to say this, but I could not help thinking that had Mr. Aspinall come back sooner, and been an active trustee, things might have turned out differently.

He nodded an acknowledgement. "It will be a comfort for his widow and son to speak to you."

"How shall I address them? Are they known by the same name, Aspinall?"

"Mrs. Aspinall and Charles."

"Are they waiting for us now?"

"In a private room."

I stood. "Then let us go."

He stubbed out his cigarette and pushed back his chair, giving a bow to Annette. "You will pardon us for leaving you."

"Don't worry about me. I have friends at the bar." She took out a cigarette, and he lit it with a small gold lighter.

Monsieur Campaner and I climbed the broad staircase to the first floor. As we reached the landing, he paused. "The family have it in mind, if there is no satisfaction from the police investigation, to take out a private prosecution against the perpetrators of the crime against Harry Aspinall. And so if there is anything you can tell us –"

"I have signed the Official Secrets Act."

"Yes, yes. I understand. I believe there was suspicion regarding foreign agitation in the Yorkshire coalfields, hotbeds of radicalism."

I would have liked to put him right, and tell him that cold beds of poverty would be nearer the mark, but I waited for him to continue.

"Surely the Official Secrets Act would not apply in the case of cold-blooded murder?"

"Monsieur Campaner, you said earlier that certain people knew that Mr. Aspinall would be arriving?"

He nodded. "A letter from Mrs. Farrar to Mr. Aspinall suggested that the cat remain firmly in the bag regarding his visit. Mr. Aspinall should have listened to his old nanny. He telephoned Mr. Dell to say that he was coming. Shortly after, he telephoned the Brockman household."

"How do you know?"

"The Bordeaux telephone exchange noted the telephone calls. The length of the first call was four minutes and forty-five seconds and the second was three and a half minutes."

"Would you be willing to let Scotland Yard have this information?"

"It is done, madam. And we have also forwarded the information to the local CID."

"Thank you. Then, let us meet Mr. Aspinall's family."

* * *

We left the restaurant and walked to a private room on the first floor.

The young man I had seen at the graveside in Rothwell stood by the window. His mother was seated in a leather armchair, so big that it threatened to swallow her. Monsieur Campaner introduced us. The family resemblance between mother and son was clear. They had the same high cheek bones, sleek dark hair and blue-grey eyes.

I can't now remember what I said, because feelings rather overcame me. It was not my place to cry. Perhaps because of my accident, my tiredness and the journey, I could not stop my tears. They cried, and so did I.

Chapter
Fifty-Two

❦

Three of us sat around the kitchen table. Mrs. Sugden had ringed a short but chilling item in the local paper.

> MURDER TRIAL EASTER ASSIZES
>   The trial of Stephen Walmsley for the murder of Helen Farrar will take place at Leeds Crown Court during the Easter Assizes. Date to be announced.

A calendar hangs on the wall, showing a date of 31ˢᵗ March for Easter Sunday. In just over three weeks, Stephen would stand in the dock. Our best hope would be to put up a magnificent defence.

"Have you heard from Mr. Cohen?"

Mrs. Sugden shook her head. "Not yet. I delivered the statements to his office." She pushed a folder towards me. "Here are copies. It was a funny business, to be asking questions of a whole street."

"Anything helpful?"

"Mr. and Mrs. Arkwright and Joan vouched for him being with them until minutes before he raised the alarm. Some neighbours had nothing to say, or didn't want to be caught up in it. There's neighbours that give times for him passing by, one listening to a wireless, one looking at the clock, wondering where her husband had got to."

"Nothing unusual?"

Mrs. Sugden pushed in a stray hairpin. "Our friend at the end house was interesting, Mrs. Waste-Not-Want-Not."

"Valerie Pennington," Sykes added.

"Aye. She made a point of saying that she didn't see Mr. Brockman. Well why would you say who you *didn't* see?"

That was a good question. "She has a grace and favour cottage, probably granted by him, but that's not a good enough reason."

Sykes wanted to know why she had a rent-free house in the first place. A movement outside, by the back fence, caught my attention. "Who's that?"

Mrs. Sugden followed my glance. "I didn't know what to do with him. It's young Alec Taylor. He came home with us on the train, worried about facing the butler's wrath for taking part in getting you back to Wakefield. He's frightened of taking the blame for tinkering with the car. I'm sure he didn't do it, but he has a good idea who did."

Alec need not have worried. Benjie Brockman would continue to care about him, buying his comics, ensuring he learned a trade. Alec may well be the reason that Valerie Pennington had the end cottage. Someone gave birth to him. If Miss Pennington had watched her son being placed in an orphanage, she deserved more than a rent-free cottage.

"He'll be safe to go back. No one will harm him. But that still doesn't explain that odd remark of Miss Pennington's."

Sykes was itching to chip in, and then he did. "My guess is that she 'didn't see Mr. Brockman' because she did see him, and is protecting him." He interlaced his fingers. "Or, she really didn't see him but she saw someone else from the house. I think one of us should have another go at Miss Pennington."

So that was a yes, a no, or a maybe. But Sykes was right that we should talk to her again. Whether she would be forthcoming with me or Sykes was another matter. She could well decide not to say another word.

We sat in silence for a few minutes, each of us thinking how best to make use of the information from neighbours on Silver Street, and how such information would play out in a courtroom.

"Are you thinking what I'm thinking, Mr. Sykes?"

"About the Wakefield CID chief inspector?"

"Yes. The neighbours need to know that justice for Stephen Walmsley would be best achieved if they give formal statements to CID. Questioning at the time was minimal, given that Stephen had blood on his hands."

Mrs. Sugden picked up the baton. "Now that they've spoken once, they'll be willing to let their tongues wag again, I'll be bound."

I gave Sykes the nod. Sad to say, sometimes a man to man chat works well. He could make the trip to Wakefield.

It was time to break the news that Commander Woodhead had thanked us for our services, and said goodbye.

Mrs. Sugden's mouth turned down at the corners. "The cheek of him, and after all your hard work and jumping on trains."

"There has been another development." I told them about meeting Bernard Campaner of the French Embassy, and Mr. Aspinall's widow and son.

Sykes frowned. "Working with the French won't do us any good with Scotland Yard."

"Pointing a tentative finger at a deputy to the Lord Lieutenant of the County did not go down well either. The encouraging part is that the French will be as happy as we are to keep cooperation quiet. They can pull strings behind the scenes in a way that we can't."

I passed him a note of the telephone calls from Harry Aspinall to the Dell house and to Thorpefield Manor, supplied by the Bordeaux exchange. "They knew he was coming. Mrs. Aspinall didn't know. I got the feeling from our conversation that there was friction about his continued links with Yorkshire, with Rothwell Manor standing unoccupied, and his obligations here only ever costing him money."

This mollified Sykes a little. "Commander Woodhead didn't want an investigation. He wanted a whitewash job and a dupe in case things went wrong. You'll be justified in the end."

I appreciated his vote of confidence.

He took out his notebook, though he clearly didn't need to. Everything was in his head. "I checked the main hotels in Leeds and Wakefield, none of them had a booking in the name of Aspinall. No one had a booking in any name for a person who didn't arrive. I spoke to taxi drivers. No one remembered him. Station Left Luggage—nothing uncollected."

It was as if Mr. Aspinall had vanished. Perhaps we would never know how he made his way to the place where he met his death.

Sykes had not finished.

"I visited the demolition firm in Pontefract. Kevin O'Donnell, nickname Giant Jack, was knocking on their door as they opened on Saturday morning, 2nd of March, morning after the murders. Did they have any work for him, he wanted to know, and he wanted to go somewhere else—be away from this area. He was philosophical when they couldn't give him work. Said he'd go to Liverpool and take his chance there. The foreman got the impression that if there was nothing for him, he'd board a ferry back to Ireland and see his family."

"So we could have lost him? Do they have an address in Ireland?"

"No address in Ireland." Sykes wore his I've-got-the-sixpence-from-the-Christmas-pudding look. "Better than that. I asked myself, where would a demolition worker go if he wanted employment in Liverpool? I looked up the trade directories, and I looked up the newspapers. There he was in the *Liverpool Echo*, an article about him."

"What's he done?" Mrs. Sugden asked.

"Surprise, surprise, he was hero of the hour. "Giant Jack stops Coal Merchant's runaway horse." He was treated in the local pub, and what's more the coal merchant gave him a job. And before you ask, I have the coal merchant's name and address."

There was a sudden burst of energy in the room. We all felt it. Sergeant Dog, who had been lying with his head on all of our feet, pushed his way out and began to wag his tail.

"Mr. Sykes, that is a breakthrough. We've no way of knowing that Kevin O'Donnell was involved but –"

Sykes was not to be discouraged. "It was them, Brockman and his butler Raynor, or Dell, or all of them. Which of them could carry a body? Not Brockman or Dell. They can push a pen. They can lift a knife and fork."

"Benjie Brockman boxed for his school. And I know they both played rugby."

"But would they get their hands dirty?"

For a few seconds, I was no longer here with Sykes and Mrs. Sugden. I was in Mrs. Dell's drawing room. She was telling me about the conversation in the library, between Eliot Dell and Gertrude. Her voice came back to me. They were talking about Mrs. Farrar, and how stubborn she was, and that she had left them no choice. And then Eliot told Gertrude that there was blood on the cuff of her coat.

She was hard of hearing. Such an account was not reliable. If I told Sykes and Mrs. Sugden, Sykes would want this made known. I thought of frail and fearful Mrs. Dell, taking me into her confidence.

Sykes was waiting for me to answer his question as to whether I thought Brockman and Dell would get their hands dirty. It distressed me to think he might be right.

"Probably not."

The most plausible explanation was that Benjie, Dell or Raynor had recruited out-of-work Kevin O'Donnell, who had then immediately left the area. "So it's a trip to Liverpool, Mr. Sykes."

"I can set off now."

"Hang on. I might be coming too."

Mrs. Sugden decided to be mother hen. "Mrs. Shackleton, think on! You've hardly slept. You're not over that shocking accident yet. And why would you want to go to Liverpool?"

"I intend to stop those orphans being sent to Canada. They're in a holding centre in Liverpool." Martin Yeats had been thorough in his researches.

Sykes's eyes widened. "Why stop them? They're going to a great new country, open spaces, fresh air, a new start."

"The youngest is four, the oldest is nine. Canada can wait."

Chapter
Fifty-Three

~

Nothing happens without completion of the correct forms, and in this case the forms must be completed in triplicate. I needed signatures from Benjie, Gertrude and Eliot Dell, trustees of the Bluebell Home. They had authorised the emigration of eight children, and they must rescind the authorisation. I was not sorry that Sykes had insisted on coming along. Since my car was out of action, we travelled in Sykes's motor. I had advised Alec Taylor to come, too, and at least let Benjie know that he was safe and well. Whatever else Benjie had done, or failed to do, he was fond of Alec.

Alec climbed out of the dickey seat to open the gates to Thorpefield Manor. "My legs have gone into cramp."

"Mine too, but from the cold!"

The first gate creaked open. I turned to Sykes, who was driving. "It's not just Alec's legs that bother him. He feels uneasy about being back here."

The police report on my accident concluded that the loosening of the steering linkage could have been done deliberately, or may have happened gradually and escaped notice. Like me, Alec believed the damage was deliberate, an opinion reinforced since he knew that Philip maintained my car. He had confided that Eliot had shown an interest in the car and spent some time taking a look at it. I thought that it was more likely to have been Raynor.

Alec opened the second gate. "I'll walk to the house." He sauntered ahead, hands in pockets.

Sykes waved an acknowledgement, and drove on, passing the main door. "I won't come in."

"That's all right. This shouldn't take long."

Like Alec, I felt slightly awkward. But now it was up to Scotland Yard and Wakefield CID to make the next move, if they chose to act on the information we had supplied.

By the time Raynor opened the door, Alec had caught up.

"The prodigal returns," Raynor said, giving him a stern look.

"Hello, Raynor. Alec needs to speak to Mr. Brockman. And is Mrs. Brockman at home?"

"She is not, I'm afraid."

Was this a "not at home to you", or a genuine not at home?

He answered the unspoken question. "She is visiting old Mrs. Dell."

In a way it was endearing that Mrs. Dell had become "old Mrs. Dell", almost in tribute to the younger Mrs. Dell who was no more. I said nothing about seeing Mrs. Dell driven away by her younger son. Perhaps she returned as quickly as she went.

"Then we'll speak to Mr. Brockman."

Raynor led us down the hall to Benjie's study, knocked and entered. "Visitors for you, sir."

Benjie's eyes lit up at the sight of us, or rather at the sight of Alec. "Where did you get to, you young rascal?"

Raynor hovered in the doorway, a frown creasing his brow. If he had it in mind to try again at silencing me, he would have to think of something quickly.

"Refreshments!" Benjie called to him.

"Not for me, thank you, Benjie. This is a flying visit. I wanted to see you and Gertrude. I believe she's visiting Mrs. Dell."

"I don't want anything, thank you." Alec looked around the room, and at the stamp albums on the desk.

"Sit yourselves down then, and you give an account of yourself, young man."

While Alec lowered himself into a chair as if it might bite his bum, I produced the papers that Martin Yeats had obtained for me.

"Benjie, you know the eight children who are lined up for passage to Canada?"

"Yes there was something about that."

As if he did not know.

"It's not a good idea for them to go. There've been outbreaks of smallpox on that ship. They would never reach Canada alive." I had to think quickly of some civil service department that would be responsible for such matters. "On the advice of the Office for Migration of Minors to the Dominions, the authority for their passage must be revoked."

"Oh well if that's the case."

"You need to sign in triplicate."

"Do I indeed?"

I passed him the forms. "You, Eliot and Gertrude."

He picked up his pen. I pointed to the line for his signature. "And today's date."

He glanced at the day-by-day calendar on his desk, and signed. "You'll catch Gertrude, but not sure about Eliot. He's had strong interest in overseas investment in our mine. He'll be gallivanting to London."

That was so annoying. He would be the tricky one.

He passed me the signed forms. "What happens to this merry band of orphans now?"

Good question.

Alec came up with the answer. "Could they be brought here, sir? There's plenty of room on the top floor."

"What do you know about the top floor?"

"Only what the servants say, sir, about how many empty rooms there are."

Benjie thought for a moment. "I don't see why not, but children need looking after don't they?"

"I'm sure that could be taken care of, Benjie."

I thought of Mr. and Mrs. Arkwright, and how they would love to be in touch with their charges again. One step at a time.

Of course if Benjie and Raynor were arrested for murder, that plan might fall flat.

I stood. "Thank you, Benjie. I'll leave you and Alec to talk. And Alec, we'll see you by the car when you're ready."

As I went out, I heard Benjie saying. "You'll be wanting your *Comic Cuts*. It's here somewhere."

I went back to the car. Sykes and I strolled towards the walled garden. Sykes looked back every few minutes, to make sure no one was sabotaging the car. We would go to the Dells' house. Once I had Gertrude's and Eliot's signatures, we would take Alec to meet Philip. There was a flat above the Battersby garage. It had been agreed that Alec might stay there, which would be an improvement on living above the stable. Now that Philip was to take over the garage, he might move into the flat too, if he could bear to leave his mother.

"Funny old place." Sykes said. "Say 'Thorpefield Manor' and you expect something grand. It's a bit neglected."

"They're hoping for better days."

"Aren't we all?"

The wind had got up quite fiercely, but the high walls of the garden protected us. Birds made the most of the sheltered spot. A blackbird pecked at the earth. A couple of blue tits perched on a branch, inspecting the bark for insects.

"Mrs. Shackleton!"

I turned to see Milly. "Hello!"

She came hurrying towards me, with a great smile.

I introduced her to Sykes. "Milly was my maid when I was here."

"Then I'll leave you two to chat. I'll look out for Alec, and keep an eye on the car."

It was too cold to sit down. We walked towards the rose bed which was all bare stems, trimmed back. "So what news, Milly? You're looking better."

"The police came from Wakefield. They searched my room. They looked in the eaves as if they knew what they would find, and I could hardly breathe, but there was nothing there. I felt so relieved, and then Mrs. Brockman appeared, and she didn't say anything but I could see she was shocked. They went along the corridor, and they were doing other searching. I was trailing after them as best I could, but they shooed me away. And you'll never guess where that stuff was."

"Where was it?"

"Mrs. Brockman's maid told the housekeeper, and she told the cook and the cook told me. It was under Mrs. Brockman's bed. And when they found it, Mrs. Brockman said, 'The maid put it there', and her maid said no she didn't and Mrs. Brockman said, 'the maid Milly'. And the police asked me and I said no I hadn't touched it."

Milly then told the police about my photograph of the items left in the eaves.

She seemed remarkably cheerful. The police officer had been nice to her.

I did not have the heart to tell her that his being nice did not mean that Stephen was out of the woods.

Alec was not long in joining us. With the restlessness of the young, he had parted quickly from Benjie.

I said goodbye to Milly.

We climbed into the car, ready for our next call.

"How did Mr. Brockman react when he heard you have a new job, Alec?"

"He didn't say much at first, and then he was all right about it." He then spoke slowly, to make every word count. "He gave me a five pound note. Have you ever seen one?"

"Yes, I have seen one."

That did not stop him describing it. "It's huge. It's white. I've put it in my sock."

'Open a Post Office savings account.'

"They'll ask me where I got it. They'll think I stole it."

"Just say who gave it to you, and that you worked for him and it was a gift when you left, a gift for being a good worker."

This cheered him. I remembered how I sometimes used to be tongue-tied. There would be something inside that needed to be said, but what were the words, and how did you put them together?

"Did Mr. Brockman say anything else?"

"He asked me if I remembered a woman who sometimes visited the Bluebell children, and brought us things."

"And did you?"

"When he reminded me. She once brought a rag rug. In the middle it said, 'ABC' in red. Round the edge, it had numbers one to ten in yellow. No one had ever seen anything like it. She said that if we stood on the letters, we would be good at reading and writing. If we hopped from number to number, we would learn our sums very well."

"That sounds a wonderful rug."

"He said she takes an interest still, and that I should visit. She lives in the village, the bottom house on Silver Street. I should tell her that I am making my way in the world."

Chapter
Fifty-Four

~

The Dell house didn't look right. I sensed Mrs. Dell was still absent.
The shutters were up at the downstairs windows. It was if the occupants planned to go away for the season, or someone had died.

"Still want to give it a try?" Sykes asked.

"Yes. You two stretch your legs and stay out of sight. If Gertrude is here, it will disarm her if she thinks I've come alone."

I lifted the knocker and let it drop, knocking three times.

When no one answered, I turned the knob. The door wasn't
locked. I stepped into the hall. "Hello! Anyone here?"

Footsteps on the stairs.

Gertrude and Eliot Dell appeared. Both wore long black motoring coats. She wore a fur headband over a woollen cloche.

"Oh Eliot, Gertrude, hello! Benjie said I'd find you here. I'm
sorry I let myself in but the place looks deserted."

Now that she was closer, Gertrude gave a cold smile. "Hello,
Kate."

"I'm glad to find you together. I can see you're just on your way
somewhere, but do you have a moment?"

Eliot opened the door to the billiard room. The only light came
through the slats in the shutters. The place felt eerie, with the dark
shape of the big table dominating the room. The chairs all stood in

a row at one side. We were not meant to sit down. And I would get nowhere with them if I used the same line as I had on Benjie—an outbreak of smallpox on the ship.

Eliot went to the window. He opened the shutters, letting a pale light into the room. The cover on the billiard table had looked black. Now it was its green self.

Eliot stayed by the window, looking out. "You have a different car."

"Yes. Apparently the steering linkages on the Short Two deteriorated."

Eliot inclined his head. "How unfortunate. And you've come alone."

"Yes, as you see." I took out the papers concerning the children's passage. "The thing is, Gertrude, Eliot, I'm here because Benjie has had a delivery of documents concerning the sailing from Liverpool of a number of children. I told him I wanted to talk to you and he asked would I bring the papers."

"What papers?"

"It's some sort of bureaucratic nicety—something to be signed. Apparently, there's a delay in the sailing and the need for a longer stay in Liverpool."

Gertrude took the papers from me and went to the window. In her long dark coat, against the pale light, looking down at the papers, she became a silhouette from a Beardsley drawing.

"I'm signing nothing. The children were in the care of Stone-gate. I expect they can be sent back there." She tossed the papers onto the billiard table. "Honestly, I don't know what this country is coming to."

Eliot said, "I'm afraid you've had a wasted journey."

"Please think again, Gertrude. Let's save something from this tragic mess."

She closed the shutters. "What tragic mess?"

It was a mistake, but I was tired of her games. "You know exactly what I'm talking about. Two murders, on the same evening, in the same place."

Mrs. Sugden had reported Valerie Pennington's words: "Mr. Brockman wasn't there." Now I knew what was behind those words. Mr. Brockman was not there. Mrs. Brockman was.

Mrs. Brockman had blood on the cuff of her coat.

Eliot shook his head. "You say that as if you are about to make some sort of accusation."

Gertrude came very close, and put her hand on my shoulder. "It would have been so good to have had you on our side. You'd be surprised how many people are coming to our meetings, ready to part with their cash. We would have let you in with first investor, privileges."

"Free coal for life?" I asked.

Eliot closed the shutters. "Some people never learn."

It is not difficult to give a withering look in the dark, but no one sees it. "You've tried to silence me once, Eliot. It would be foolish to try again."

"How can someone so very charming also be so deeply annoying?"

I stepped away from them. "In the same way you were so very clever, and so very stupid."

He grabbed my wrist. I let out a cry of pain.

"Oh dear," Eliot said with mock sympathy, "I hurt her bad wrist, just as she was going to be even more annoying."

I had rattled them and was not about to stop now. If I didn't come out soon, Sykes would come looking for me. I pushed for an admission.

"Which of you killed Harry Aspinall? I'm sure his widow would like to know."

Gertrude slapped my face. "I've wanted to do that for such a long time. You are so smug. Don't want to consider adopting an orphan, but happy to rescue eight, and what? Leave them on my hands? Pity you weren't born a boy. You could have been a fireman, rushed into burning buildings, rescued people, and left them on the pavement. Harry Aspinall liked to have his name on letterheads and do nothing. For three generations they had done nothing except live on their reputations as philanthropists. I was the one let Helen Farrar rent the shop for next to nothing, not Harry. And if you want to know who killed him, it was I. Eliot merely had the presence of mind to bash Helen Farrar on the head. It wouldn't do to have two identical murders. And do you think either of us wanted to kill them? Do you imagine that was in our minds when we got up that morning?"

"Yes I do think that, or you wouldn't have taken a gun. It was wilful, Gertrude. There's no excusing it."

"We faced bankruptcy, and saw a solution. Wouldn't you do the same?"

Eliot let go of my wrist. "She wouldn't do it, but only because she doesn't know what it means to be on the edge. She is a nothing-ventured kind of person."

They were talking about me as if I were not here, as if I were already beyond troubling them. "I'm not alone. There are two men with me." Alec wasn't quite sixteen but I could stretch a point.

Eliot went to the window again. From what he said, I realised there was no sign of Sykes and Alec. "I'm surprised you got yourself another Jowett, so soon after the last one let you down."

He reached for Gertrude's hand. "Come on. Leave her. No one believes her story. We'll say we never saw her, had already left. Oh and before you think of telephoning for help, the telephone has been disconnected."

Gertrude sighed. "Eliot, dear, Kate will never give up. It's typical of her to barge into someone's house, not because she should but because she can."

"What then, Gertie?"

"Nothing serious. Just a fall down the cellar steps, fatal of course. We never even knew she'd come into the house. We had business in London, gave the servants a week's holiday. When the house is open again, you'll have no idea why her car is outside, and how she got in."

As if he couldn't resist his moment of triumph, Eliot said, "And we don't want to miss our train. Investors are falling over themselves to buy shares."

"And will you let Stephen Walmsley be hanged for murder?"

"Possibly for two murders."

He clapped a hand over my mouth, and twisted my arm up my back. Gertrude grabbed my other arm. I kicked as best I could, but he lifted me off my feet as they dragged me along the hall and down a passage. Within a minute, he was pushing open a door, with darkness on the other side. He assumed no one would hear me scream, and moved his hand from my mouth.

I screamed.

The stone steps looked deep as the stairway to hell.

One shove, and I was bouncing down hard cold steps, every fibre of my body crying out against the pain. I tried to slow my descent, and to break my fall. The crack I heard was my arm, and then everything went black.

From a long way off, I heard voices that seemed not human.

"Is she dead?"

"If not, she soon will be."

Chapter Fifty-Five

~

Mrs. Shackleton ought to have come out of the house by now. You should have gone in with her, Sykes told himself.

He had walked the grounds on the south side of the house. Anyone in an upstairs window would have seen him, but he saw no one. There was a large vegetable patch and greenhouses. Beyond was farmland. Separating the Dell land from the farmland was a country road.

Although the downstairs windows were all shuttered, he went and peered through a crack.

He had told Alec to stay out of sight, and listen for Mrs. Shackleton coming out. That would be their signal to leave. Sykes made his way back to the gate they had first entered.

And then he heard a car engine, but from round the other side of the house. Several moments later, Alec came running.

"They've taken her."

"Who has?"

"I hid, and watched. I saw them loading something into the boot of the car, something big, and now they've gone. It was her."

Sykes went to the door of the house and banged. He tried to open the door, but it was locked.

Alec's voice was urgent now. "I'm sure they've taken her. It was Mr. Dell tampered with the steering on her car, and now he's taken her."

"Did you see her?"

"No. It was something he carried in his arms."

Sykes leapt into car and drove round the side of the house towards the lane, stopping just long enough for Alec to jump in. Racing along the lane as fast as the car would allow, he passed hedges and ditches, trees and fields with such speed that they might be on a reel being turned at speed in a picture show.

And then he came to a fork in the way. There was nothing to choose between the roads leading off either side of the lane. They were of similar size, and equally deserted.

Which way, which way?

"Right," said Alec.

Sykes, who had just begun to veer left, turned the wheel, pushing the car as hard as it would go.

Mr. Dell had a bigger car, but he was not racing as if a life depended on it.

In the distance, a train rumbled. The sky ahead filled with new clouds rising from where the train must be. The sound grew louder. Alec saw it first and shouted for him to stop. Afterwards Sykes thought that Alec told him the name of the train, but he wasn't listening. He only knew that he would have to stop, or drive into the side of a railway carriage.

Carriage after carriage passed by until the train had passed. And then Sykes knew, either he had lost the motor on this road, or they had taken the wrong turn at the beginning of their journey.

"Why did you say "right"?" he asked Alec.

"Well it was one or the other, and you asked me."

"You picked wrong. We've lost her."

Chapter
Fifty-Six

~

At first, the darkness seemed total. My head throbbed. I did not move, except for shivering, being unsure how much of me was broken. Something bitter as an ice wind wrapped itself around my body, shooting icicles into my bones. The pain was excruciating. Gingerly, I reached over and touched one arm, one leg. It was when I tried to move my left arm that I let out a yell of pain. So that was the worst. It needed some support. I diagnosed a broken arm, unsure which bone had cracked.

I cringed as I became aware of a soft, scraping sound. Something walked onto my leg. I screamed. The thing quickly moved on.

As my eyes grew accustomed to the dimness, I realised the darkness was not total. Light spilled from what must be one of those half windows some cellars have. Because of the pain in my left arm, the only way to stand was to roll onto my right side and push myself up onto one knee, then both knees, shift one leg, and then the other. Having achieved that, I decided against standing and shuffled to the wall. Sitting with my back to the wall, I brought my left arm close to my chest, pulled off my scarf and took I do not know how long to make a sling.

I could hear the sound of silence, a kind of low hum. By concentrating on minutiae, I would pass the time until Sykes found a way in. He must by now have heard their motor as they left.

Becoming aware of the smells, I thought there must be food here. Cheese, ham, sour milk. Of course there may not be food. Smells linger.

What I could not understand was why Sykes and Alec failed to find a way in, to search for me, to call out. Perhaps they had. Now I wondered had I passed out for a few crucial minutes.

If they were searching, they must know to look in a cellar. Painfully, I got to my feet. Staying close to the wall, I edged my way towards the glimmer of light that seemed to come and go. Perhaps this was an optical trick, or the sun disappearing behind a cloud.

Gertrude and Eliot must still be here, otherwise Sykes would have come to find me.

Fear was in abeyance, but in the hope of attracting attention, I screamed. This had its disadvantage. If Gertrude and Eliot were still in the house, they might come and finish me off.

Greed had brought them to this, greed and a sense of entitlement. They were not very good at murder. The attack on me was clumsy. If I died, an amateur could solve the crime. A detective from a sixpenny novel would solve it.

As a reward to myself for this thought, I screamed again.

That would be my pattern. Scream, take a long pause, and scream again. Save my voice, save my throat, save my sanity.

Edging my way round, I knew I was coming closer to the half window that, when I lay on the stone-cold floor, seemed distant as a star. And then suddenly I was there. At windowsill level was a large sink. With the hand of my good arm, I steadied myself. Doing so shot darts of pain through my wrist.

Screams of pain are often quiet. I indulged in one of the hair-raising kind.

It was my reward to see a pair of men's black shoes. The shoes stopped. I screamed again, wishing I had found something long enough to hit the window, to break it. Above the shoes were black trouser turn-ups, the calves of legs. The person bobbed down, knees in my direction. Lastly came a face. The face jutted forward, close to the glass. I saw him. He saw me. Raynor.

Part of his plan was to appear benign, in his look, benign and concerned.

He shouted something that I could not hear.

He would have been the one to put the body on the train, and now it was my turn. He had come to finish me off.

I blinked, and he was gone.

Now that I was at the sink, I realised that I had a burning thirst. I turned on the tap and put my head under it, gulping water into my mouth, letting it run onto my temples, and then down my neck which was horrible. The idle thought came to me that perhaps icy water running down one's neck in a freezing cellar might make death seem perfectly acceptable.

I heard nothing more, and in those moments of nothingness, wondered whether there might be a side door, another way out, a place where the coal came in. If there were such a place, I might find it by touch before Raynor got to me. And where was Sykes?

But even as these thoughts came, I heard the creak as the cellar door swung open. Footsteps came steadily nearer and nearer. I must be living in slow motion, and perhaps I would go on living in slow motion after death.

There was a light, a swinging light reflected on the far wall, a lantern perhaps.

In spite of my plan to look for a door or coal cellar, my feet had taken no notice of my brain. If I could keep my broken arm steady, I might hit out with my other hand.

And then he was standing in front of me, looming over me.

"People will miss me. You won't get away with it."

"My dear Mrs. Shackleton, of course they will. The world will miss you. I will miss you even though I know you so slightly. Now let me help you."

This was clever. This might put a person off her guard.

He took a roller towel from the wall by the sink. "This will make a better sling."

It took a moment to realise he was not going to try and strangle me, but made a better sling than mine.

"Now will you take my arm, or shall I carry you?"

"I can walk."

Stay calm, I told myself. The moment will come. You can walk but you cannot run. There will be an escape. It will not end like this.

He talked. He held my right elbow, and he talked.

"Mr. Brockman told me you were coming here. I thought you would be all right. Alec was with you. Where has he got to?"

"I don't know."

"Have they taken him?"

"I don't know."

He would learn nothing from me. I hoped Alec was safe, and Sykes too.

"Did they send you?" I asked. "Benjie, Gertrude, Dell?"

"Heavens no. Do believe me. I am here to help."

"They killed Harry Aspinall and Mrs. Farrar."

Raynor said nothing.

"Did you know that, Raynor?"

"I wondered. I had begun to think that a possibility, once Mr. Brockman told me the identity of the man on the train."

"Why didn't you say?"

"One hopes one is wrong. But why did you come here?"

"Didn't Benjie tell you? I wanted their signatures in triplicate, so that the eight orphans could be brought back from Liverpool."

"You should have asked me. Forging signatures is one of my skills."

We had reached the top of the steps, without my remembering the pain in my arm.

He left a note on the front step, secured with a pebble. "Just to say you are safe, in case whoever is searching for you comes back."

There was no sign of Sykes's car.

Raynor helped me onto the back seat of Benjie's car, and covered me with a motoring blanket. "I cast your astrological chart for you, Mrs. Shackleton. It alerted me to the fact that today was not propitious. Also, you are advised not to take on any new ventures at present, or to make hasty investments."

Well that was good to know.

Chapter
Fifty-Seven

❧

Raynor drove me straight to the hospital where I was treated by the most gentle of doctors who assured me that I had been fortunate. I was fit, and had "fallen well".

That might be thanks to listening to Harriet, and assisting when she practised her ju-jitsu. Some instinct must have taken over during that terrible tumble down the stone steps.

I did not feel that I had fallen well. My whole body ached. Bruises mapped my arms. My right elbow was swollen.

"You got away with a fractured wrist, Mrs. Shackleton."

I had got away with my life, but did not say so.

"What happened?"

"I was pushed down cellar steps by two former friends."

"I say, that's a bit rich." He glanced at the nurse, giving her a nod. "It's the kind of thing we must report."

For once, I did not have to go to the police. The police came to me, in the form of the silent CID chief inspector, Mr. Emsley. So much had happened since he sat with me and Dad two evenings ago that it felt like a lifetime.

Mr. Emsley took my statement. When I told him that Gertrude Brockman and Eliot Dell had admitted murdering Harry Aspinall and Helen Farrar, he paused in his writing. "Did anyone else witness this admission?"

"No. But the gentleman who brought me here, Mr. Raynor, he –" I had a terrible reluctance to say the words "rescued me". Mr. Emsley kindly filled in my blank.

"He came to your assistance?"

"Yes, he did."

"Mr. Raynor has given us a statement. Now are you able to sign yours?"

"Yes. I'm right-handed."

Chief Inspector Emsley made no comment about my statement. He had the evidence of his eyes as to the treatment I had received at the hands of Gertrude and Eliot. What I described as an attempt on my life, they would brush off as the ramblings of a woman who found her way into an empty house.

He watched me sign. "Now can I take you anywhere, Mrs. Shackleton? Mr. Sykes is waiting along the corridor and Mr. Raynor is still here, but if you wish me to take you somewhere, or to telephone –"

"Thank you. I'll speak to Mr. Raynor, and Mr. Sykes will take me home."

Sykes had been full of annoyance with himself for chasing off after Eliot Dell's car, and then losing it. He was only too eager to make amends.

* * *

The cast on my arm went from just above the knuckles to below my elbow. With help from Mrs. Sugden, who cut out the sleeve from a very old raincoat and fastened it over my arm with tape, I was able to risk taking a bath. The belt from the raincoat made a temporary sling. As a nurse, I would have told a patient not to do any such thing.

Mrs. Sugden hovered on the landing, tapping on the door every few minutes to make sure I didn't slide under the water and undo the doctor's good work.

I was resting on the sofa, too tired to climb back up the stairs, when the despatch rider arrived from the French Embassy, wheeling a Gnome Rhone motorcycle onto the garden path. Mrs. Sugden opened the door. After unpeeling layers of clothing, the rider turned out to be an elegant young woman. Her name was Catherine.

Seated on an armchair by the fire, with sausage and mash on a tray, she told us that she had first ridden a motorbike during the war, and the love of it never left her.

The letter she brought from Bernard Campaner informed me that communications had been made to the British government at the highest level, praising "the Kate Shackleton Investigation Agency" and regretting the false start that shrouded early enquiries into Mr. Aspinall's death. There was also a hand-written note about stock exchange interest in the Bluebell Mine, and a commitment to help ensure justice for Stephen Walmsley.

Mrs. Sugden wanted Catherine to have a good night's sleep. I was happy for her to take my bed. That gave me a good reason to stay put on the sofa.

She chose to snatch two hours' instead, and had brought her own alarm clock.

I urged her to sleep for longer, but she refused. This was not entirely out of concern for her welfare. I did not want her to crash on the way back and lose the precious bundle of paperwork that I hoped would damn the guilty and free Stephen Walmsley.

Much as I now felt I could trust Chief Inspector Emsley, I wanted to cover all possibilities for saving Stephen and ensuring that the guilty would be brought to justice. Even as I thought that, I felt sick to my stomach about Gertrude. A horrible dizziness came over me. I had asked Mrs. Sugden for pen and paper. My hand shook as I took the pen. The room started to spin.

"Lie back," Mrs. Sugden said. "Give yourself time to recover. That bath was too hot."

"I need to add a note for Catherine to take with our paperwork for Monsieur Campaner, telling him that Gertrude and Eliot confessed to me."

For that moment, my strength fled. I couldn't think how to begin. "I need to tell him what they said, and what happened."

"And it makes you sick to think of it, and you've been through the wringer. I'll type it while you shut your eyes. Your Frenchman doesn't need chapter and verse, just the facts."

* * *

As it happened, the courier did not hear her alarm. She woke after four hours, annoyed at the delay.

I was glad Harriet was there to wave her off. The sight of a young woman setting off on a motorbike to ride over two hundred miles was something she ought to see. Barring some accident, our painstakingly gathered statements and my letter would be delivered safely.

* * *

"Is our case nearly finished?" Harriet asked.

"We have done all we can—or almost."

"What else is there to do?"

"Oh not a great deal, some loose ends."

The loose ends included interviewing Kevin O'Donnell, nickname Giant Jack, and discovering whether Eliot Dell and Gertrude had been found and questioned.

When the telephone rang, Harriet went to answer it. I heard her saying, in her best telephone voice, "Just a moment, I will bring Mrs. Shackleton to the telephone."

I was shifting myself from the sofa when she came back in. "It's Chief Inspector Emsley."

This might be what I was waiting for.

He spoke in a flat tone of voice. "The two people in question had gone from the house when you arrived. They were on their way to Manchester for a meeting with potential investors, and from there to London."

"But you saw what happened. And they were seen leaving."

"There are conflicting accounts. Mr. Dell's bailiff was nearby and confirms that they left before you arrived."

"And you accept that?"

There was a long pause. "I'm sorry, Mrs. Shackleton."

So was I. And so would be Stephen Walmsley, still in his cell, awaiting the trial that loomed closer.

Chapter
Fifty-Eight

~

At Benjie's request, Raynor booked a first class carriage to transport Sykes, Mr. and Mrs. Arkwright, Milly and me to Liverpool Lime Street, and two first class carriages to bring us and the orphans back. They would stay at Thorpefield Manor. Eliot Dell and Gertrude had wriggled out of sight. Not knowing where they were or what they were up to left me feeling uneasy.

Raynor drove over to bring Sykes's and my rail tickets. He could have put them in the post, but this way we could talk.

"Raynor, if you know where Gertrude and Eliot are staying, tell me."

"That's what Mr. Emsley of CID would like to know." He was unruffled. "These things have a way of working themselves out."

"So far the workings out have led to murder and attempted murder."

"That is rather difficult, but the police are still investigating. The house has been searched. The Lord Lieutenant asked to see Mr. Brockman. I drove him there. The sadness in his eyes after that meeting was almost unbearable. We do not know how this will end."

"The word 'badly' comes to mind. I hate waiting on events."

"It is no consolation, but Mrs. Brockman and Mr. Dell are doing a fine job in recruiting investors. It will be my job to ensure that those investors stay with us, whatever might happen, especially if we are amassing orphans as we go along."

* * *

We all caught the train in good time. Sykes and I sat opposite each other, near the door. The Arkwrights and Milly were by the window. The engine settled into its soothing rhythm of clank and hum. My painful wrist throbbed in tune. I was wearing a plaid cape that was easier to deal with than a coat.

I had confided in Raynor about my intention to seek out Kevin O'Donnell, but we agreed to spare Benjie the pain of any disclosure until we knew more.

Sykes fully expected that he would seek out Giant Jack, and I would go to the children's holding centre, with our documentation, and bring back the orphans. He took out a cigarette.

When I said, "We'll do it the other way round, Mr. Sykes," his cigarette lighter stopped in mid-air.

"Are you mad? You want to tackle a man who's the size of a mountainside, and leave me to gather up kiddies?"

Sykes did not need to know that Raynor had forged two out of three signatures. He would be less than happy about that. Nor would I tell him my deeper reason for not gathering up the children myself. Going into the holding centre would break my heart. The wartime images in my mind are sufficient for a lifetime's nightmares. For the present, in my weakened state, I could take no more.

"There are good reasons why you should pick up the children. You are a dad, and you will know how to reassure them. Red tape is involved, which means officious officials will make the transaction as difficult as possible. You only have to adopt the 'I am every inch a policeman' look and they will roll over. I, on the other hand, with my arm in a sling and a bruise on my cheek would have to expend a great deal of energy trying not to look pathetic."

He lit his cigarette. "And why should a woman with a broken arm —"

"Wrist."

" — and bruises confront a great stoit who can stop a horse and cart with his little finger?"

"I'll be no threat to him. If we're right, and he was the one who did the lifting and carrying, and put the body on the train, he'll know that at the very least he could face prison. At worst, he is an accessory to murder. He's bound to be a Catholic, and will want to confess, if he hasn't already. I'll coax him into telling the truth."

"Then let me be standing by, round the nearest corner."

I knew that Sykes felt bad about making the wrong choice at Eliot Dell's house. He saw that as his first big mistake in all the time we had worked together, and was being extra cautious now.

It was a tempting idea to have him standing by. Yet for Sykes, there would be no nuances. Kevin O'Donnell would be culpable or blameless.

Sykes was still inclined to argue, so I put a stop to it. "I have to do this, and not just for the sake of regaining confidence after tumbling down those stairs."

He gave a kind of growl. "You didn't tumble, you were pushed."

"That is why I must interview Mr. O'Donnell myself. We should never plan our next move based on what went wrong before."

In the face of such impeccable logic, Sykes recognised defeat.

* * *

The obliging taxi driver opened the car door, helped me out and waited outside the Burkes' house. Fortunately Mrs. Burke knew her husband's rounds inside out. He had come home at dinnertime. She had given Bonnie, the horse, her drink of water, oats and a carrot. Now himself was delivering to the big houses on Princes Avenue and Princes Road, all round there. I climbed back into the taxi, idly wondering what himself had for his dinner, or whether Bonnie was the one who really mattered.

For discretion's sake, I asked the taxi driver to stop at the top of Princes Avenue and wait for me there. I walked down Princes

Road, to where I had seen the horse and cart. I sat down on a low garden wall, to wait.

The wiry coal merchant came out of a house on my left. He was about to pick up another bag when I interrupted him.

"Mr. Burke!"

He paused, looking not displeased to take a break. "Aye that's me."

"Mrs. Burke told me I'd find you here. I'm a friend of Josh Whitwell who took Mr. O'Donnell's photograph." I held the envelope with the picture I had copied and mounted—Giant Jack next to Mrs. Whitwell. "When I told Josh I would be in Liverpool today, he asked if I would bring it for him."

He sniffed and spat out coal dust. "Well he's famous across Liverpool. He's had proposals of marriage and offers of work, but I got in first."

"So if it's all right with you, I'll have a word with him. Not to propose." As I stood, my cloak fell open. "The proposal can wait until my arm mends."

He laughed. "Chat away, queenie. Do Kev good to have a break."

Kevin had come from the house next door. Mr. Burke spoke to him, and pointed to me.

He approached cautiously, taking off his cap, twisting it in his big hands, black with coal dust. He was too big to sit comfortably on a low wall, but did so, stretching his legs.

"You've been in the wars, missus."

Not wanting to waste time, I said, "Eliot Dell did this when he threw me down his cellar steps and left me for dead."

He knew the name, but made out he didn't. "Eliot Dell?"

"You applied to him for work after you'd finished the demolition job on the children's home. I'm wondering if you wish you hadn't."

"What's that to you?"

"I've brought the photograph Josh Whitwell took of you."

He looked at the envelope but made no move to take it. Perhaps he thought this was not a photograph, but blood money, or a blackmail note.

Holding the envelope in my left hand, I withdrew the picture and showed it to him. "It's a fine likeness."

A look of relief came over the red face that was smudged with coal dust but he said nothing.

He stared. "Someone stole my soul after this was taken."

I looked from the picture to him, and saw what he meant, but contradicted him. "I would say your soul is intact."

"What do you want, missus?"

"Not to cause you trouble. How did it come about that you helped Eliot Dell?"

"I didn't help him, not with—It wasn't like that."

"Then tell me. Trust me. I'm guessing you weren't there when the murder happened."

Had he been there, Valerie Pennington would have seen him. He was too big to miss.

"What's behind your asking?"

"Just to know what happened."

"Who will you be after telling?"

"Talk to me and I'll do what I can for you. Talk to the police and there'll be no end to this."

He sighed. "My pay went flying. Bets, sweepstake, the boozer called out for my wage packet. That kind of job sends a feller doolally. Watching a grand house fall, when there's souls sleeping in alleyways. We all knew kiddies had been turned out. My foot flattened the face of a little rag doll. My sister was after a dolly like it. Whatever demon got to me, it emptied my pockets."

"So you went looking for work."

"Honest work."

"You were unlucky."

"Foolish." He picked up the envelope with the photograph, and put it down again. "The mammy will love this, if I see her again, this side of the grave."

Now he was overdoing it. "The work you took on?"

"The boss at the farm on Dell's land got me lifting the last of the rhubarb. I was set to go on the tramp after that. Mr. Dell said he had something to go onto a train, bound for the London markets. Only it was hush-hush because killing wild boar breaks the law."

"There are no wild boars."

"That's what he told me, a wild boar. Here's something for your trouble, he said. He gave me two gold coins. Said wild boar fetched a good price in London. I felt sick when it hit me that I was carrying a man. I put Dell's blood money in the sack, put the poor fellow on the train, praying for his eternal rest, and I set off on the tramp. God guided me to Liverpool."

I understood why he would make a run for it. An Irish labourer who had drunk and gambled his wages would make the perfect dupe.

"Did Eliot Dell drive the van?"

"No. He sat in the back with me. It was dark. He didn't want me to know too soon what or who was in that sack."

"Did you see who was driving?"

"Probably some poor sod as hard up as me." He looked towards the cart, where the coal merchant had set off along the street.

"Where did the van set off from?"

"By a barn on the farm where I'd done the work."

So Eliot Dell and whoever was with him had managed to get Harry Aspinall into the back of a car. He must have parked behind the shop, out of sight.

"Would you tell your story to the police?"

"You know where I'd end up. I'm not a violent man. Here they call me Giant Jack. At home I was the gentle giant."

"Take your likeness, Kevin. Good luck to you. Live well."

He put the photograph in his pocket. "What's your name?"

"Kate."

* * *

The taxi driver was relieved to see me. He was standing by his car, looking about. "I thought you'd done a runner."

"That's not likely."

"Why not? You've one arm but two legs."

"Let's make one more stop, before you take me back to the station. I want to go to the French Consulate."

I would send a secure message to Bernard Campaner. He should have the full story, but with nothing to incriminate Kevin O'Donnell.

The driver had opened his window. As he drove along a broad street towards the docks, I could smell the River Mersey. Second thoughts floated in on the breeze.

I am so guided by my own official secrets act that when we arrived at the consulate, I changed my mind. "We'll go straight to the station."

If Campaner did not have enough information by now, he never would.

* * *

Sykes was standing under the station clock, waiting for me. We had five minutes before the train left.

"Where is everyone?"

He grinned. "On the platform."

"That's a relief."

We walked towards the barrier.

"You should've seen the joy on the bairns' faces when the Arkwrights appeared. They looked half-starved. We'd to find them something to eat."

Sykes showed our tickets and we hurried to the platform. "What about O'Donnell, how did you get on?"

"He's blameless."

"But did he do it?"

Chapter
Fifty-Nine

❧

When our party of adults and children arrived at Thorpefield Hall in two taxis, the staff assembled by the front door to meet us. Benjie Brockman had donned his old military uniform. He saluted as Mr. and Mrs. Arkwright led four boys into the house. Milly followed with two girls. A couple of young ones had fallen asleep in the taxi. Raynor carried one, and Sykes the other.

"Where will you put them all?" I asked Raynor.

"Two rooms are spruced up. They'll be in there together, and there's the old nursery."

Milly holding the two little girls by the hand, said, "I feel happy and sad at the same time. Happy for the children, but no one is saying anything about Stephen."

"Don't give up."

"I never will. And the housekeeper says I can look after children."

I congratulated Benjie on giving the orphans a home. "Only for now, you know. There have been misunderstandings. Gertrude will be making arrangements."

He was a little out of date. We had just rescued the children from Gertrude's arrangements. I wondered if Benjie fully understood what was going on, or whether his mind played tricks in order to protect him.

"And we've had offers of help from the village. People are very good. Valerie—Miss Pennington—brought rugs for their rooms. The chap who looks after the pit ponies brought a box of toys that he found."

Now that he had done ceremonial duty by welcoming his visitors, Benjie was anxious to return to his study. He asked me to come with him. His stamp collection was on the desk.

"If the children are good, I may let them see my collection."

"And what about your coins, Benjie? Did you find the two that you missed?"

"I never did you know, but they'll turn up I'm sure. Gertrude seemed to think that Alec stole them, but she's wrong. He's gone, you know, gone to be a proper mechanic as he calls it."

"The man he works with is a friend of mine, Philip Goodchild. They'll get on very well. And I'm sure Alec will come and visit you."

"Do you think so?"

"Yes."

I would see to it that he did, just as Benjie had suggested Alec visit Valerie Pennington. "Benjie, what were those coins, the missing ones?"

"George III guineas, dubbed the spade guinea because of the shape of the shield."

"Two the same?"

"Yes. I was going to do a swap. Fellow collector I correspond with, he wanted one in exchange for a military guinea."

"Well perhaps yours will turn up, or perhaps Gertrude might have another thought about where they are?"

He gave me an odd, slightly quizzical look. "I wondered that too. Funny you should have the same thought."

"Where is she today?"

"She and Eliot are doing a grand job, raising investments. She telephoned just before you arrived. They are arranging a meeting with important investors in London." He closed the lid on his stamp collection. "She thought you might invest, you know."

"I'm advised by a very cautious bank manager, Benjie, and I follow his judgement. But to be honest, I forgot to mention it to him."

He laughed. "You always were a bit of a card, you know. If you change your mind, just say. Fully subscribed or not, there'll always be a slot for Gertie's oldest friend."

That was kind of him, even though untrue on both counts.

I had heard someone come in, and thought Sykes had grown tired of waiting. Raynor appeared at the door. For once he looked slightly flustered, which at first I put down to his having the sudden additional duty of shepherding a couple of four-year-olds.

"Sir, there's Chief Inspector Emsley here to see you. I told him you have someone with you and when he heard who, he says perhaps you will both be interested in what he has to say."

Since Mr. Emsley had, if reluctantly, accepted Gertrude and Eliot's version of events at the Dell house, I felt a sudden animosity towards him. Whatever he wanted to say now would not bode well.

"Show him in," Benjie said. "While you're about it, see if Mrs. Shackleton's chap would like to come in. I've spotted him walking past the window. I'm sure our grounds aren't so very fascinating."

Raynor had already thought of this. "Mr. Sykes has declined. He is enjoying the fresh air."

Benjie often surprised me. He had never met Sykes, but made the connection. Just as I had Benjie marked as a man with his head in the clouds of his collections, he would be suddenly astute. I wished I could remember whether he had always been like that, or whether he was feeling his age.

Moments later, Chief Inspector Emsley entered. He took the chair offered by Benjie, while giving the impression that he would have preferred to stand.

"It's good news and it's bad news, sir. The good news for him and his friends is that we will be releasing Stephen Walmsley."

I blinked. I listened, waiting for him to say it again, just to be sure.

"There has been a lot of interest in his case, from various quarters, leading to the conclusion that a trial may not be in the public interest. The charges against him have been withdrawn, after new information has come to light."

What I most wanted to know was what new information, and where it came from, and was this really justice for Stephen, or might some dark cloud cast a shadow across his future?

"What new information?" Benjie asked. "And is the lad innocent?"

Being a man who preferred as few words as possible, Emsley answered only part of the question. "In my view, only babies are innocent, sir, but new evidence casts doubt on the advisability of prosecuting Stephen Walmsley."

This man would get on very well with Sykes. "How soon will he be released?" I asked.

"He has been released. He was met at the prison gates by representatives of the Miners' Union." He sighed.

I guessed there had been some fanfare, perhaps including the Temperance Band.

Benjie picked up a pencil. He tapped his blotter. "I suppose he'll want his job back."

"That I couldn't say, sir."

The relief swept through me with such power that it was unnerving. Until that moment, I hadn't realised how much I dreaded Stephen going to trial and being unable to hold his own against a hostile prosecution barrister. It took a moment for me to catch my breath.

"Inspector, you said you have good and bad news."

"At present we have no other viable suspects for the murder of Helen Farrar and Harry Aspinall."

So the local CID had finally admitted that the crimes were linked, and the two murders were committed by the same perpetrator or perpetrators. That was a start.

Chapter Sixty

❧

After Stephen Walmsley's release, silence prevailed. If Wakefield CID was still investigating the murder of Mrs. Farrar and Mr. Aspinall, they were not telling me. Scotland Yard had signed me off with a thank you and a cheque. That would satisfy a mercenary. It did not suit me.

My case was in the hall, and the taxi booked.

Mrs. Sugden voiced her objections. "This is madness. You can't go to London with your arm in a sling."

She had a good point, but I had a better one. "It's that or start climbing up the curtains."

"Take someone with you then."

"Are you offering?"

"I am not. You won't catch me going to London, not unless I'm summoned by the King."

That lifted a weight from my shoulders.

"At least let me cancel The Savoy. Stay with your aunt or stay with your cousin."

"The Savoy is very good at arranging help for residents with an arm in a sling."

She looked so crestfallen that I had to tell her. "I'm meeting a friend there. She and I have a lot to talk about."

Annette Kerner was more an acquaintance than a friend. If anyone could tell me what was happening at Scotland Yard, it would be she.

I checked my watch. Before catching my train, there would be time to visit Mr. Cohen, the solicitor who had so superbly submitted a defence for Stephen Walmsley.

Since being without a car I have got to know a friendly taxi driver, Stanley Wilson. He was happy to wait on Park Square, while I called on Mr. Cohen.

* * *

Small and squat with a slightly squashed face, Mr. Cohen has a warm smile and an amiable manner. I thanked him for his work on behalf of Stephen Walmsley.

"That's our job done then, eh?"

"Yes, as far as the wrongful charge is concerned. What I would like to know is why everything has gone so quiet. I know it will take time to re-investigate and to build a case, but do you have any idea how long, and when there may be other arrests?"

"I'm no more privy to these matters than you are, Mrs. Shackleton. All I can assume is that the evidence isn't strong enough to bring a case. What you told me about the items in the eaves of the house, that can be explained. The shoes may have been left behind by a guest. Mrs. Brockman's ownership of a pistol does not make her a murderer, even if the type of bullet matched one found on the shop premises. Pistols are made in vast quantities, more's the pity. The occupant of a grace and favour cottage—readier to say what she did not see than what she did see—would make a poor witness. Is there anything new that you can tell the police?"

There was nothing new. I clutched at the straw offered by Bernard Campaner of a private prosecution.

Mr. Cohen should have had the grace not to laugh, but his lips formed a pillar box shape and a puh-puh-puh sound came from them as his shoulders moved up and down.

"I am not an expert in French law, but I do know that what they call *citation directe* wouldn't be brought in the case of a felony in France, only for a misdemeanour or a petty offence. And they would have more sense than to try such tricks here."

"What would be needed to take a private prosecution?"

"A dossier would have to go to the Public Prosecutor. There would need to be new and compelling evidence. The chief police officer of every district is bound to give information to the director with respect to indictable offences alleged to have been committed in his district. Your French friends may not even gain entry to the British labyrinth. If they did, a modern-day Charles Dickens could make a novel of it."

His words hit me like a blow. My arm began to itch intolerably. The bruise on my face throbbed so hard that I wondered if my cheekbone was cracked. Had Campaner known this all along, and simply dangled the prospect of a private prosecution so that I would share information with him? If so, I had been totally naïve.

My time with Mr. Cohen was at an end.

I had a train to catch.

"Don't look so glum, my dear Mrs. Shackleton. Your friend probably doesn't understand English law. Only a very few of us do. You did the correct thing in communicating the facts as you knew them. The family had a right to know what happened to their loved one. And I'm sure that the French Embassy played a part behind the scenes. Without your information finding its way into the right hands, Stephen Walmsley would not have been freed."

Chapter
Sixty-One

My taxi stopped outside The Savoy. The taxi driver ceased to be helpful after he deposited my case on the pavement, taking my tip and saying he had to keep moving or he'd hold up the traffic.

The commissionaire came across to take my luggage. As he held the side door open for me, I froze to the spot. Coming out of the hotel through the revolving door was Gertrude. For a split second, an invisible thread held us in each other's gaze as the revolving door continued its movement and Eliot appeared.

The commissionaire waited patiently for me to move.

Eliot paused, tilting his head. "Well, well. Fancy meeting you. If you are here for our first meeting, you've missed it. Sit in on the repeat performance in an hour. Meeting room on the first floor, sign on the door." He nodded at his own magnanimity. "Excuse me. Breath of fresh air."

Gertrude had taken a few steps and was waiting for him. They turned back and looked at me. I held my ground and stared back, watching as they walked off arm in arm.

A porter took my suitcase from the commissionaire.

It took an effort to sign the register. Mrs. Sugden was right. This was madness. Only the thought of meeting Annette Kerner kept me here. It sickened me to think of Gertrude and Eliot walking free, prospering, sure of themselves, and untouchable.

But I would not let them make me change my plans. They wouldn't dare try anything here.

One look at my arm in a sling and the porter pressed for the lift. We stopped at the first floor. The room opposite the lift had a sign on the door.

BROCK-DELL INVESTMENTS

BLUEBELL MINE

So I was not only in the same hotel. Fate led me to the very floor on which they would make their glib presentation of the prospects and profits to come from the Bluebell Mine.

I did not need to attempt unpacking. Good as his word, the manager had arranged for a member of staff to come and do that for me.

I went back downstairs to wait for Annette.

She beamed with pleasure at having got me here at last, as she put it. Our waiter opened the champagne and poured. We toasted female detectives.

"Even with broken limbs, we triumph!" She raised her glass again.

"You don't have a broken limb."

"No but I spent three weeks in a drugs den, until I could stand my own stink no longer."

"Mr. Woodhead?"

"Who else? But I am here to tell you that the commander has retired to the country, to spend more time in his garden."

"So that's the lie of the land."

"I thought you'd want to know. You're still on the list of wanted women for the right sort of investigations. You would have been anyway. In a place so big, the left hand doesn't always know what the right hand is doing."

She did not volunteer any more information.

Instead, she talked about the sort of cases she enjoyed, working for rather grand people, who remained nameless, but who got themselves into bother now and again, "Particularly the young people whose parents are most anxious to guard reputations."

"We move in very different circles, Annette."

"Ah and before I forget –" She produced a fat white envelope from her elegant bag. "You are not allowed to refuse this, as you'll see from the writing on the envelope."

It was handwritten, and I saw straight away that the penmanship was not English.

For The Benefit Of The Orphans

"It would take rather a long time to count, and so you may want to put it in a second envelope and have it kept in the hotel safe."

For some reason, my heart began to pound—a feeling I could not explain. This felt like an indirect way of paying me for my information about the murder of Harry Aspinall.

"Is it from Mrs. Aspinall and her son? Are they still in London?"

"Oh no. As far as I'm aware, they went back to France with the poor man's body. Couldn't wait to be away from here."

"Who then?"

"I'm not allowed to say his name, but he is very charming and diplomatic, and is acting for the person most senior to himself."

"Bernard Campaner?"

"You don't see me shaking my head."

As far as I knew, I was as much in his debt as he in mine. Had it not been for the intervention at higher levels than our CID and Commander Woodhead, Stephen Walmsley would be in the dock.

After I had done as she suggested, and deposited the money in the safe, she came up to my room, to help me change. I can manage with one arm in a sling, but it takes such a long time.

"What's the matter, Kate?"

I told her about my episode at the Dell house, and my sojourn in the cellar. "And they are here, Eliot Dell and Gertrude, conducting their business, in this hotel, on this floor."

"Good heavens! And you have the nerve to stay here?"

"Gertrude once said that I don't give up, and she was right. Let them think I am here to stay on their trail."

"They might try again."

"Then they will be showing their hand, and this time may not get away with it."

"All the same, I'm going to ask at reception when they are leaving. If it's not very soon I shall move in here with you."

"You will not!"

It did not take her long to return, with the news that Mr. Dell and Mrs. Brockman would be leaving directly after their next meeting.

"Come on then, Annette. I want to walk along the Embankment. If we see the pair of them, I shall stare them out. Did you ever do that as a child? You'd stare at your friend until one of you blinks?"

Bright sunshine reflected on the sweet and smelly Thames. We watched a pleasure cruiser, a Tyne collier barge and a small motorboat gliding and chugging. A child waved to the passengers on the pleasure cruiser and some waved back. No sign of Eliot and Gertrude.

By the time we came back to the hotel, a kind of fury had grown inside me. Gertrude had been willing to sacrifice the children, scatter them to the winds, send them across oceans. She and Eliot had committed murder, and now they were presenting themselves as respectable business people. Trust your money to us. Sink your funds into the deepest mine in Britain, perhaps the deepest mine in the world.

"Where are you going?" Annette asked, as I began to climb the stairs.

"Into the meeting."

"For heaven's sake, you'll have us thrown out of the hotel."

"Worse things happen."

I charged up the stairs. She was a few steps behind me, talking, urging caution, but I wasn't listening. With no idea of what I would say or I do, I walked along the corridor.

DC Martin Yeats was standing by the door of the meeting room. I felt like screaming. Not only had they got away with murder, but they had police protection.

"What are you doing here?" I demanded.

"I was about to ask you the same thing."

The door opened. I would have gone in, but someone was coming out. In fact, several people were leaving the room, headed by Chief Inspector Emsley from Wakefield CID. He stared at me. His mouth opened, but no words came. It was quite something to be able to astonish such a self-possessed man.

Behind him came Gertrude, handcuffed to a detective constable. The look on her face was of puzzlement, and disbelief. It reminded me of a time decades ago, when her pony refused to jump across a stream. She never understood when things did not go her way. Eliot followed, handcuffed to a burly constable. He gave me a look of pure hatred.

When they had gone, Martin Yeats said, "Well, what are you doing here?"

"Pure coincidence."

He glanced from me to Annette. "I'm not sure I believe in coincidences."

Had Annette known something was going to happen, I wondered, that arrests were imminent? Perhaps that explained why she was so keen for me to visit.

Martin began to walk along the corridor, towards the stairs. "There's something, someone, you should see."

Chapter Sixty-Two

～

We did not speak until we reached the second floor. Martin cleared his throat. "Mrs. Brockman adopted a child yesterday, a baby by the name of William. There is a nursemaid in an adjacent room, quite oblivious to everything."

He was going too fast. "Martin, I knew that Gertrude planned to adopt." There was no point in saying that she was adopting her own child, hers and Eliot Dell's. "But tell me, when was it decided to arrest the pair of them? I'd given up hope."

"Sometimes evidence builds, and builds."

Annette chipped in. "Thanks to Kate Shackleton and cohorts!"

Martin gave the slightest incline of his head. "Mr. Dell and Mrs. Brockman have been arrested on suspicion of murder. They're to be escorted north and questioned in the presence of solicitors."

Oddly enough, I no longer held their attack on me against them. It paled when set beside their other crimes. Attacking me was a kind of madness. They must have known there was no longer a way out. They vented their rage, and then continued to sleepwalk through the nightmare of their own making.

Their turning point came when Harry Aspinall refused to comply with their plans and wishes. After that, there was no going back, and no redemption.

"Does Mr. Brockman know that his wife has been taken into custody?"

Would this be a great shock, or had Benjie known? Somehow I thought not. Raynor would have protected him.

"Mr. Brockman will be informed by a local officer shortly."

"I'd like to see little William."

Annette tapped my arm. "Kate, I'm not a great one for other people's babies. I'll wait for you downstairs."

Martin seemed relieved. "The adoption papers are signed by Mr. and Mrs. Brockman. The society would consider taking the child back if necessary."

The baby lay in a Moses basket. The nursemaid beside him was a middle-aged woman, her black hair streaked with grey and with a severe centre parting. I thought she may not want me near her charge, but she was pleasant.

William looked up. He had a scrunched up little red face and slightly pointy ears.

I reached out my hand. He grasped my little finger in his tiny fist.

Oh Gertrude, what have you done? She had talked so blithely about adopting a baby that would be intelligent and with no bad blood.

I hoped little William would never know the true history of his parents, and that Benjie would not look at those pointy ears and think of Eliot Dell.

Martin sighed. "It's going to be rather awkward for the local officer to tell Mr. Brockman that his wife has been arrested, and then to ask about the future of the child."

"Let me make a telephone call."

Martin looked alarmed. "Not to Mr. Brockman? He is in ignorance of all this."

"I'll speak to his butler, Mr. Raynor."

Something told me that the baby might fit in well at Thorpefield Manor. Perhaps the Bluebell Mine would prosper too, when those who would have raided its profits were absent from the scene.

Chapter Sixty-Three

~

Easter Sunday came on the last day of March that year, and a fine day it was too. Good Friday is always a day off in Yorkshire, which makes for a long weekend.

Philip Goodchild and Alec Taylor closed the garage for four days. They hired a charabanc to go to Scarborough, where I had booked rooms at the Crown Hotel. Philip and Alec would take turns to drive. Benjie was persuaded to go, and to take the eight children, the baby, the nursemaid, Valerie Pennington, Harriet, Milly, Stephen Walmsley, Mr. and Mrs. Arkwright and Joan.

Raynor worried about the cost. The mine would do well, but that was in the future. I assured him that the holiday was thanks to a well-wisher, but did not name the well-wisher as the French Ambassador.

Sykes and Rosie went to stay at the Imperial Hotel, Blackpool over the Easter weekend. Keen ballroom dancers, they intended to spend most of their time at the Winter Gardens, reprising the success of their younger years, when they won many prizes on the dance floor.

I decided to stay at home with Sergeant Dog and my aged cat, Sookie. I would walk in the woods, read, and persuade my broken wrist to mend.

Mrs. Sugden thought this my best idea yet. As I lay on the sofa, thinking about going for a walk, she brought in a tray. "That's it, you rest. Here's a cup of tea, and a slice of my rhubarb pie."

She can be very sensitive about her baking. "I'm sure it's very good, but no rhubarb pie for me."

Author's Note

The question writers are often asked is "where do you get your ideas?" The simple answer is, everywhere. If one is lucky, different ideas then come together. I was interested in the way investigations can become skewed by a false trail, or by a detective becoming obsessed with a particular line of enquiry. At the time of writing, there was a great deal of discussion about "fake news", leading me to think of fake news in the 1920s. The letter that opens this book was inspired by a forged letter that contributed to the downfall of the Labour government in the 1924 General Elections. Known as the "Zinoviev letter", it purported to be from a Ukrainian-born Russian Jewish revolutionary and politician, urging British Communists to incite revolution.

There was a special train, six nights a week, between Christmas and Easter, setting off from Leeds Central station to King's Cross, transporting up to 200 tons of forced rhubarb to London. It ran until the early 1960s. The idea of that train with its cargo of scarlet stalks intrigued me. Trains are such a familiar trope of Golden Age crime fiction that I was tempted to commandeer one.

Formerly a triangle of land of about thirty square miles, the forced rhubarb growing area now covers about nine square miles. In 2010, twelve farmers within the Rhubarb Triangle successfully applied to have Yorkshire Forced Rhubarb added to the European Commission's Protected Food Name scheme. Those who know the area may recognise some of the places in this story. Thorpefield is fictional.

London-based Annette Kerner, known as the Mayfair Detective, began her work as an operative during the First World

War. I have taken the liberty of borrowing her name and a little of her history. I also borrowed the name of the vicar of Holy Trinity in 1929, the Reverend Mr. H S Branscombe. I like to think that Ryder Cup team members Al Espinosa and Leo Diegel were accompanied to Leeds by Mrs. Espinosa and Mrs. Diegel.

The initial inspiration was none of the above. That came from the way the children of the poor fare in twenty-first-century Britain. The opposite of justice is poverty.

Acknowledgements

Many thanks to Staff at Leeds and Rothwell Libraries and to Simon and Susan Bulmer, Stephanie Carncross, Sylvia Gill, Ralph Lindley, Janet Oldroyd-Hulme, Anthony Silson, Noel Stokoe and Roy Sumpner.

Once again it's a pleasure to thank Emma Beswetherick and the team at Piatkus as well as copy editor Robin Seavill. Jenny Chen and the team at Crooked Lane pulled out the stops to ensure a speedy passage across the Atlantic. Thank you.